THE GIRL AND THE UNEXPECTED GIFTS

A.J. RIVERS

The Girl and the Unexpected Gifts
Copyright © 2023 by A.J. Rivers

PROLOGUE

Them

I HAVE ALWAYS LOVED SNOW GLOBES.

The delicate glass. The sparkling snow. The perfection so finely crafted and preserved within. The tiny house and imagining how beautiful it was inside. The cozy warmth and the scent of sweets and cinnamon. The trees delicately dusted with perpetual snow, densely clustered together with the promise of a trail through them perfect for a romantic walk or a carriage ride. Or the glorious Christmas tree, exquisitely decorated with glowing lights and glittering details. I could lose myself staring into them.

But it seems that is always the way.

Losing yourself in perfection. Losing yourself for it.

I craved that kind of perfection. I stared into the one in my hand, wishing I could crawl through the fragile bubble of glass and feel the cold of the snowflakes on my face. I ran my fingertips along the smooth, cool surface wishing it would let me go inside and live in the peaceful beauty forever.

My snow globes aren't just for Christmas. They stay on display throughout the year, reminding me that the ultimate beauty and pristine perfection can be just shards of shattered glass away.

The glittering new snow globe set aside, the distraction out of mind, it's time to return to the unfinished project spread across the festive plastic tablecloth across the dining room table. Shimmering silver wrapping paper. The thick kind unfurled from a massive roll that seemed like it could last a lifetime, but seemed to disappear into the ephemera as piles of gifts appear beneath the tree. For now, only a few gifts were ready to be wrapped. With seasonal music playing in the background and the smell of hot cider mulling on the stove, it was a picturesque Christmas scene. Only the small smear of blood across the paper marred the perfection.

But that was gone with just the light swipe of a hand.

CHAPTER ONE

"**O**H, GOOD L—PLEASE BE CAREFUL," I SAY, HOLDING MY HANDS up as if I'm going to be able to catch Sam and Dean if they come tumbling down from the attic. "This. This right here is the exact reason I am so thankful this house was built like this. It's treacherous enough with you coming down an actual set of stairs. Can you imagine if there was one of those ladders that comes down out of the ceiling?"

"Like the one at my parents' house?" Sam calls out from behind the pile of boxes he's trying to carry down without being able to see around them. "I used to get stuff down from there all the time."

He takes a slightly unstable step and the already suspect structural integrity of the tower of boxes diminishes. He swerves to accommodate the tilt and makes it down the last couple of steps unscathed.

"See?"

I roll my eyes. "Yeah, well, you probably carried one box at a time, and if I know you as well as I think I do, you probably laid down on your stomach through the opening and dropped a lot of stuff down rather than carrying it all the way down the ladder."

My husband shrugs. "It was efficient."

Dean is trying the same feat Sam just accomplished and giving it just about the same performance. Too many boxes. Not enough visibility. He makes it down with a slightly more pronounced wobble than Sam and I hit a lunge with my hands above my head to catch a box labeled "holiday throw pillows" as it topples down so he doesn't step into it, fall down the stairs, and ruin Christmas.

I tilt the box back and forth between my hands, examining it as I step out of the way so Dean can safely reach the bottom.

"This is a big box. I didn't realize we had this many holiday-themed throw pillows," I say.

"We didn't. That's why I put it up there," Xavier says, coming down the stairs holding a tree topper in one hand and a cluster of giant plastic candy canes to line the sidewalk with the other.

"You put a box of pillows up in the attic just so we'd have to carry them down?" Sam asks.

"Yes. It's Christmas tradition."

"To hide pillows?" Sam asks, exasperated.

"To bring them down from the attic, Sam. How is the box going to start developing its Christmas storage smell if it isn't in storage?" Xavier asks.

"We already have the Christmas tree up and decorated," I say. "What's with the extra topper?"

"I need one for the tree in my room," he replies, walking around us and heading for the living room.

I look at Dean. "He has a tree in his room?"

"Apparently," Dean says.

I really shouldn't be all that surprised. This Christmas season hasn't gotten off to the smoothest start, and without the traditions that mark transitions like fall to winter or Thanksgiving to Christmas, it throws Xavier off kilter. It may seem to many like he's already that way, but once you get used to him, you realize Xavier has a state of normalcy just like everyone else, and like everyone else, he's vulnerable to being knocked off track when that normalcy isn't maintained. It is by no means the same kind of normalcy, but it's his base level. Maintaining that base level can be a very delicate game sometimes, but others are much more obvious.

I knew this holiday season wasn't going to be easy for him before Thanksgiving even rolled around. To Xavier, there is a very clear delineation between the seasons, and they should not bleed into each other. He goes to great lengths not to hear a single Christmas carol, eat Christmas-themed candy or chocolate, wrap a gift, or drink eggnog before Thanksgiving. It is still autumn, and the Thanksgiving holiday should be cherished as the time of thankfulness for the bounty of the harvest that it is, according to him. But come the time the dishes are put away and the dinner has been officially declared leftovers, the switch has been flipped and it is Christmas.

The seasonal pajamas come out, he pours a giant glass of egg-nog, and it's time to decorate the Christmas tree. Our entire extended chosen family, including my father, Bellamy, Eric, and little Bebe, are all together for the Thanksgiving holiday and then get to kick off the Christmas season together. It's a streamlined process that gets him right from decorative corncobs and cornucopias to holly and stockings in an instant. Within the next couple of days the house will fill with the smell of gingerbread as he produces this year's line of gingerbread men around the world.

I'll admit, it's become a treasured tradition for me as well. After many years of barely celebrating Christmas at all, I've gotten attached to the cozy, festive feeling of being here in Sherwood like I did when I was a child. Now the family I share the holidays with is larger and more complicated, but there's something really special about our traditions and celebrations together. Even if I do have to be prepared for a razor-thin margin between the two holidays.

But this year, it hasn't worked out that way. Dean and I have both been working on challenging cases that kept us apart for Thanksgiving, and Bellamy's entire family came down with a flu that lasted more than two weeks and almost made Xavier attempt a full ban on them for the entire holiday season. He does not enjoy being sick. And no one around him enjoys him being sick. I am pretty sure if Bebe wasn't a factor, he would still petition for Eric and Bellamy to not be allowed to enter the house until after the new year. I'm actually completely sure about that.

A rash of thefts and rowdy behavior uncharacteristic of Sherwood has kept Sam busy and my father dropped off the radar again for several weeks. I don't know what he was doing. I'll never know what he was doing. I won't ask and it definitely won't come up in dinner conversation. As far as anyone else in the world knows, he was around the whole time just like always. That has been life with my father. It's taken time to come to terms with the reality of who my father really is. There will always be questions about him and what I really went through with him in the years after my mother's murder, but I've settled into a place of not really needing to ask those questions or wait for the answers.

It all added up to a strange, rocky beginning to the holidays and now we're trying to make up for it. We're more than a week behind at this point according to the great clock of Xavier, so we're trying to stuff a lot of Christmas into this weekend. The others aren't here, but the four of us have been handling getting the house prepped for the season and trying to inject some festivity into what has been a challenging last few weeks.

I've been trying to force myself not to think about the note that appeared at my house just before Halloween. It came on the heels of my confrontation with the man responsible for a staggering string of deaths among women spread across several states. It was a complex and confusing case I almost got very wrong, and that note was chilling punctuation.

I didn't save you for you. I saved you for myself.

I know exactly what the note refers to. I knew the second I read it. The tense moment in a dark, desolate rest area parking lot when a car went past, driven by a person I couldn't see. It gave me just enough time to get my bearings so I could survive a showdown with a killer. I didn't have the luxury of questioning who was driving or what their motivation was. In the chaos that followed, I didn't think about where the car might have gone and why the person didn't stop. The only thing that mattered was the man on the other end of my gun and the backup officers coming to take him.

But it goes beyond the mysterious driver. That moment was no more one of serendipity than the note was a Hallmark card. I know it has something to do with the series of attacks on me and the strange occurrences that have plagued me over the last several months, possibly far more. From being followed around Sherwood to finding items on my car, I have absolute proof someone is watching me. The violent attacks that left me in a coma for weeks never get far from my mind.

But that's exactly what I've been trying to do. Keep them out of my mind. At least for now. I tucked the note in the back of a drawer in my office so I can try to focus on enjoying the holiday season.

We carry everything into the living room and arrange the boxes by where the decorations will eventually end up. The Christmas tree is already up and for the most part decorated. I'm sure we'll find a few more baubles and shiny things to add to it, but the foundation is there. We've also put up a few of the little decorative collectibles I remember being up from when I was a little girl and this was my grandparents' house.

This was the closest place to a consistent home I had when I was younger. My childhood was defined by moving around and constantly grasping for some sort of familiarity. The result was a patchwork quilt of fractured memories some of which I still can't confidently place. But there are some concrete experiences I can hold on to, and almost all of them happened here in Sherwood. This is where we would come for stretches of many school years, where we would spend weeks in the summer, and every Christmas.

Thinking of that and seeing Dean in the living room where I used to gleefully unwrap gifts under the watchful eyes of my parents and grandparents brings a twinge to my heart. I love those memories. The holidays here were always filled with joy and magic. Even when there was turmoil going on at the periphery of my life, I didn't know. When I was here, I had the chance to be just purely happy.

But even then, I had the somewhat nagging awareness that my family didn't look like the ones in Christmas movies on TV or the covers of holiday cards. There were the parents and the grandparents, but I was the only child in all those memories. I had no siblings. No cousins. It was just me.

I didn't know until I was well into my adult years that I did have a cousin, one I never had the chance to celebrate a childhood Christmas with. Who I never got to giggle with while trying to sneak down the stairs to get a peek at presents or open stockings alongside. The family photo albums have no candid snaps of us asleep in our seasonal pajamas in front of the TV or playing with new toys.

There's an emptiness I feel when I think about those lost moments, memories that we should have together. I got the opportunity to know our grandparents. I remember the breakfast my grandmother cooked for me every Christmas morning that always included her glorious cinnamon rolls that I have tweaked to make my own and now bake every week at least. I remember my grandfather sitting in his chair in the corner of the living room, just gazing at the Christmas lights like a little boy.

One time I asked him about that, and he told me that when he was young, they didn't have electric lights like that on their Christmas tree. At the time, I took that to mean he didn't have electricity when he was a child, and the world was black-and-white like in old movies. It wasn't until I was older that I realized he definitely had electricity in his house. They just didn't use strands of multicolored light bulbs to decorate their tree each Christmas. Instead, his parents insisted on remaining traditional and lighting tiny candles they attached to the ends of the branches.

Highly not recommended.

I hold on to the memories of running down the steps on Christmas morning to see the presents under the tree and my newly filled stocking, mesmerized by the appearance of the gifts after having snuck down to peek at, over what felt like just a short time before. I'm sure now it was actually hours, but to me as a child, it was all magic. It hurts that Dean never had that chance. Not just that he didn't get to celebrate Christmas with us, but that he never met our grandparents. He didn't even know his father, so he never had the opportunity to be a part of the family.

It makes it even more important to me now that we do as much as we can together. It makes my heart swell to see him carefully pull the fragile components of our great-grandmother's nativity out of its newspaper wrapping that still has advertisements from when my grandmother was a little girl and arrange them on the side table. It has me thinking more about this house and the one a few blocks away, left vacant by Sam. It's the house I remember him living in when we were young. In a corner of my brain, a hazy one that is filled with the confusing false memories produced by my coma, it's where I have a new chapter with Sam after signing my grandparents' house over to Dean and Xavier.

In the rest of my brain, I am fully aware that everything that "happened" while I was in the comatose state was just dreams fueled by Xavier's stories along with Sam and Dean talking to me. But even knowing that, I hold on to what I still consider memories very closely. They aren't real, and yet they feel so authentic. One of those that I treasure most is transferring the house over to them and knowing they have a place to call home when they are here in Sherwood.

"There's still a couple hours of light out," Sam says, hoisting one of the cardboard boxes up. "Do you want to get some of these outdoor decorations up?"

"Sure," I say.

We each pick up some more of the outdoor decorations and head outside. It is a fairly mild afternoon, so we're able to stay out for a couple of hours putting up lights and getting oversized ball ornaments, the plastic candy canes, and other lawn decorations in place. As I step back and watch three of the most important men in my life laughing and joking together as they prepare the house for the holidays, I know in my heart that memory is one I want to make real. I need to talk to Sam about the idea.

I've told Sam about a lot of what I experienced when I was unconscious, but not everything. I haven't mentioned that particular part of that dream to him. I didn't know how he would feel about it, and I'm still wondering that now, but I can't stop myself from thinking about it. It's obviously a major decision for him as much as it is for me, and I want to at least bring up the idea.

"The wicker furniture looks so summery," Xavier says. "There should be some red cushions or something on it."

"You don't have a box full of those around?" Sam asks facetiously.

"No, but I know how I can," Xavier says, taking out his phone and giving a dramatic swipe across the screen with his finger.

I have a feeling he's online shopping. The fact that he can get just about anything in the world he wants without having to go into a store or interact with any other human being is one of the greatest innovations in the history of humanity, according to Xavier. He uses it liberally.

"Hey, babe," I say, walking up to Sam and slipping my hand into his. "Want to go for a walk with me?"

"A walk?" he asks.

I nod. "I want to show you something."

"Sure," he says. "Dean, we're going for a walk. If you guys go inside, can you bring all this stuff with you?"

Dean waves over his head as he grapples with a length of artificial garland he's trying to position perfectly over the living room window.

Sam and I walk down onto the neighborhood sidewalk and start our stroll. The sun has started to set and like it tends to do in the winter months, dusk is gathering quickly. As we walk along, the yards around us start to come alive with Christmas lights and decorations. In recent years the holiday inflatables trend has become a very big thing in Sherwood. I remember houses tastefully draped in white lights was standard for Christmas around the little town when I was younger. A few people added some excitement by clinging to the retro multicolor lights. Some started choosing lights that danced and that seemed to open the floodgates.

But it has really reached a new level these last couple of years. I have a strong feeling that a lot of the responsibility can be placed squarely on Pamela Song's shoulders. Formerly Pamela Welsh, Pam is my high school classmate and an employee at the property management company that oversaw the ongoing care and rental of my grandparents' home. She also has the unfortunate distinction of being part of one of my more disturbing cases. It was actually her position at Lionheart

Property Management that put her in the path of a destructive, psychotic person who nearly took Pamela's life right in front of me.

Pamela and I didn't have the best relationship growing up in Sherwood. In fact, there are still plenty of people around who will talk about our heated rivalry. Apparently, there was major tension over Sam's affections when we were teenagers. I don't personally remember there being any kind of conflict over Sam specifically. I just remember her being generally unpleasant and never being friends. That unpleasantness didn't change much during our adult interactions when I first moved back to Sherwood. But things had started to mellow, and then being involved in the same traumatic event that could have ended it all for both of us did have a certain way of bringing people together.

This is why when Pamela decided to spend some time in Richmond, she contacted me. I've spent a good amount of time there over the years working cases, including a horrific explosion in the bus station that claimed the lives of a lot of people—and was set by a mad bomber trying to get my attention. That wasn't the kind of information Pamela was after, however. She was more interested in restaurant recommendations and sightseeing tips.

Since there's a lot of both in Richmond, I probably gave her more than she ever wanted to know. When she came back several weeks later brimming with excitement over her experiences, she had taken me up on quite a few of the tips I'd given, but it was one particular event that truly captured her heart.

The Tacky Light Tour.

I've heard of similar activities in different cities, but I obviously have a soft spot for the one in Richmond. I have no idea how it got started, but anybody who has spent a holiday season in the city has, whether advertently or inadvertently, seen the effects of the craze. Each Christmas season, people all across the city and suburban areas surrounding it deck out their houses and yards to truly obscene degrees. The brighter and more garish, the better. Official listings are published, and countless families make a holiday tradition out of touring around looking at the various houses. There are even limo companies and party buses that bring groups around for festive entertainment.

It is certainly something to behold. And when Pamela came back from her time in Richmond, she was clearly a devoted convert. She did her best to describe the entire thing in all its glory to anybody who would listen, but it's difficult to really capture that kind of over-the-top tackiness. But she's been doing her best to bump up the decorations throughout the community and is pushing hard for our own official tour. I've heard this may be the year it happens.

If that is the case, the houses around my neighborhood starting to overflow with lights, densely packed inflatables, and even themed walk-through areas are definitely clamoring to be a part of it. I am enjoying walking around taking it all in so much that I don't mind taking a larger loop around the neighborhood rather than just cutting straight over to the house. Once we've explored for a while, I now notice the cold starting to kick in, so I detour us down the side street until we are walking along the block where Sam used to live.

"What is it that you wanted to show me?" he asks as we are getting close.

"This," I tell him, gesturing at his parents' house.

He looks at me with a confused expression.

"I've seen it," he says. "Many, many times."

I frown. "Have you?"

He chuckles. "I think so. I grew up pretty near here."

"I know," I say. "Have you been thinking at all about what you might want to do with it?"

"What do I want to do with it?" he asks. He looks back at the house and gives a half-shrug. "I don't know. I really haven't thought about it all that much. It isn't the easiest decision to make."

"I know," I say. "We've talked about it. I was just wondering if you had come up with any other ideas? Or if you may have gotten any interest in it?"

"Is there something you're not telling me?" he asks.

"I'm not sure what you're thinking, but I can promise you it's not that. I told you that while I was under, I had a series of lucid dreams. In one of them, somebody had made an offer on your parents' house. They wanted to buy it and fix it up for their family to live in. You were really struggling with the idea of that, because somewhere in the back of your mind you thought maybe that would be where we were going to grow old together.

"But at the same time, you said that you were happy living at my grandparents' house and that we had built our life there, so you felt silly even considering not going through with the sale. Anyway, it's a lot of details that don't really matter. But what matters is we finally decided that you and I were going to move back into your parents' house. You came over here when I first came back and eventually, you just kind of didn't leave. We never really talked about it. But maybe now it's time that we talk about something new," I say.

"And what happened to your grandparents' house?" Sam asks.

"Well, that's the thing. I wanted to bring you over here to show you this and talk to you about it, because this particular part of my dream has really stuck in my mind. We decided to move into your parents' house, so I signed our house, my grandparents' house, over to Dean and Xavier. I know both of them have rooms in our house that they consider theirs, but that's not the same thing as having a true home base when they come to town to visit.

"Besides, that house should have been a part of Dean's life. It's part of his family legacy. My grandparents are his grandparents, and just because he didn't have the opportunity to get to know them doesn't mean he shouldn't feel close to them. Having that house could give him some of that connection."

"What about Xavier's house in Harlan?" Sam asks.

"They kept it," I tell him quickly. "It wasn't about them moving into Sherwood permanently. They still maintained their normal life and their house and everything, but they have been spending more and more time here with us. I like having them around and I don't consider them guests, but I think it's hard not to feel like a guest even when you are family if you are staying in someone else's house. Dean even admitted he tends to not spend as much time here, or rushes from one thing to another when he's here, because of the feeling that he's taking up space or getting in our way.

"Having that house to call theirs and have it available to them at any time would let them feel completely at home and comfortable no matter how long they were going to stay in town. And it gave Xavier another place to decorate for Christmas," I say.

Sam stares at the house again. He opens his mouth a few times like he's going to say something, but nothing comes out. Finally, he looks over at me.

"That's a lot to take in," he says.

"I know. 'Just think about it. Let it digest and see how you feel. We'll talk about it again."

He squeezes my hand and smiles at me. We don't say anything else as we're walking back down the street the other way so we can take in the houses on the other side of the street. I don't need to. I'm glad to have told him about it and to know he's thinking about it.

CHAPTER TWO

WITH THREE WEEKS LEFT UNTIL CHRISTMAS, FESTIVE PREPARA-
tions are well underway throughout Sherwood. To get more
people into this spirit and bring everyone together, the Chamber
of Commerce planned a new holiday celebration down on the village
green. A massive Christmas tree has been set up in the center, and this
evening there is a little artisan market with a grand lighting of the tree
as its highlight.

Sam, Dean, Xavier, and I get bundled up and head down to the
green to check everything out.

I already know we're going to have to park a bit away. Sam's department had been tasked with setting up road blockages and putting up No
Parking signs all around the area so no one would be able to drive right
up and park along the curb. Instead, we park a few blocks away and walk
in. The chill in the air makes this feel like a bit of an inconvenience, but
when we approach the village green and see how beautifully it's been set
up, not having cars parked close by makes complete sense.

The whole area has been crafted into an old-fashioned Christmas village. The nostalgic feeling is unexpectedly emotional as we walk past the lights hung up at the edge of the green to welcome visitors in. Even from the entrance, the enormous Christmas tree is impressive.

"Wow," I whisper. "This is really amazing."

Edith, one of the ladies on the planning committee who is stationed at the welcome table just inside the entrance, smiles at me.

"Thank you. I think it turned out even better than we expected. So many community businesses and organizations turned out. And we have quite a few local vendors. There are even some crafters and vendors from outside of town. You'll have to be sure to stop by the food booths and try some of the treats. I got a chance to sample some of the apple cider doughnuts fresh from the fryer and just rolled in cinnamon sugar."

Sam lets out an impressed whistle. "Well, I know where I'm headed."

Edith smiles. "Oh, they were spectacular. You'll love them."

We thank her and venture further into the green, immediately enveloped in the festive feeling of the event. It seems like most of the town has turned out to see it. People bundled up in their best seasonal outerwear look excited and filled to the brim with holiday cheer. I'm already enjoying just taking in what everybody around us is wearing.

For some visitors, tonight was an opportunity to get dressed up in their finest winter coats, gloves, and expensive-looking scarves. For others, this event presented itself as one giant ugly Christmas party. I see sweaters that light up and flash like decorated Christmas trees. Women dressed as Mrs. Claus. Children in all forms of sparkly, cute outfits. But it's the novelty hats and scarves that are really getting me. One woman walks past with a scarf that looks like a strand of Christmas cookies wrapped around her neck. Her hat is white and a 3D version of one of the cookies is stitched at an angle on the top like it's dunking into a glass of milk. Another is designed like a gingerbread house with white piping like icing and embellishments like candy.

Dean shakes his head and chuckles. "Crazy what people come up with these days."

"I've never seen anything like that," I say.

But as we approach the artisan section of the vendors, I discover their source. A large booth sitting at the corner of the main aisle features expertly designed displays of the clever scarves and hats along with a few decorations like what looks like a throw pillow in the shape of a Christmas pudding.

"Look, Xavier," I say, pointing it out. "Another throw pillow."

He turns toward the display and gasps, his hand going to his chest. I didn't know he had this much of an affinity for pillows, but I'm learning things about Xavier all the time. He takes one step toward the booth, then pauses, his eyes still locked on the displays.

"It can't be," he murmurs.

"X? Buddy? You okay?" Dean asks. His hand reaches around to his pocket. In the event of a Xavier-related emergency, Dean always has peanuts somewhere on his person. Xavier's heart condition has been pretty well managed in recent years, but we always make sure to have salty snacks around just in case.

Xavier's eyes move over to the banner hanging along the side of the draped table and his eyes widen to the point that I'm expecting to see connective tissue.

"It is. Oh… my… Why would she be here?"

"What are you talking about? Who?" I ask.

He points at the sign. "Cupcake Makery."

"Cupcake? Isn't that the designer you're so into watching all the time?" Dean asks.

He stops searching for the peanuts, which I figure means there's some significance to this booth that goes beyond clever Christmas cookie scarves.

Xavier draws in a breath, the air seeming to pull him up to a greater height. He holds it in for a second and then it bursts out. "Yes!"

He takes off for the booth.

When I get to the booth, Xavier has his hands clasped in front of him and is staring at all of the creations on display. The displays themselves are brilliant. Scarves like the cookie one I just saw are folded on a tilted baking sheet. One made specifically out of gingerbread men is coming out of a mixing bowl. A rack in the corner has hats and scarves that look like decorated Christmas trees and the space underneath is filled with wrapped gifts. A clearly hand-painted faux fireplace set up at the back of the booth has stockings hanging from it, each of them stuffed with plush Christmas characters.

"Hi there," a woman says as she walks toward Xavier with a smile.

She's wearing a pink skirt with a black crinoline, a pink top, and an ear warmer with a cupcake stitched over each ear. Thick-rimmed black glasses accent heavily made-up almond eyes.

"Cupcake," Xavier says in a low, almost reverent tone.

She smiles and it all comes together. Xavier is fanboying.

This is a phenomenon I have never seen, and I can't help but take a step back and just watch the whole situation unfold. The woman holds out a pink-gloved hand toward Xavier.

"You can come in," she says.

He puts his hand in hers and she guides him forward. Rather than just being set up as a table piled with items shoppers can step up to browse and the space behind it reserved for the artisan, this booth is the size of at least two and shaped like a tiny store. The woman is walking around it with Xavier now as he tells her about watching all her videos online and owning her pattern books.

"Who is this person?" I ask Dean in a half-whisper.

"She goes by Cupcake. I don't know if that's her real name. I kind of want it to be. She's a crochet designer who does all stuff like this. She posts tons of videos online of her making stuff and Xavier loves watching them," Dean explains.

I look back over at Xavier and Cupcake and watch as they whisper conspiratorially to each other. They look like old friends sharing secrets, laughing, and trying on various items throughout the booth. She loops a scarf that looks like giant peppermint candies around his neck. Xavier's face beams with delight. He reaches into his pocket to get cash, but Cupcake shakes her head.

"No. That's a gift. I recognize you. I've seen the comments you left me on my videos. They mean a lot. I wish you had sent me a direct message so I knew you would be here," she says.

Xavier is beside himself. "You've seen my comments?" He looks over at me, his eyes wide. I have never seen him like this. "Emma. She's seen my comments!"

"I heard," I say.

He gestures for me to come over and dramatically sweeps a hand toward me. "This is Emma." He repeats the sweeping hand motion toward the dark-haired woman. "Emma, this is Cupcake."

I look at her waiting for her to give me a different name to call her. She doesn't, so I have to figure that is either actually her name, or it is the persona she has adopted for herself and the only name she goes by. Either way, from what I've seen of her, it fits. I smile at her.

"I've never seen Xavier quite like this," I tell her.

"I'm really glad you came tonight," Cupcake says. "I always love meeting my online friends."

"I didn't even know you were going to be here," Xavier says. "What are you doing in Sherwood?"

There is just the slightest twinge of something in his voice when he says it that it could come across as an insult, but I know he loves this town. He's just surprised to see somebody with the apparent illustrious online presence as this one setting up a vendor booth at a tiny Christmas village like this.

"It was actually kind of a last-minute decision," Cupcake says. "I was taking a few weeks to visit some family a couple of towns over, and I heard this was going on. I absolutely adore Christmas and thought it would be fun. I hadn't planned on doing any in-person markets this season because I'm so busy with doing all my online content, but I just couldn't resist. I contacted the organizers, and they were happy to let me set up. So, I had a couple of friends from home come pack up everything in my inventory room that would fit the theme and send it to me, then I spent the last week prepping."

I look around at everything at her booth. "You did all this in a week?"

"Not all of it, but a lot of it," she says. "I used to just stitch for fun, then I really fell in love with it and started selling my pieces online and at markets. I didn't pay very good attention in school when they tried to teach us to make a plan before we made big changes in our lives, and I took the leap of quitting my day job way before I should have. When your entire income is suddenly dependent on how many things you can make and sell, you learn to stitch pretty quickly."

"I can imagine," I say. "I really love your pieces. They're so much fun."

"Thank you," she says. "That's why I got started doing it. I noticed there was a big hole in the market. Actually, it was just a me-shaped hole I thought at first. I moved to a cooler climate and my wardrobe was woefully unprepared. I started looking around for things to keep me warm during that first fall and winter, but I couldn't find anything I really liked. Everything was very generic. And," she lets out a full, genuine laugh, "that is one word I would never use to describe myself.

"I figured I was either going to have to settle for the boring things I could find around or I could make what I wanted myself. I learned to crochet a long time ago from my grandmother, so I thought I'd just whip up a few things that fit more with my own style. I don't have any formal training, so there was a lot of trial and error when it came to those first designs. And when I say trial and error, that whole error part is emphasized. Underlined. Italics. Bold. All of it. But eventually I got into the groove and started making things I loved. Then realized other people loved them, too. And Cupcake Makery was born.

"Obviously, I love designing and making things, but my favorite part of it is connecting with other people who love crochet. It's funny, when I first started my video channel and other social media, I thought I was going to have customers coming to see what I was making and put in orders. But I found that I was getting a lot more other makers visiting than customers. Some of them were trying to figure out my patterns, some of them were following my tutorials, and others were just watching because of a love of the craft. I started interacting with them more in comments and through live videos, and it's really become a group of friends," she says.

"Is that you how you see it, Xavier?" I ask.

"No," he says without missing a beat, still gazing at Cupcake.

Well. Okay, then.

"Babe, I'm going to grab something to eat," Sam tells me.

I nod and he walks away toward the collection of food stands set up on the other side of the green. The tree is at the center, rising up from a platform covered with prop gifts and decorations. There are several photo ops positioned around the area, and families and couples are lined up to snap the ideal shot for their Christmas card or scrapbook.

Several people come to Cupcake's booth to admire her items and Dean steps up beside Xavier.

"Let's go see what else is around," he tells him. "We'll swing back by here."

"Make sure you do," Cupcake says, touching his arm.

I notice he doesn't flinch. As we walk away, she turns to the group of new customers and starts showing off the various items she has. She invites them to come walk around the booth but doesn't welcome them the way she did with Xavier. I'd had a brief moment of wondering if it was all an act, if she was being that sweet and gushing because Xavier was obviously enraptured with her and she thought it was good business sense. But he didn't buy anything, and she was being kind but not overt with this new group. She had genuinely recognized Xavier from his comments and was happy to see him.

This in and of itself is a fairly impressive feat considering I've seen the picture he uses online, and it is not the best one to ever be taken. Social media is not Xavier's thing and he only has the profile on the video site so he can watch people whisper and crochet. I am a Special Agent in the FBI and have come up on some scary, messed up people throughout my career. Even still, I am not ashamed to admit there are few things in this world that I find quite as unnerving as when I walk into the library in Xavier's house to find him sitting in the pitch darkness with his computer in his lap as he watches people whisper about true crime stories. That one will stick with you for a long time.

As we walk across the green toward the vendors selling food, I find myself looking around, taking in all the faces that pass me. It's instinct, compulsion to be aware of my surroundings and remember the people in every place I go. It happens without me thinking about it, without me trying to make those imprints in my mind. But I try to tell myself to stop. I'm trying to let my guard down and not be so on all the time. I'm not here working on a case, I have to remind myself. I'm supposed to be here enjoying my time with my family. This is the Christmas I've been looking forward to, and I just want to savor being in the holiday spirit together.

Making our way past the massive Christmas tree, I try to pay attention to Xavier's rambling on one side while I look at the carefully designed display of fake gifts and props arranged around the tree. Someone went to great effort to make this look like a many-times magnified version of someone's holiday living room. Even the gifts are arranged so that they look randomly placed, but clearly aren't, the shapes, sizes, and patterns perfectly coordinating so that the entire image is cohesive while looking natural and welcoming.

"What do you think, Emma?" Xavier asks.

I have no idea what he's asking about. Clearly taking in everything around me doesn't extend to what he's saying.

I stare at him blankly, hoping the words will find their way to my brain.

"He wants to write crochet patterns," Dean supplies.

"Oh!" I say. "I think that's a great idea."

"And start a channel for my own videos."

I think that's a less great idea, but I'm not going to say it. Xavier could be extremely compelling for people to watch and listen to. He could also be completely confusing or forget to say anything as he's stitching so it would essentially turn into just hours of him crocheting with no commentary. But maybe there's a market out there for that.

"Sam has a churro," Xavier says. He tilts his head to the side. "Sam has several churros."

He sounds like the state fair version of a Dick and Jane reader from when my father was in elementary school. I follow the direction of his unflinching stare and see Sam coming toward us with one hand gripping a cardboard drink carrier and the other holding, quite accurately, several churros. We walk toward him and when we meet he holds the churros out toward us. The smell of cinnamon and sugar is always a surefire way to woo me, and the added sprinkles of green and red sanding sugar for a festive touch is enough to get my heart beating to the tune of "Jingle

Bells" and my mind off thinking about what could go wrong in a place this open with this many people walking around.

I take one of the churros and a cup of hot cider from the carrier. The combination isn't one I would have ever thought of, but it's insanely delicious as I bite through the freshly fried dough and follow it up with a swig of rich hot apple. Some may argue this is more of a fall combination than it is Christmas, but I am one who will lean toward spice and fruit no matter the occasion.

But I'm also not going to turn down one of the peppermint hot chocolates I see at a nearby stand and I have my eye on a booth that promises homemade macaroni and cheese with pulled pork on top. It is a very good thing Sam and I have been jogging together every morning. I've been spending more time in the field recently and that means I need to be able to keep up. Without those jogs, eating like this would definitely be a tick in the advantages column for the criminals.

But after spending my younger years sharply, almost obsessively focused on a clean diet and aggressive training nearly every day, I long ago made the commitment to myself that I was going to let myself live a bit. I'm not going to stop enjoying food. Therefore, I jog.

It's nice having that time with Sam in the early morning hours as well. He might not realize it since he's far from a morning person, but it's good to have that quiet hour to connect and just be together. I've told him he doesn't have to come along with me if he doesn't want to, especially in the cold he hates so much. But he refuses to let me go by myself. He doesn't admit it, but I know it's because he is still worried I'm going to be attacked again.

We enjoy our snack as we make our way over to another section of vendors. This type of event is my favorite way to do Christmas shopping. I would much rather pick out something unique and interesting for people than go to the nearest mall and roam around tossing things in my bags for whomever might come to mind later when I look at them. I would highly recommend to anyone who may ever come into contact with Xavier that they never bring up any sort of personal support for the concept of a gift closet.

Shopping through little artisan markets and craft fairs, though, always lets me find fun things that are special just for the recipient. I know whatever I pick for each of the people in my life, they are going to know it was just for them. By the time I've gotten through my churro and my cider cup has been discarded in a recycling container, I have already bought a handmade reusable shopping bag and put three gifts in it. Christmas morning is officially underway.

"Emma, look," Xavier says, pointing at a display of angels at one of the nearby booths. "I'm going to pick one for Dean's room."

My lips roll in and I press them together to keep from laughing. Two of the spare bedrooms in my house were claimed by Xavier and Dean the first time they came to stay with me. They are decorated much the same as they were when I was young: one full of buttery yellow and cream accents, and one full of angel statuettes.

I don't know why the angels are there, when she started collecting them, or why that is the only place in the house where I can ever remember there being angel decorations other than the one that was on top of the tree at Christmas and the one in the nativity scene. Whatever the reason, the second Xavier saw that room, he turned right back around and walked out of it. He has no issue with angels as a concept. He has a serious issue with them staring at him while he's trying to sleep.

He retreated straight across the hall to the yellow bedroom where he said he could feel like a cozy kernel of movie theater popcorn. Dean, by default, got the angel room. And is still there. He has never asked me to take the angels away. I leave them because that's where my grandmother had them. They were put back that way by the property management company when the last rental family moved out and Pamela was staging it to show again. I decided not to change it when I moved back in and let them know their services would no longer be needed. It reminded me of when I was a little girl. Even though I can't remember most of the angels, I know my grandmother touched every one of them and that they were placed back in that room based on pictures the company took when they took over the house from my father.

"Hey, babe," Sam calls me from another booth.

I go over to it and find him holding a windchime. "What do you think of this?"

"It's beautiful," I tell him.

"It reminds me of the one my mom had when I was a kid." He looks over at me. "Do you remember that? It was in the corner of the front porch."

"I remember," I tell him. "It always sounded so nice when we were sitting out there."

He smiles softly as he looks down at the decorative chime draped across his palm. There's so much nostalgia in his eyes, I can't help but smile myself. I'm not going to push him for his decision about the house, but I can see he's getting sentimental. He's really touched by the thought of going home, even though he's been avoiding it for a long time.

Sam puts the windchime down and walks to the next booth, but I follow right behind him and buy it, asking for the vendor to package it up and mail it to me so Sam won't see it until I give it to him Christmas morning. Whether he decides he wants to accept my idea of moving to his parents' house and handing over ours to Dean and Xavier or not, he needs that chime.

"Emma!"

I finish paying for the chime and putting down my address, then look in the direction of Dean's voice. He's standing in front of a row of games set up in the middle of the green, waving a beanbag over his head. I make sure the artisan who made the windchime has everything he needs, then head for my cousin.

"What are you doing?" I ask.

"Being festive," he tells me. He tosses one of the beanbags to me. "Join me."

I laugh and step up beside him. The bean bag he tossed me looks like a Christmas ornament and we are standing several yards away from a corn hole board cut out to look like a Christmas tree. There are holes where there should be ornaments and one at the tip where there would be a topper. I look down at the white bucket sitting near Dean's feet and see another bean bag shaped like a star.

"Alright, is there some sort of order we're supposed to do this in?" I ask.

"We're supposed to start from the bottom and work our way to the top, just like really decorating a tree. The star is the last one," he says.

"Perfect."

We laugh our way through several games before venturing further into the food area to sample more of the treats. Evening is settling around us, making the lights hung around the green look brighter and even more beautiful. There's a chill in the air that makes everything feel even more Christmasy and I want nothing more than to settle in for a season of just having times like this with the people I love.

CHAPTER THREE

Them

T HERE'S SOMETHING SO SPECIAL ABOUT AN ARTISAN MARKET AT Christmas time. I had never really been the type of person to get excited about exploring craft fairs or farmers' markets during the rest of the year. But for some reason as soon as the holiday season rolled around, I wanted to find as many little markets and gatherings like this as I possibly could. They felt like being in another time in the best way. But that really was all of Christmas. At least, when it was unfolding the way it should be.

The whole season felt like going back in time for a little while. People really latched onto tradition and suddenly felt extremely attached to the way things used to be. Candlelight became a perfectly acceptable and even preferable alternative to electricity among people who have full house generators to prevent ever having to go without power. It was a beautiful thing. Just like my snow globes.

Walking through this market stirred emotions deep within me. Everything around me was steeped in nostalgia, like I was wandering through one of my own memories even though all the cheerful banners up around the open green area in the center of town proclaimed this to be the very first year this event had occurred. Obviously, I had never been before, yet it felt so familiar.

The emotions got stronger the further I walked into the crowd. The smell of the food cooking. The sight of the sparkling decorations and glowing lights. The sound of laughter. It surrounded me, closing in on me.

Thoughts of last Christmas rose to the surface. They blended with what I was seeing, like a droplet of white paint dropped down into a pool of silver. I remembered that holiday so clearly. Every moment of it I felt so close I could reach out and touch it. I could still taste the hot cocoa, still feel the cool on my cheeks. I could still hear the Christmas carols. I still felt it all.

So much had changed since then.

There were so many people there at the event it seemed like the rest of the town must have been completely empty. Most of the people faded into the background like they were just part of the decorations, but some of them stood out to me. I was drawn to watching the happy couples roaming around, holding hands, creating their own memories within the bubbles they created with each other.

I caught a glimpse of a small group of people I could only describe as a family. One of them was a pretty blonde woman. She wasn't spectacularly beautiful. She didn't stand out to me because of extraordinary looks or an outlandish outfit that set her apart from everybody else. There was just something about her, a presence that demanded attention. I found myself watching her more than anyone else. I walked through the event following her with my eyes, curious about her life and the people she chose to have around her.

At one point, I saw a tall, strong looking man go to her and the others with treats. There was something about him that looked familiar. I knew I had seen him before. It took watching them for a few moments for me to realize I had seen his face on one of the displays wishing the town a Merry Christmas from prominent members of the community, including that man. Sheriff Sam Johnson.

I could have just continued to meander through the event for the rest of the night and been happy, but I knew I didn't have that much time. I was there for a reason. My mind traveled to the package I was holding. No one around me seemed to have even noticed it. There really wasn't any reason for them to. Nearly everyone there was carrying bags and boxes with them. It was one of the main reasons for the event, after all. Vendors and artisans were set up around the green hoping to attract customers eager to spend their holiday shopping budgets on their products. It meant most of the people who attended that night would go home with treasures that would end up tucked under Christmas trees or into stockings.

That was the intended destination for the package in my hands as well. Only, I didn't need to bring it home first in order to accomplish that.

I walked around to the back of the Christmas tree set up in the center of the green. The way it was arranged, and the elaborate backdrop behind the platform created the ideal cover as I slipped into place. Everyone around was anticipating a glorious lighting soon. All the attention would be on the tree. The organizers of the event had made sure that attention wouldn't be wasted. The display was truly beautiful. There were many fake gifts set up under it along with magnified versions of toys and other gifts. Just looking at it, I could practically hear a fire crackling grand amidst the cold Christmas Eve snow.

I reached into the bag I was carrying and pulled out a box wrapped in thick, shiny paper. I slid it under the tree and walked away. Without even a glance over my shoulder, I sank into the crowd again and left. Someone was going to be drawn to that package. It was exactly the way I intended it to be. Obvious. It was meant to catch someone's attention so they couldn't resist picking it up and finding out what was inside.

As much as I wanted to stay and see everybody's reaction, I knew it would be better to observe from afar.

CHAPTER FOUR

"**H**EY, WHAT TIME IS IT?" DEAN ASKS AS WE FINISH EXPLORING the vendor booths along the final stretch of the market. "It should be just about time for the illumination, right?"

I glance at my phone. "Um, yeah. Getting close. We should probably head over there if we want to grab a good spot to watch it."

"So, what's going to happen?" Xavier asks as we walk toward the tree.

"For the illumination?" I ask.

"Yes."

"You've been to an illumination before, haven't you?" I ask.

"I've seen people illuminate things, but not a formal one, no," he says.

"Oh. Well. They're going to light up the tree," I say. Xavier stays silent, obviously waiting for me to say something else. "And then we look at the lights."

We walk around the back of the platform and he glances to the side. He points at the gifts beneath the tree.

"That one's different." He doesn't miss a step and just continues walking along beside us. "The grand illumination is watching someone light a tree and then looking at the lights?"

"Yes."

"And then we go back and see Cupcake."

"Sure."

"Alright."

It was a response of acceptance. Apparently, the illumination is not the highlight of the evening to Xavier as it is to the rest of us. We position ourselves to one side of the platform so we have a good view of the tree but aren't right in the crush of everyone trying to be front and center.

"How's this for everybody?" Sam asks.

"Good," I say.

"Why is that gift different?" Xavier asks.

"What gift?" Dean asks.

"Do you want to move over some?" Sam asks.

"The silver one. It's not like the others."

"They aren't all alike."

"Stay here? Or shift over some?" Sam asks. "Can everybody see?"

"They all fit with the same theme," Xavier points out. "They all have the same color scheme. Then there's that one. It doesn't fit. And it's a different size scale than the others. It doesn't fit."

"Are we moving?" Sam asks.

"This is fine, honey," I tell him.

"That's probably why they put it in the back," Dean says. "They realized it didn't really fit in with the rest of them, so they just put it back there."

"But then why would they put it under the tree at all? It isn't like they had a quota for the number of boxes they had to put there. Though, I suppose they might have. They could have taken the average amount of money spent on Christmas gifts, translated that into number of gifts based on average consumer pricing for various age groups, then used that to create the different piles of gifts to illustrate various constructions of families. And that little silver one is the outlier to demonstrate those who stray from the commercial norms and imbue meaning on the season through less materialistic means," Xavier says.

"That's lovely, Xavier," I say.

I do have to admit, it is strange.

Out of the corner of my eye, I see a little boy tugging on his mother's arm as he points at the out of place silver gift. She jiggles his hand to signal her disapproval of his behavior, but he doesn't quiet down. It seems he has been far too transfixed by the gift that seems oddly real in comparison to the beautiful but obvious props around it.

The mother is so wrapped up in the conversation she's having with another young woman she doesn't get her son fully under control before he pulls away from his mother, runs up to the platform, and grabs on to the gift.

"Victor!" the mother shouts, looking horrified as she puts down the packages she was holding with her other arm and rushes over to her son.

But he isn't about to relinquish his hard-earned treasure. Gripping the shiny silver package tight against his chest, he takes off running, bobbing and weaving through the crowd until he gets to the other side of the platform. He drops down and slithers beneath the black skirt around the edge.

"Victor!" the mother screams again.

I want to commend her for the fact that there's more fear in her voice than anger, but I'm not about to get involved in this situation. Seemingly everyone in Sherwood is gathered around watching her son go completely rogue and become the reason Santa Claus retires in a direct-to-TV holiday movie somewhere. This can't possibly be a fun situation to be in. With no other parent figure coming to help her, a nearby woman I recognize as Jean Carroll, one of the members of the Chamber of Commerce events committee, rushes over to try to offer her assistance.

On the surface, it seems like a friendly and even compassionate offer, but the reality is Jean is probably mortified that the event she worked so hard to build with the other committee members is being upstaged by a spoiled child incapable of controlling his impulses around shiny Christmas presents. They try to beckon Victor out, but the little boy doesn't appear.

Suddenly, a scream explodes from under the platform. The little boy's mother's face goes pale and she drops down, shoving herself under the platform skirt as well. Her feet appear again a few seconds later and she wriggles out, dragging her son along with her. Sam steps in to push back the nosy onlookers and provide assistance, helping the woman to her feet. When he gets the young boy out, he's still gripping the box. Sam looks at it and his face hardens.

Victor finally tumbles into his mother's arms and Sam takes hold of the box. A few people start to murmur, then move quickly away from the platform. I hear a couple of screams as if someone has just heard something horrifying. Sam looks over, catching my eyes. He bobs his head backwards to indicate I should come over to him. Handing Dean everything in my arms, I hurry over to Sam.

"What's going on?" I ask. "Was the kid hurt while he was under there?"

"No," Sam says. "He's okay. At least physically. He went under there and opened the box. We may need to get the perimeters secured and not let anyone leave until we've spoken to them."

I shake my head, not understanding. "Sam, what's going on?"

Sam hands me the box and I look down into it. My stomach turns when I see what appears to be a human heart nestled among tissue paper inside. Tucked next to it is a gift tag.

My heartbeat.

All of the holiday spirit I had tried so hard to maintain drains out of me. Everything in me instantly clicks back to special agent mode. From one moment to the next I go from Emma Johnson, wife of sheriff Sam Johnson, to agent Emma Griffin, FBI.

"I need everyone to pay attention to me," I call out over the increasingly curious crowd. "Everyone is to stay exactly where you are right now. Until an officer or I tell you that you can go, you are to stay here. And please keep your voices down."

"What's going on?" somebody calls out.

"What happened?"

"Is something in the box?"

The members of the crowd yelling out questions and trying to get closer causes another rush of sound to swell up through everyone gathered near the platform. I stand firm and hold my hands up to get their attention.

"Everybody quiet down. As of right now, we are looking at a potential criminal investigation. Your cooperation will determine how quickly and smoothly this is able to go. Everyone is to stay where they are and remain quiet." A hush falls over the dense group of people and the milling around that had started turns to just shifting in place. "Thank you. We will be back with you."

I turn and go back to where Sam is standing. He is just getting off the phone with dispatch.

"I've called in some help, just in case this isn't a hoax," he says.

"Perfect," I say. "We're going to need to move. Those people are restless. We need to make sure nobody leaves and keep the chatter down to a minimum. Try to seal off the green as much as possible."

Dean and Xavier push through the crowd to get to us. Dean's' eyebrows are knitted close together, concern etched across his face.

"What's going on?" he asks. "What happened to that little boy?"

"Nothing happened to him," I say. "He's fine. At least, physically. The box he took off the platform held what we believe to be a wrapped human heart."

"Holy shit," Dean mutters.

"Dean, I need you to go to his mother and try to keep her calm. Make sure she understands how important it is not to talk about what's going on with anybody who's here. We're going to need to keep this situation under control and ask if anyone saw who placed this gift," I say.

I take a breath and brace myself. I already know there are no security cameras around the village green, so there will be no footage of who left the package under the tree. It already feels like we are at a disadvantage in the investigation. We're going to have to rely on what everybody here tonight saw to figure out where the box came from, and more importantly, who the heart in the box belongs to.

CHAPTER FIVE

W HILE DEAN COMFORTS AND REASSURES THE MOTHER OF THE young boy, Sam begins to move through the crowd talking to everyone. He is very much the face of Sherwood. A fourth-generation sheriff, he is immediately recognizable to everyone living in the community, and represents reassurance and order. Though most of the people around the community know who I am, I have nowhere near the kind of influence here that I do in other places.

When I am in Sherwood, Sam is the one with the sway. The people of the community trust him. They rely on him to give them peace of mind and help them to feel secure in the town they love. Seeing him here is particularly impactful this holiday season. It wasn't too long ago that Sam nearly left the department altogether so he could handle the disappearance of his cousin in Michigan. At the time, he didn't know if he was going to be able to take the time he needed in order to help his aunt search for his missing cousin, but wasn't willing to compromise that personal and family obligation. He was willing to leave the career he adored in order to do what he felt he needed to do.

Fortunately, the mayor didn't want to remove him from office. He was granted family leave with the understanding that he could come back to his position whenever he was able.

This is the first large community event since he has fully resumed his duties as sheriff. Putting his uniform back on and having his picture taken for the banner offering his Christmas greetings was an emotional moment for Sam. But I know it was also extremely impactful to the people of the community. Both those who passionately support him and are beyond relieved to have him back, and those who felt hurt and even betrayed by his choice to step away at all.

If there's anyone who is going to be able to manage this large of a group in an open-air environment like this, it's going to be Sam.

While he works to control the crowd and keep their movements to an absolute minimum, I further examine the box. I don't want to touch it too much. While I have my sincere doubts there's going to be any sort of recoverable fingerprints or DNA available, especially considering it has been grabbed several times since being placed on the platform, I understand the importance of preserving evidence.

I take a few pictures of the box from different angles. I'm particularly interested in the wrappings themselves. If I can find identifying features within the wrapping, it can help to direct me. Something as seemingly simple as the type of knot used to tie a package can offer critical details that could lead me to the person responsible. But this box wasn't tied. Like what most people would expect from a traditional Christmas gift, the wrapping paper was secured with pieces of tape. It would be difficult, though not impossible, to use tape like that and not inadvertently lift the ridge pattern of at least one or two fingers.

In fact, most people tear off pieces of tape and put them on the tips of their fingers to keep them accessible while they fold the paper. With any luck, forensic examination will be able to isolate fingerprints that can be·run through databases to search for a match. That having any kind of benefit is dependent, however, on the person who left the heart under the tree already having their fingerprints on file. Without those records, there would be nothing to compare to until we have a suspect.

It doesn't take long for the other officers to arrive and I turn the heart over to the medical examiner. She'll bring it to her office for preservation and a full examination. I turn my attention to searching for the wrappings. The young boy and his mother have been led away from the situation by the psychologist who works for Sam's department. He will bring them to the office to interview them. While I doubt he will get any kind of particularly useful information out of them that we don't already know, getting them out of the situation will help us to keep the rest of the crowd better under control and reduce the emotional intensity that can quickly get out of control.

With them away from the site, Dean comes back over to me.

"What now?" he asks.

"Is Xavier alright?" I ask. "Where did he go?"

"He's fine. Cupcake came over to find out what was going on and she brought him back to her booth with her. Apparently, she has a stash of yarn and hooks, and they are going to stitch," he says.

I let out a breath and nod. "Good. Alright. We need to go to all the vendors and look at the packaging they have. Everything. Items they brought prewrapped, any kind of props or decorations that involve gift-wrapping, and wrapping materials they have on hand. I need to find out if any of them have the kind of paper or gift tags that are on that box."

"Let's go."

This is not how the end of this event was supposed to go. As late evening slips into night, the chill gets deeper and the crowd that had been so festive is becoming miserable and angry. Cold, tired children are crying, and frustrated adults are pushing back against officers just trying to maintain control so we can make sure we contact every person present. It's not feasible for us to get full statements from everyone here tonight, but we have to collect and confirm contact information from all of them so we can follow up.

Without any form of surveillance footage available, the only thing we have is the observations of the people who were at the event when the package was put in place. The hope right now is that someone will have seen something, whether they recognize the significance of it or not, and we will have a springboard to go off of. Checking the vendor booths for the type of wrapping present on the box turned up nothing. While some of them offered gift-wrapping services for the items they were selling tonight, none of them had the silver paper. In fact, most providing any kind of wrapping are relying on white or brown butcher paper and twine, some with custom embellishments, some completely plain.

After hours of initial investigation there at the green, we leave cold, exhausted, and raw. I'm left hoping this isn't a murder. Whoever did this purposely intended on it being uncovered in the midst of what was supposed to be a joyful, festive celebration. It's disturbing, but not just because of the way this heart was left. Someone with this much drive for attention is unlikely to only do it once. The instinct deep in my gut tells me we're only at the beginning.

CHAPTER SIX

’M AT THE MEDICAL EXAMINER'S OFFICE EARLY THE NEXT MORNING, hoping she has more answers for me. Fortunately, Keegan O'Hare is neither a procrastinator nor a late sleeper. By the time I get to the office, she has already done an initial examination of the heart.

"I can definitely confirm this is a human heart," she says. "I can make an educated estimate of the age of the person who it belongs to, but you have to understand that isn't an exact science just with visual observation. There are many different factors that could go into the appearance of the heart. Disease, issues at birth, overall health and fitness level. All of those can dramatically impact the appearance of the heart. But, if I was to make a guess, I would say this is the heart of someone in their late thirties to early forties. Healthy. Fairly fit."

"Great. That does narrow it down some. Anything else? You mentioned disease. Can you see any signs of anything like that? Something that might show up on a medical record?" I ask.

Keegan shakes her head. "No. I didn't see any signs of disease, but there's some trauma."

"Evidence of stab wounds?" I ask.

"I wouldn't go that far," she says. "There are cuts and knicks, but they appear to be post-mortem. They aren't from the cause of death, but from the removal of the heart from the body."

"So, likely not someone who has done this before," I say.

Keegan gives a slight shrug. "Or they just never developed a particular skill at it. It's much more difficult to remove organs from the body than people think. I am convinced most people who either plan to kill or find themselves suddenly having killed someone automatically think they are going to be able to quickly chop them up or take out body parts so they can conceal them. They think it's going to be a quick project and they'll be able to go undetected.

"Only, they don't realize just how well put together the human body actually is. Not that my knees would agree with that on particularly rainy mornings, but for the most part, the human body has pretty good structural integrity. It isn't easy just to dismantle it. And it definitely isn't easy to take it apart without causing damage to the various components. That's what I think happened here. Whoever did this didn't know the simplest ways to access the heart. It's unlikely they are sophisticated in anatomy. So we can definitely rule out that it was intended for transplant; like I said, most likely removed immediately post-mortem.

"I'm going to run some tests to see what else I can find out about it. I'll keep you updated."

"Thank you."

I leave Keegan's office and go right to Sam's. Ruth behind the reception desk looks at me with a sad smile when I walk through the door.

"I'm guessing you aren't visiting just as the sheriff's wife?" she asks in a way that at one time would have bothered me, but now I find endearing. "Possibly bringing some of your cinnamon rolls?"

"Unfortunately not," I say. "I'm here about what happened at the market last night."

She presses her lips together and draws in a breath. I can see in her eyes she's imagining the scene. I know she was there, so she heard what was happening and watched as the chaos unfolded. Luckily, she wasn't close enough to actually see the heart in the box.

"Go on back," she says. "I think he's in his office."

"Thanks, Ruth."

I go into the back of the station to Sam's office and find the door most of the way closed. Pressing it open, I lean my head in to find him sitting behind his desk, his head in his hands.

"Babe?"

He looks up at me with eyes weighed down by exhaustion. He barely slept last night. We got home extremely late and he tossed and turned for two hours before taking a blanket and going to watch TV in the living room to try to get him to sleep. By the time I got up, he was already working out in our home gym. This is getting to him. Sam adores Christmas. He always has. He's the type to light up like a little child as soon as decorations start showing up in stores. One of the few things he and Xavier really share is their excitement of counting down as the holiday season approaches.

Though he definitely enjoys the holiday, for Xavier, I think the countdown is more about preparing for the next seasonal transition and getting the satisfaction of checking items off a list. Waiting to see a specific sequence of holiday-themed commercials is among his most treasured traditions. For Sam, however, the countdown is pure excitement.

Now, that excitement has been dampened. Anything painful or difficult happening around the holiday season is challenging for him, but something this horrific is truly going to chip away at him.

"Hey," he says, managing to sound happy to see me. "Did you find out anything from the medical examiner?"

"She was able to confirm it is definitely a human heart," I say. "And she believes it was from a healthy adult. There aren't any signs of disease, but there also isn't any evidence to indicate cause of death. She's going to do more tests and get back to me with as much information as she can. One thing she did mention is that there is damage to the muscle that looks like it's from when it was removed from the chest cavity, post-mortem. With that in mind, it seems like we're looking for someone who doesn't have a lot of experience."

"I don't know if I should take that as a good thing or a bad thing," he says. "On one hand, it means they probably killed that person and it was their first. But on the other, it means they might not have their DNA or fingerprints on file, making them even more difficult to locate."

"But we're going to," I tell him. "We're going to find who did this. And that starts with finding out who that heart belongs to. We should start with missing persons reports. Now that we know the heart came from an adult likely between their late thirties and early forties, we can narrow the search to the missing people who fit that demographic. It's only one step, but it helps."

There was a time when searching reports of missing individuals in the area would require sifting through written records and digging through case files. It's moments like these when I'm especially grateful for the many ways technology has streamlined the process of investigating crimes. It will never replace intelligent minds and true skill, but it can simplify tasks and save tremendous amounts of time in situations when every single second counts.

We input the information we got about the heart from Keegan and use that to narrow down the options from the missing persons database. The specifications that the heart came from an adult heading toward the middle of their life rather than one just at the beginning of adulthood eliminates quite a few of the candidates. From there, we start to compare other details with what we have in the profiles of those who are missing.

"Look at this one. Galen Winters. Thirty-nine years old. Last seen jogging around the lake. That corresponds with what Keegan said about the heart being healthy," Sam says.

"Yeah," I say, "but this says his family reported him missing fairly quickly and were concerned about him because he needed to take medication. He had open heart surgery a few years ago. That's something that would have showed up."

He makes an acknowledging *hrm*. "You're right," he says. "I missed that."

"This one would be the right age now," I say, pointing out the profile for Carlin Ferris. "But he went missing almost ten years ago. We can't completely eliminate it, obviously, but I think the chances of his heart just now being removed from him and showing up under a Christmas tree are pretty low."

"Probably," Sam admits. "But there's DNA on record for him from an old arrest, so we can have that compared to the heart just to be sure."

"I'll let Keegan know," I say.

I want to have a pile of possibilities to go through, but there's only a small handful of people who are missing around the area we specified and fit the demographics. Because Sherwood isn't a big community, there are very few missing persons reports floating around at any given time. We have some, such as Carlin Ferris, who have been missing for a considerable amount of time, but people don't often just disappear out of this town. That's why we expanded the search to include reports from all the neighboring towns and even some just beyond those.

It broadens the radius and puts us in the position of having to venture into other jurisdictions if we get a hit, but it increases our chances of figuring out who this person is. The possibility is good that they didn't live in Sherwood. It would be much more obvious if someone was missing from around here and so far, there haven't been any new reports and no one has come forward to express any concern about friends or family members.

With none of the missing persons reports panning out, Sam and I turn our attention to the strange gift tag included inside the box. It's already been processed and recorded in evidence, so now it sits on the table of the conference room we're using for the investigation with a tiny tag of its own attached to it.

"My heartbeat," I read. "That's it. There's no name. Nothing. It's just so odd that a gift tag would be inside the package with the heart. Tags like this are usually attached to the outside. Why would someone put it inside? And what was the point of it at all? What do those words mean?"

"I wish I knew," Sam says. "For now, the best we can hope for is that the forensics team was able to lift fingerprints or any kind of DNA from it. I'm waiting to hear from them about it. I'm not holding out a tremendous amount of hope, though. When they talked to me after their initial review, they said it didn't look like they were going to be able to get much off of it. It wasn't in the best condition coming out of that box."

"Minor understatement," I say, looking at the blood soaking into the cream-colored cardstock of the tag.

I let out a sigh.

What does it mean?

CHAPTER SEVEN

T HE LATE MORNING AND AFTERNOON ARE DEDICATED TO MEETING with people who were at the village green last night so we can process their statements. I already know that the vast majority of them won't have anything to tell us. There were a lot of people there and most of them weren't even close enough to the platform where the giant Christmas tree was set up to even see what was going on.

They weren't aware there was a problem until they heard the screaming and then my warning for them not to go anywhere. I still want to make sure someone speaks to every single one of them. Sometimes the most critical piece of information uncovered during an early investigation comes from somebody who doesn't even realize they have that information.

It's very possible one of the people who wasn't near the tree and didn't see the box could still have seen who put it in place. Or maybe they saw someone acting suspiciously before or even after the box was discovered. Right now, our goal is to narrow down the possibilities. We need to find some sort of path to follow in hopes of it ending with the person who is responsible for this.

I've already interviewed more than twenty people when I decide to take a break for lunch. I head back to Sam's office and poke my head around the door.

"Hey babe, how about we run up to Pearl's for…" I start, but I trail off when I notice his expression. This time, he doesn't look so happy to see me. Instead, his eyes bore into mine from across the desk and I realize he has his desk phone held up to his ear and the expression is likely not actually directed at me.

"What's wrong?" I ask, walking across the room toward him.

"We'll be right there," he says. He ends the call and hangs up the phone before walking around the desk and heading for the door. "Come on."

"What's going on?" I ask. "Where are you going?"

"You're coming with me," he says.

I fall into step beside him, and we go out the back of the building to the parking lot and climb in his cruiser. As soon as we're out of the parking lot, his lights and sirens are on.

"That was Percy Nash from the Claremont Hotel," Sam tells me as we peel off down the street.

The Claremont is a very new addition to Sherwood. It's a very nice, very chic hotel that just went up downtown. Many people around here aren't happy to have it around, saying it ruins the small-town feel of the community and is going to start attracting far more people than they want to deal with. Others think it's exciting and have cited the influx of jobs in the area as one of the best supports.

"What's going on at the hotel?" I ask.

"They have a Christmas tree in their lobby," he tells me.

I don't need him to tell me anything else. That was plenty.

When Sam and I get to the hotel, Percy Nash is already waiting outside. He looks tense and uncomfortable in his expertly tailored suit. He reminds me of so much of somebody, but I can't put my finger on it.

"Sheriff," he says when he sees Sam. "Oh, thank goodness. I just didn't know what to do. One of the guests noticed it and brought it to my attention."

"Did you open it?" Sam asks as we walk into the hotel. I immediately notice uniformed officers standing post on either side of the doors just inside the lobby.

"No," Percy says. "I told everybody not to touch it and I called you first. I thought you should be here for when it is opened depending on what might be inside.

"Do you have some reason to know what's in the box?" Sam asks.

"Not at all," Percy says. "But I can tell you the package was not under the tree yesterday when I closed down for the night."

I raise an eyebrow at that. "Isn't this a hotel? What time do you close?"

"We don't allow for twenty-four-hour check-ins here. There is a cut-off at midnight. After that, the hotel is secured and no one else is permitted in until early the next morning."

"So, it was either put into place overnight after you closed up the hotel tonight, or this morning," I say.

"Yes," he says.

By now, we've gotten across the lobby and to a back corner where a staircase swoops upward to the next floor. In the curve of the bottom landing is the Christmas tree. There are elaborate gilded decorative deer positioned on either side and I immediately notice the silver box tucked nearly behind the three. The wrapped package has been put in such a place that it doesn't look like it is supposed to be part of the display. There are no other boxes or other pretend gifts under the tree, making this one stand out even more.

"Wait for the crime scene unit to come and photograph it before opening it," Sam says. "I would appreciate if there is a secure area where it can be opened without anyone seeing."

"Absolutely," the manager says.

It doesn't take long for the crime scene investigation team to arrive and thoroughly photograph the area. They make sure to capture every angle of the tree and the gift before anybody touches it. Wearing gloves, Sam picks up the package. He bounces it slightly up and down, looking almost like he's a little child trying to figure out what he got for Christmas. He is trying to gauge what may be inside, but there is none of the Christmas morning excitement in the gesture.

"There's definitely something in it," he says. "It's not just an empty box."

We take the box into an empty office, and I request a roll of wax paper from the hotel kitchen. When it's brought to us, we spread it across the table to provide a clean and uncompromised surface that can also be rolled up and brought into the station for further investigation if any fibers or other minute evidence happens to fall onto the table.

With the photographer standing close by to ensure each step of this process is properly documented, Sam slides his finger beneath the pieces of tape on either end of the box. With the edges popped up, he pushes the box through from one side so it comes out the other. This box is significantly larger than the one that contained the heart.

"It's cold," he reports, pressing his hands to the sides of the box.

"How cold?" I ask.

"Not like ice, but definitely a chill."

The box has another piece of tape securing the flaps closed and Sam slices through it with his pocketknife. He pauses for just a brief instant before opening the flaps. I'm standing beside him when the box opens, revealing a pair of lungs nestled in a nest of tissue paper. There's another gift tag rested in the box with them.

"The air I breathe," I read.

"Emma," Sam says calmly. "I think it's time to call Eric."

My call to Eric formalizes what Sam and I already know. The FBI will step in to manage this case, with me at the lead. It's much easier to wonder if the local law enforcement is going to be cooperative with me during an investigation when that local law enforcement is my husband. My next call is to Dean to let him know what's going on, and then I head for Keegan's office.

She doesn't look quite as enthusiastic to see me as she did this morning. Brushing her hair back from her face with the back of her arm, she lets out a heavy sigh.

"Emma," she says. "I haven't had time to get the test results back on that heart. I know you already have another organ for me."

"I know. But you should have had the chance to at least look over the lungs, right? Can you tell if they were frozen?" I ask. "The box they were wrapped in was cold to the touch."

"I can't be positive until I'm able to examine a tissue sample under a microscope, but I don't think they were frozen. Likely refrigerated."

"How likely do you think it is these lungs are from the same person the heart is from?" I ask.

"That's not something I can tell just by looking at them, obviously, but I can tell you that the lungs appear healthy and they seem to be from a person in the same age range as the heart. They also show some of the same damage from their removal as the heart," Keegan says.

"So you can't be positive, but…"

"I think it's a very strong possibility," she says.

"Okay. Thank you. Let me know when you find out anything else."

"I will," she says.

Back at the hotel, I ask the manager for the surveillance footage from the lobby. The vast majority of hotels these days have good camera coverage of public areas, and this hotel is no different. Unfortunately, upon watching it, the footage shows only a specific angle of the lobby, capturing the front desk and the doors, but cutting off the back portion. Another set of cameras is in place in surrounding hallways where there are guest rooms, but the tree itself is not captured on the footage.

"Why do you think this person chose this hotel to leave another box?" Sam asks. "It isn't as public as the market on the green. And it wasn't put in such an obvious place this time, though it was pretty easy to see."

"I think it's purely a matter of staying out of sight. In both instances now this person was able to move through the area and leave the packages without being noticed. Even with the security system in place here, there isn't any footage of the tree. We can look at all the other cameras and trace the people who move through the hotel, but there's no actual footage of the tree or the box being left. I think that's very intentional," I tell him.

He considers it. "So they're leaving these packages where they'd be the least visible, but they'd be easily found. Immediately obvious and out of place."

"That means they are either familiar with the area or knows someone who is," I continue. "There might be some other significance to the locations, but I don't want to over-complicate the investigation by trying to apply excessive meaning. There's already plenty to consider and we need to focus on what we have rather than trying to come up with other angles," I tell him.

"Fair enough," Sam says. "So, what now? Where do you go when you have organs, but no body?"

"You look at what they were in instead," I say. "The packaging for both is the same. I want to know where it came from. If we can find out where the boxes and wrapping were purchased, or at least narrow it down, we might be able to track who bought it."

CHAPTER EIGHT

'M WELL AWARE AS I START MY RESEARCH INTO THE PACKAGING that I'm likely embarking on a massive wild goose chase. It isn't like wrapping paper is a rare commodity. Especially at this time of year. But I have to hold out hope that there could be something notable about this particular type of packaging that could steer me in the right direction.

After all, none of the vendors throughout the market were using anything even similar, and I can't remember ever having seen this particular type of paper at the massive displays in the department stores. I hope it will be as simple as snapping a picture of the paper and running it through the image search app on my phone. I like to think of it as the high-tech bloodhound that lives in my pocket.

This time, the bloodhound didn't find the right trail. There are images of the paper on the internet, but it essentially comes up with the result of "wrapping paper" and "silver Christmas gift." It takes a bit more creative search engine use to eventually narrow down that result.

"How's it coming?" Dean asks, coming into the living room with a cup of coffee in each hand.

He hands one down to me and sits beside me.

"Thank you," I say, taking a deep sip. "Oh, that's good. What did you do to that?"

"There's one of those soft peppermints in the bottom," he tells me. "Xavier's trick."

I nod. "Sounds like it. Where is he, by the way? I saw him at breakfast, but he wasn't here when I got back."

"He's hanging out with Cupcake, if you can believe it," Dean says.

"Wow. He's really branching out," I say. "Do you think he..."

"No," Dean says, shaking his head. "I don't think it's like that. I don't know if it has even fully processed in Xavier's head that she is, in fact, a woman, and his fascination with her could be interpreted that way."

"Are we sure he even understands she is a fully realized human being and not just a character that exists online and when he is in her presence?" I ask.

Dean smiles as he takes a sip of his own coffee. "Now that, I'm not so sure of."

"Alright, well, as long as he is accounted for, I don't need to worry. So, I can focus on this riveting bit of evidence."

"Wrapping paper?" Dean asks.

"Wrapping paper. Which I thought was going to be a massive failure, but is actually turning out to possibly be something," I say. "This paper isn't just mass produced and available everywhere. I didn't think it was. I figured I would recognize it. It's pretty distinctive. What I found is it is a specialty option released on a very limited basis by a fashion designer. It can't be purchased through any conventional channels online. I found a few rolls on eBay, but other than that, it has to be purchased through specific retailers.

"I was able to identify five stores within a thirty-mile radius that are authorized retailers. I'm going to contact them and ask for records of all of the purchases of the paper. They should be able to scan the bar code they use and their computers would document every unit that's been sold and when. From there it's just a matter of tracing payment methods. We should be able to find out who bought all of the rolls of this particular paper in the area."

He raises an eyebrow. "Seriously? We're tracking wrapping paper?"

I shrug. "We work with what we've got."

The first store Dean and I visit isn't a great start to the trail. A tiny gift boutique tucked along a row of equally tiny and adorable shops in a tourist town that feeds off the popularity of nearby caverns, Trinkets and Treasures hasn't quite caught up with the rest of the world when it comes to use of technology. They have clung to the use of their traditional cash machine rather than having a computerized point of sale system. This means they keep track of sales with receipts they collect at the end of the day rather than allowing a computer system to do it for them. They strongly discourage use of cards, but when they need to use one, they have a reader that attaches to their phone.

The juxtaposition between that kind of operation and being an authorized retailer for high-end designer wrapping paper is a hard one to wrap my head around until Dean reminds me that wealthy people tend to have a fondness for the quaint and unique. This isn't just a shop. This is an experience. They come here and get to feel like they've ventured back to a simpler time. Rather than shopping at some big box chain store or one of the flashy destinations down the street, they feel like they are getting a more authentic, personal experience right here in this little shop.

Whether that's actually true or not doesn't seem to matter.

Fortunately, the search gets far better from there and the rest of the shops are able to confirm they have systems in place that track sales of specific items, especially specialty items such as that paper. They aren't able to give me the information immediately, but I give them all my contact information and they promise to get in touch when it is available.

I'm leaving the last store when I get a call from Keegan. She tells me to come by her office and she will fill me in on what she has found out about the heart and lungs so far. I drop Dean off at the house so he can get back to work on his own case and be there when Xavier gets home, then make my way to the medical examiner's office. Keegan looks far more put together than she did the last time I saw her. A fresh coat, newly styled hair, and probably a considerable caffeine flow have perked her back up.

The fact that she has some actual information to give me and won't have to deal with me bugging her for something likely doesn't hurt.

"I'm about to order lunch," she tells me. "Are you hungry?"

I haven't eaten since breakfast, so I take her up on the offer to order something for me from the little Italian place down the street and while we wait for it to arrive, we sit down in the lounge. She rests back in her chair and seems to take a couple of deep breaths.

"You okay?" I ask.

Her eyes snap over at me. "Yeah. I'm good. I just like the opportunity to get out of the thick of things sometimes, if you know what I mean."

"I think I do," I say. "So, what can you tell me?"

"Don't you want to wait until our food gets here?" she asks.

"You know, as accustomed to this whole thing as I am, if I have the choice, I really do prefer my lunch conversations to not be about internal organs that are no longer internal. Why don't we get this part of the conversation done with, and then we can chat about something more pleasant when the food gets here?" I suggest.

She gives a nonchalant shrug. "Whatever works for you." She picks up a folder she'd put down on the table in front of her and flips it open in her lap. "Alright. I ran some tests on both the heart and the lungs. Microscopic evaluation confirms the heart was frozen at some point before it was discovered, but was thawed by the time it got to me. That makes it much more difficult to pinpoint when it was removed from the body. The lungs, on the other hand, have not been frozen. They were deeply chilled, but the cells don't show the characteristics of having been frozen. That could place time of death at potentially very different points."

This immediately strikes me, and I realize what she's saying.

"Different points of death. The heart and the lungs aren't from the same person?" I ask.

"No," she says. "I ran quick genetic testing on both organs, and it showed the heart belonged to a male while the lungs belonged to a female. It's not a lot of information to go on, but at least it's something."

I lean back in my chair and cross my arms. "It's definitely something," I say. "It's confirmation we are looking for two corpses instead of one."

Keegan looks up as the receptionist comes in with a couple of large bags and boxes from the restaurant.

"Oh, thank you, Betsy," she says. "You could have just called for me. I would have come up there to get this."

"It's not a problem," Betsy says. "Hey, Emma."

"Hi, Betsy," I say. "How are you doing?"

"Doing fine. Did you have fun at the market the other night?" She cringes a little. "Before everything."

"I did. It was really well put together. Were you there?" I am a little bewildered that she would ask if I had fun if she only thought I was there to investigate.

"Yeah. I actually called out to you. I tried to get your attention a couple of times, but I guess you didn't hear me," she says.

"Oh, I'm sorry. I definitely didn't. I would have stopped to say hello if I had," I tell her.

"No worries. It was really busy there. I actually ended up leaving after just a little while because there were so many people. I was getting a little overwhelmed. I'm actually glad. I wouldn't have wanted to be there when all that was going on," Betsy says.

"I don't blame you. I'm sure it's not exactly the type of Christmas memory parents would want their children to have," I say.

Betsy gets a solemn look on her face. "I better get back to the desk. You ladies enjoy your lunch."

As she walks away, I think about what Betsy said. She was right there trying to get my attention, yet I didn't even notice her. A person I have known, albeit with a fairly large gap in the middle, since I was in high school and she was a teacher just a handful of years older than us. By the time I got back here to Sherwood, she had changed direction in her career, but I still knew exactly who she was when I saw her. Yet, I wasn't able to filter her out of the busyness of the crowd that night.

I'd put effort into not tuning into everything around me and it had worked, but it also illustrated just how easily someone can move among others without registering. Whoever left these gifts could easily have assimilated into the group and simply went about the motions of enjoying the market the way everyone else was, detouring only for a second to leave the package. Because they weren't doing anything overt and overly dramatic, they didn't call any sort of real attention to themselves.

In my conversations with the people who were there that night, and what I've been able to gather from the statements Sam and his officers took as well, nobody close to the platform noticed anybody behaving strangely. Nobody stood out as unusual or out of place. And nobody noticed anyone either carrying around that package or leaving it behind before it was found. Whoever this is, they are skilled at being invisible while right in the middle of everything.

I hear back from the shops about the wrapping paper that evening and the next day. To isolate each of the individual instances of that paper being purchased over the course of the last six weeks, which is how long it has been on the market. From there, I seek a warrant for the financial information for those who have paid with cards rather than cash. Tracing purchases made with cash is far more difficult, but I'm hoping the stores have reliable surveillance footage that could show the people who made those purchases.

It's going to take some time for me to get that information, and I don't know where to go next. I come home that evening to two bowls of my favorite Christmas candy and a massive amount of cookie dough. The guys want to make Christmas cookies, hoping it will help me to cling to at least some of my happy Christmas feelings. I appreciate the effort and I do my best to let myself get distracted, but I have a hard time not thinking about these potential murders. It bothers me to my bones that I don't know who these victims are. Not only does it mean that they are left without their identity, it makes it extremely difficult for me to even start to unravel what might have happened to them.

CHAPTER NINE

M Y WARRANT REQUEST GOES THROUGH QUICKLY AND I AM PLEAS-
antly surprised the next day when the financial institutions will-
ingly turn over the details of the card numbers used to purchase
the paper. I've encountered more than my fair share of situations when
I've had to grapple with banks, credit card companies, social media platforms, and even cell phone services to try to get critical information for
investigations. Having the information they provide me allows me to
get to work narrowing down the list of customers who bought the paper.

I sit at a large table at the Sheriff's Department with the printouts of
the information spread out in front of me. Highlighter in one hand, I go
through and streamline everything until I am able to compile profiles
of the individual purchases. While I am connecting names to the credit
and debit card users, Ruth from the desk shows up at the doorway.

"Emma?" she says.

I take off the reading glasses I've just recently started using at the advice of my eye doctor to ease the tension headaches I've been getting more frequently since my attacks.

"Hey, Ruth. Did you need something?" I ask.

"There's someone here who asked to speak with you," she says.

"Me?"

"Yes. She specifically wanted to speak with you."

"Alright. I'm coming," I tell her.

Ruth walks in front of me out to the waiting area at the front of the department and I see a woman with wide eyes shifting her weight slightly back and forth like she's trying to get nervous energy out. I notice she's carrying a roll of the same silver wrapping paper I've been tracking down.

"Here she is," Ruth says, holding her hand out toward me.

"Hi," I say, extending my own hand toward the woman. "I'm Agent Griffin."

"Hello. Ashley Houston."

"What can I do for you, Ashley?" I ask.

"I heard you are looking for people who have the type of wrapping paper that was used on the box that had the heart in it at the market the other night," she says. "My aunt was one of the vendors and she told me you came by and were checking all of the booths for that specific type of wrapping paper. I have some and I wanted to let you know in case it might help you narrow things down."

"Oh," I say, a bit surprised. "Yes, actually, that does help. Would you mind coming into the back with me and telling me when and where you bought that paper? Having a signed statement about it would really help me."

"No problem," she says.

Ashley takes a few minutes to tell me about buying the paper, shows me the roll and allows me to document it, and helps me to locate her individual purchase out of the information that was given to me by the shop. Now that I have her personal information, I can easily cross-reference the other shops and confirm that she only purchased this one roll of the paper. She signs her statement and leaves the department, but her showing up has done more than just give me evidence of one person with the paper.

I have purposely been avoiding speaking publicly about this incident, including the importance of the paper. But, obviously, discussions about it have spread beyond people who were at the event the other night. This means whoever is responsible for the two packages knows we have taken note of the paper and are attempting to track it. This confirms to them that we are actively pursuing a possible case. But it could also give them more details that I want them to have. There are some circumstances that are different, but I rarely like to show my cards to a perpetrator.

The truth is, every case starts with an investigator at a disadvantage. By the time we know or at least suspect a crime has been committed, we are already several steps behind. It's my job to catch up to the perpetrator and get ahead of them. Giving away too much about an investigation, including the types of evidence that we have gathered and who we may be interested in talking to, or looking further into provides the perpetrator with information they can use to better elude my chase.

And if they are intending on continuing their string of crimes, which I can only hope this person is not, having those details allows them to modify their approach in a way that can confuse and distract investigators.

But there's nothing I can do about this particular detail now. It's gotten out that the paper is something we're looking at, so all I can do is continue to lean into it and hope it gives me something.

I spend the rest of the day continuing to narrow down the purchases of the paper. Two more women Ashley knows show up at the department to let me know they have some of the paper, allowing me to eliminate them up from the lists. I'm able to further narrow down the possibilities by the timing of the purchases. Some of the paper was bought the day after the heart was located, making it impossible that it was the paper used.

I am able to watch surveillance footage of several more of the transactions, helping me to identify purchasers who paid with cash. Late in the afternoon, I start contacting others on the list. They show me rolls of intact paper, never taken out of their packages, or ones with only small amounts used. The ones who can't produce the paper or seem to have used a considerable amount answer questions and provide evidence of where they were when the heart was found.

This isn't perfect. As has already been established, the heart was frozen prior to being wrapped up and left under the tree. I can't find any reason to think any of the people I question about owning the paper would do something like that.

I still have their names on a list and permission to contact them, my philosophy of never fully eliminating anyone without unshakable evidence intact. But I soldier on. As I am going over another set of purchases, I realize one shop had a strangely dense flurry of sales of the paper on one specific day. The other shops may have sold one or two rolls on any given day except in those instances where a single person would purchase more than one. But this shop, the quaint Trinkets and Treasures I thought was a dead-end from the moment I walked in, sold twelve rolls, all within a ten-minute span across eight transactions.

Digging into these transactions shows the people who bought them all live in the next town over, apparently within the same neighborhood. Intrigued, I do a little more research and find that the neighborhood is actually a housing complex where many students of the local college live while they are studying. I reach out to them and arrange to meet up tomorrow.

CHAPTER TEN

THE HOUSING COMPLEX IS ONE OF THOSE NEIGHBORHOODS THAT'S supposed to be sleek and ultra-modern but can easily come across as industrial instead. All the buildings look essentially the same with only small signs bearing simple names to differentiate them from each other. The buildings are arranged in a spoke pattern around a central hub consisting of a large pool, a smaller wading pool, a playground, and a green space offering grills and a picnic pavilion.

The effect is at once welcoming and somewhat creepy. I know there are a lot of people who appreciate this type of controlled, minimalist approach, but I am getting tremendous Stepford vibes out of it. At the same time, I can see how it would appeal to a certain demographic. No lawn maintenance. A central place to get together with people that doesn't require hosting them in your own home. This is the kind of place that would also have various planned events and activities for residents throughout the year, further incentivizing living here.

It would be nice for a couple just starting out or a young family. It also reminds me a lot of dorm living, making it perfect for the college students who apparently take up a good portion of the units. It's one of those units where I arrive for my first meeting of the day.

A girl who appears to be in her late teens or very early twenties opens the door in a pair of fleece pajama bottoms featuring a repeating pattern of a moose wearing a Santa hat, an oversized white sweater, and matching moose slippers. Her hair is also fully styled and she's wearing a full face of makeup. She welcomes me inside and another girl comes out of the back of the apartment wearing something similar, but with a Grinch theme. I'm getting the impression this is the current college girl aesthetic.

They show me to the living room and I sit on a pale blue couch that has a bright Christmas quilt tossed across the back. A tree stands decorated in the corner and somewhere they are burning what seems like an abundance of pine and cinnamon candles.

"I'm Presley," the girl who opened the door introduces herself. "And this is my roommate Nancy."

"Hi," I say. "I'm Special Agent Emma Griffin. I really appreciate you letting me come over and talk to you this morning. I'm not going to take up much of your time."

"It's alright," Nancy says. "We want to help if we can."

"And it's exciting to meet a badass woman police officer," Presley adds.

"I'm actually not a police officer, I'm in the FBI," I tell her.

She grins. "Even more badass."

I can't help but smile. "Thank you for that. Anyway, like I mentioned on the phone, I am leading a potential murder investigation out of Sherwood and a detail of interest that has come to my attention is a particular type of wrapping paper."

"Oh, my gosh," Nancy says. "I know what you're investigating. That heart that was found wrapped up under the Christmas tree. People were posting about it online."

Presley's hands come up to cover her mouth. "Nope. That's just...." She shakes her head hard. "No."

"That is what I'm investigating," I tell them. "The wrapping paper that was used on the package is very distinctive. I tracked all the purchases of that paper that happened in the general area since it was released and I found that multiple people in this housing complex bought the same type of paper right at the same time. I'm just curious about that."

"The silver wrapping paper?" Presley asks.

"Yes."

"I can show it to you," she says.

She gets up and walks down the hall leading off the living room. I follow after her and she leads me into her bedroom. This room is also decked out for Christmas, a strand of lights wrapped around the top of the wall and a display of snow globes arranged on the top of the dresser. I look down at them, taking in all of the little scenes inside. I notice a few of them seem to be from tourist destinations.

"Are you a collector?" I ask.

"Of what?" Presley asks from inside the closet. She peeks out and sees me standing next to the dresser. "Oh, the snow globes. Yeah. My dad has been getting them for me since I was little. He traveled a lot for work and he always used to bring me back one from the city he went to for whatever it was he was doing."

She disappears back into the closet for a second, then comes out with two rolls of the paper in her arms. One of them is still wrapped in its original plastic and the other has been used. I know from the transaction history that these are the only two rolls she bought.

"Did you find it odd that multiple people seemed to be buying the same wrapping paper at the same time? Within just a couple of minutes of each other?" I ask.

"No, not really," she says. "We were all together. It was a group of girls from this complex. We decided to go Christmas shopping together and we all just kind of fell in love with this paper. We all bought some."

Now it makes more sense that there are so many people from the same neighborhood with the paper. Just to confirm, I ask her the names of the other people she was with that day, and she rattles off the list of the other people I'm planning on speaking with this afternoon. There's one more name on my list, but it's a man, so I can assume he wasn't a part of the girls' day shopping trip.

"Are you the one who used the paper?" I ask.

Presley nods and heads back for the living room. She points out a small stack of gifts behind another wrapped in brighter-colored paper.

"I also used some for my mom's present, but I already mailed that to her," she says. "I think I have a picture of it."

She reaches for her phone, but I hold up a hand to stop her. "That's alright. Thank you for your time."

I leave that apartment and don't even have to get back in my car to get to the next. It's one building down, the ground floor unit to the left. I have a similar conversation with the girl inside, then drive to another of the sets of buildings. This apartment is on the top floor and I take the steps, much preferring to climb through the levels with the open space around me and being able to see everything over the last time I was in a stairwell.

The girl who opens this door looks almost like she forgot I was coming. After a second of staring at me blankly, she cringes.

"The FBI agent. Right. I'm so sorry. My mind is all in a thousand different places today."

We stand there for another awkward second before she blinks. "Um. Right. Come in."

She steps back and I walk past her into the apartment. After she closes the door, I extend a hand to her. "Agent Emma Griffin."

"Kylie Pearce," she says. "Nice to meet you. You can sit down. Can I get you something to drink?"

"If you have coffee, it would be amazing."

Kylie laughs. "I just finished my second-to-last semester of college. Of course, I have coffee. I was cramming so hard for finals that I half considered just giving it all up and becoming a barista with the skills I've developed."

I laugh. "A viable second option in life." I sit down and look around at her version of Christmas decorations. It's been an interesting glimpse into these girls' lives seeing how they surround themselves with holiday cheer while they are on their own. Presley and Nancy were a bit scattered. The girl in the second apartment, Helen Mar, was something I'd call eclectic. It looked like she'd taken something from every member of her family and brought it with her so she could have them with her for the holidays. All the different aesthetics and eras crashed together into one explosion of Christmas. Now I have Kylie's very classic approach.

This is the kind of apartment I wouldn't be surprised to find out was partially decorated during a visit from her parents. She hasn't gone quite as far along the spectrum as Nancy and Presley in terms of her outfit, but she also isn't nearly as put together as her holiday décor.

"I'm going to do my best not to take up too much of your time. I know you're probably looking forward to getting some high quality doing nothing time in since your semester just ended."

She rolls her eyes. "If only. I'm working during the break. Administrative assistant at the school to supplement my financial aid package. Yay."

She gives a meager celebratory dance and I laugh.

"Nothing wrong with that. And it looks fantastic on your resume. Anyway, I mentioned over the phone I'm investigating a potential murder case in Sherwood."

"You did mention that. That's horrible. What happened?" she asks.

"Well, that's what I'm trying to find out. One of the elements of the case I'm focusing on has to do with silver wrapping paper. It's a very specific pattern and I tracked every person who purchased it in the stores around here."

"I did buy some silver wrapping paper while I was shopping with a bunch of the other girls who live around here. There are a lot of us," she says.

"I noticed that," I say. "Is that something the school facilitates, or is it just that it's convenient to the campus, so everyone gravitates here?"

"Well, they have ads in the student life center and during the orientation week at the beginning of each year they set up an information booth to talk about this place. They offer special rates for students, and it's pretty close to campus, so it's pretty popular." She gives me a questioning look as she comes back into the room with coffee.

"Is there something about the wrapping paper I should know about? We all thought it was really pretty and the owner of the shop said it was limited edition, so we got it."

"Have you used any of it?" I ask.

"I used all of it," Kylie says. "I'm not going to get a chance to go home for Christmas this year, so I sent my family their gifts a few days ago. I ended up using the whole roll of that paper plus a little bit of some others I had lying around. I might have some scraps left. I keep the little bits for art projects. I make cards with them and stuff. Want me to look?"

Without waiting for me to answer, she goes to a closet in the hallway and pulls down a large plastic storage box. When she opens it I see it's full of the little bits of wrapping paper and tissue left behind after wrapping presents. Some have torn edges like they were actually salvaged from when somebody tore into a gift. Even from the distance I can see bits of paper from every major holiday, birthdays, retirements, and other events. It seems like Kylie gathers these little bits from every occasion she can, and likely accepts some from people when they have them on hand as well.

She brings the box over to the coffee table and sits down on her knees next to it so she can sift through all the remnants. She pulls one out and examines it, puts it back in, and selects another. She examines it for a second, then holds it out to me.

"There we go. I knew I had some of it."

I take the piece of paper she holds out to me even though seeing a little sliver of it doesn't really tell me much of anything.

"Okay. The girls you went shopping with. Do you share any of the same classes?"

"I have a couple with Presley and others with Helen. I've had some with Skylar, she was on the trip with us, too. The others I don't have any classes with, I just know them from around the complex. We all end up hanging out around the pool or doing things at the clubhouse if we're not studying, so we've gotten pretty close," she tells me.

"That's great. The friends you make in college are really some of the most important friends you'll ever have. My two best friends in college are still my best friends. And now they have a baby and are getting married." As I stop speaking I hear the silent reverberation of the words I just said come back at me from the blank look on Kylie's face. I cringe. "Wow. I don't think I have ever sounded so old in my entire life."

Kylie laughs. "It was kind of afternoon special of you. But I can dig it."

I raise an eyebrow at her. "You can dig it? Now who's the old one?"

"Hey, linguistics are fluid. They are constantly adaptable to those using them and frequently come back into fashion as young people reclaim the passage of time and honor the people who came before them." She looks very serious for a second, then grins. "Or so says my English professor from freshman year."

"That was impressive. I was about to say you should meet my friend Xavier. He would have eaten that up. Or he would have argued with you using a similar approach. It would be highly unlikely most people would be able to follow him either way, so equally delightful," I say. "Alright. I have a few more people to talk to around here, so I'm going to go. Thank you for the coffee," I take the final swig from my mug, "and for showing me that."

"Sure. If you're going to talk to Helen, Nancy, and Presley, they are in that direction," she says, pointing toward the set of buildings I just came from. "Molly lives in the building next door to here. She lives in a single like me. And Cory and Lila live together in the building directly across from the playground. It's easy to get turned around in here. Everything looks exactly alike if you're just looking at the buildings. I tried to go into the wrong apartment a few times when I first moved in."

"Great. Thanks." I start toward the door, then stop and check the name of the last person I was planning to talk to. "How about Kade Murray?"

She frowns. "Kade Murray?".

"Yeah. Do you know him?" I ask.

She shakes her head. "No. Not that I know of. Is he another student?"

I happen to know by surveillance footage Kade Murray is somewhere around middle aged. That doesn't automatically discount the possibility that he goes to her school considering how many more adults are going to college later in life these days, but I don't think that's the situation here. Even those adults who do make those choices rarely decide to pack up and head to the nearest college-living neighborhood to hunker down with their fellow students.

"I don't think so," I say. "But he lives somewhere around here. The Triangle Building?"

"Oh. Yeah. That one is actually at the very front of the complex. Paradoxically, not a triangle."

This is a moment when I'm glad Xavier is at home. I don't need to watch this girl crumble under his scathing explanation of how she used a word incorrectly. He thinks he's being helpful. He's not.

"Hmmm. Maybe it was named for a Mr. Triangle?"

And this is a moment when the silence around me is almost aching for one of Sam's horrifically bad jokes. This one would definitely have something to do with him just "being obtuse."

"I don't know."

"Alright. Well, congratulations on your semester and I hope you can at least still enjoy some of your holiday season even though you're working." I look at a carefully constructed display of Christmas village houses and snow globes arranged on a table against the wall. "Looks like you're all ready for it."

She nods. "After we went shopping, all of us helped each other decorate for Christmas. Most of us aren't able to go home this year, so we're trying to kind of keep each other's spirits up. We've been each other's dates to a lot of holiday parties already. And we're having one here at the complex next week. It's not quite the same as being able to wake up to family on Christmas morning or have that leftovers dinner your mom always makes the day after, but it's better than just riding it out alone."

I don't know if I should say 'that's the spirit' or not. It was at once cheerful and the saddest interpretation of the holiday season during young adult years I've ever heard. I wave and head out, following her directions to the next apartment.

Now that I know the girls helped each other decorate, I'm not as surprised by the pristine, sparkling white decorations filling the home of Molly Garson. She isn't as welcoming as the other girls have been. I wouldn't say Helen was warm and friendly, but she at least invited me inside as soon as she opened the door and chatted with me a bit about school and her plans for the holidays. There just wasn't a lot of emotion and excitement in our interaction.

Molly, on the other hand, seems affronted by my mere presence. Rather than opening the door all the way, she opens it just enough to make her face and one shoulder visible, stuffing her foot into the gap to give herself control over it opening any further.

"Are you the cop?" she asks.

"Not a police officer," I say for the second time today. "FBI. Agent Griffin. We spoke on the phone earlier."

"Yeah."

It's just a word. Not really an acknowledgement or an answer. Just a sound.

"Like I mentioned, I need to talk to you about a case I'm investigating. Is now a good time?" I ask.

Learning to be patient with people like this and not immediately lash out the way I want to is one of those aspects of the job I've been trying to work on over the last few years. Being back in Sherwood with Sam has certainly softened me in a lot of ways, but at my core I'm still the person I've always been. And that person is already tired of this girl's shit.

"Depends on what you want to talk about," Molly says. "I didn't kill anybody."

"I didn't mention anybody getting killed," I say.

"Yeah, but why else would the Feds come knocking around here? Somebody has to be dead for somebody calling themselves 'Agent' to show up at my house. You people aren't going to come for a bunch of kids getting drunk and acting stupid, or some stupid rumor drama at the college."

"What kind of stupid rumor drama?" I ask.

"What is it you want to talk about? Because I don't like feeling like you think I did something and it's seeming to me like it's about to be a bad time for talking," she says.

"How about we go inside?" I ask.

"We can talk right here," she counters. She looks around like she's indicating all the apartments in the building. "All of us here are like family. Anything you need to say to me, you can say it so they can hear."

She laughs at this point, but it's not the kind of laugh I like hearing in a conversation.

"Is there a reason you're being hostile?" I ask.

Like it almost always does with someone who is pushing back against me for no reason other than not liking my shield, the question takes Molly aback. She wasn't expecting that kind of reaction from me and now isn't sure how to respond. She takes a beat, then pulls herself back together. She hasn't lost any of the sharpness, but now she knows she's not impressing me and the sass is tempered.

"I didn't do anything wrong and I have a federal agent questioning me," she says. "That's enough to piss anyone off."

"First, I'm not questioning you. That's a very different thing and you would be very aware of it if it were happening to you. I'm just here asking you a few questions because I'm sifting through the details of this case and trying to eliminate details as extraneous. It's standard practice. Happens in just about every investigation. Second, I've spoken with several other people and none of them have had an issue with it. You're the only one who seems offended just by the fact that I'm standing here. Which makes me wonder what is causing you to have a completely different reaction than everyone else."

"Maybe they're just naturally more cooperative than I am," she says.

"Then consider this a personal growth moment. It will look good on your next essay. You were right. I'm here because we discovered some body parts that are very likely from a murder. It happened a few days ago in a town called Sherwood. Are you familiar with it?" I ask.

"Are you here about the guy who got his heart cut out and put under a Christmas tree?" she asks.

"You heard about the case," I say, taking note of the fact that she referenced the victim as a 'guy' when the detail of the heart belonging to a male is something that hasn't yet been released to the public.

"Yeah. I didn't realize they'd get the FBI on it. Aren't there police in this Sherwood place?"

"Yes."

She rolls her eyes and shifts her weight. "Look. I haven't been to Sherwood. I don't know how my name came up in this, but tell me how to get it out of it, because I'm not interested in being wrapped up in some gruesome shit I have nothing to do with."

"I hear you went shopping with several other girls from around the complex recently," I say.

"I don't know if I'd say we went shopping together. It's not like we wore matching outfits and piled up in the same car to go to the mall. I mean, they might have, but I was up at the caverns that day. I was wandering around the shops and ran into them," she says.

"It doesn't sound like you are very friendly with them," I say.

"We hang out when there's a reason to, but we don't have a lot in common."

"Were you at the caverns alone that day?"

"No. I was with my boyfriend," she says.

"Do you remember buying silver wrapping paper?" I ask.

"Silver wrapping paper?" she asks with an incredulous scoff. "What kind of questions are these? Did a dude get his heart cut out because he bought gold bows and someone doesn't appreciate mixing precious metals?"

"Just as a reminder, someone really did die, and I am trying to find out why and who caused it. I'm just asking for a little bit of cooperation. I know you bought the wrapping paper at Trinkets and Treasures. What did you do with it?" I ask.

"I don't remember buying any wrapping paper that day," she says.

"There's a record for every transaction that's made in the store and the owner can isolate just the transactions that involve purchasing a specific item. When she searched for that wrapping paper and I reviewed the financial information, it showed your debit card was used to purchase two rolls of the paper within a five-minute window of the other girls purchasing the same paper."

The surveillance camera in the little store is designed to take photos at regular intervals every three seconds at normal times and only changing over to video if it is triggered by the operator of the system. Most of the girls were captured in these staggered photos, but Molly and one other girl weren't in them. They must have moved in and out of frame quickly enough to miss being captured. That means I can't tell her I saw her make the purchase of the paper, but the financial record is enough. I was put off by the seemingly archaic technology used by the owner, but I am pleasantly surprised by how much information they were actually able to give me about the transactions.

"I don't know what to tell you, but I don't remember buying anything at that store. I don't even celebrate Christmas. Not in the authentic sense, anyway."

I'm not sure what that means, considering wrapping things with shiny paper and stuffing them under a festooned tree or into giant socks isn't exactly following a star through the desert to a stable.

A couple of years after the first Christmas I spent with Xavier I got a package in the mail in August that was wrapped in brown paper stamped with images of farm animals and shepherd hooks. "Merry Christmas" was written across the front.

Considering my career path and the types of people I have come across during said career, I was not thrilled about the prospect of opening it. But the snow globe inside, a scene of several little snowmen smiling happily together on a tree-dotted hill, was a far more delightful gift than the hand I once received in a box on the porch. Inside was a card wishing me a merry Christmas and it was signed Xavier. When I asked him about it, he explained that according to scholars, following the wording of scripture would have placed the birth of Christ in August. Interpretations of the history of the Wise Men also mean it would have likely taken two years for them to make the journey that is often portrayed as just one night. Therefore, this was my official Christmas gift for two years before. My authentic Christmas experience, "without the heavy sacrilegious implications."

This from the man who wears Santa Claus pajamas and drinks eggnog like it's a food group for one month out of the year. To put it into his words, "And therein lies the difference between authenticity and tradition."

I told him I'm good with just sticking to tradition, but after that I've been a bit wary of people referencing their authentic observations of just about anything.

"You seem to have a considerable amount of Christmas decorations for someone who doesn't celebrate the holiday," I point out, nodding into the small sliver of space I can see between the door frame and the door.

She rolls her eyes. "The others did that. They think it's cute."

No further explanation. I don't particularly want more.

"I suggest you either remember that paper and what you did with it, or get in touch with your banking institution to report a very isolated fraudulent charge, because the computer records clearly show the purchase. I'll be checking back in with you."

I step away from the door and Molly slams it without another word.

Shaking my head, I continue on. My next stop is the outlier. Kade Murray, the only male and about twice the age of the others who purchased the wrapping paper at the same time. On the surface, it seems very strange, but I'm trying to keep my mind as open as possible. Assumptions are poison to an investigation. Recognizing and understanding the difference between assumption and instinct is a critical skill for anyone who investigates.

This open-mindedness slips just a little when I knock on Murray's door and there's no answer. I spoke to him earlier this morning and he said he would be available today. I knock again and there's still silence, but on my third knock I hear a muffled voice coming from inside telling me he's on his way. The door opens and Kade Murray looks out through the sides of the towel that hangs down over his face from where it's draped over his head. Locks of wet hair cling to his forehead.

Another towel held around his hips with one hand and a lot of confidence make up the entirety of the rest of his outfit.

"Sorry, I was in the shower," he says. "Can I help you?"

"Agent Emma Griffin," I tell him. "We spoke earlier."

"Did we?" he asks. Something seems to click and his eyes widen briefly. "That's right. We did. I'm sorry. Um." He glances behind him, then back at me. "Can you give me just a minute?"

"Sure."

He disappears into the apartment again. I'm sure he's going to get dressed, but I couldn't help but notice that despite his wet hair, there were no water droplets on his exposed chest, stomach, or arms.

Kade comes back to the door, but instead of letting me in the apartment, he steps out with me.

"Mind if we talk while I check my mail?" he asks. "I'm expecting some important papers."

Nothing like getting rejected from entering people's homes twice in a row. But I can't force my way in and there's really no reason to anyway. I'm just here to find out about the paper.

"Sure," I respond again.

He grins and we walk down the cement steps toward the bank of mailboxes positioned a few dozen yards from the entrance to the breezeway.

"You didn't give me a lot of details when we talked earlier," he says. "You just said there were a few questions you wanted to ask me pertaining to an investigation. What's going on? I have to admit, you have me a little spooked."

"Is there a reason you should be spooked?" I ask.

He looks at me sideways and forces a laugh. "That's a good tactic, there."

"Not a tactic. Just a question," I say.

"No. I mean. It's just I've never had an FBI agent want to talk to me before. I don't even like it if a cop pulls me over because my taillight's out. I don't do great with pressure. Leave me in a stew room long enough and I'd probably confess to being the shooter on the grassy knoll."

"Bit of a throwback reference, there," I say, mirroring the structure of his earlier comment to both put him at ease with the familiarity and ensure he knows I'm paying close attention to what he's saying.

It's not always the words you choose to say that make the most difference in how someone responds in a conversation. It's the way you say them. It's a basic concept, but one that many people forget.

"Well, you don't have to worry. I'm not here for that. I'm curious about a particular roll of wrapping paper you bought," I say.

The more I say that today, the more ridiculous I feel. There are some pieces of evidence that are sharp and compelling, that drive an investigation forward. I've hunted witnesses and suspects based on blood spray, on damning video evidence, on stumbling words that slip out and tell secrets. And now I'm tracking down people who bought wrapping paper a few weeks before Christmas.

I have to keep reminding myself of the heart nested in the tissue paper, the lungs from a second person. Two human beings without names or faces. People reduced down to a single organ and a disturbing gift tag that references its function but doesn't give any meaning.

Kade opens his mailbox with a tiny key dangling from his ring and pulls out a stick of envelopes and fliers.

"Wrapping paper?"

He doesn't look up. He's too invested in sifting through the mail apparently in search of the papers he mentioned.

"You bought it at Trinkets and Treasures," I say.

"Oh. Near the caverns. Yeah, I remember that." He lets out a short laugh that sounds almost shocked. "Wow. How did you know that? I guess Big Brother really is watching."

"Not exactly. I used purchase records. The ones from the store show exactly when you bought it," I say.

"I suppose that isn't quite as oppressive. But it still smacks of our corporate overlords trying to take over our lives," he says.

I really want to think he's kidding. I genuinely want to believe this man just has the kind of sense of humor that doesn't really fall into place when it's supposed to but is coming from a good place. There's still the jaded bit of the back of my mind that believes he doesn't think birds are real and worries about tipping off the edge of the planet if he isn't careful.

"Well, if it makes you feel better, I don't think the type of wrapping paper you choose is of drastically high interest to the powers that be," I say.

"Except," he gestures up and down my body with the handful of mail. "You're here."

He's got me there.

"I'm more interested in what happened to the paper after you bought it," I say.

"It's still sitting in my closet," he says. "I've been procrastinating with my shopping this year and haven't gotten around to wrapping anything."

"Fair enough. Can you show it to me when we get back to your apartment?"

"I guess," he says.

"What brought you up to the caverns that day?" I ask.

"I go up there all the time," he says. "I've been going since I was a kid."

"Oh, so you're from around here," I say.

"Yep."

"These apartments don't look like they've been around very long. Any reason you decided to move into them?" I ask.

He gives me a smirk. "What you're actually asking is why I live in a neighborhood with a bunch of college kids."

"Now that you mention it, I am a bit curious as to why your purchase came right at the time that seven girls who live in this neighborhood also made purchases."

"If you expand your search, I bet you'll find that a lot more from this complex than just those seven were shopping in that place and the others around it that day. It's a popular place to shop, especially at this time of year. They have special shopping events and stuff all the time during the holidays," he says. "It's always packed."

"Were they having one of those special days when you bought the paper?" I ask.

"Probably. I don't know for sure. Like I said, I go up to the caverns all the time. I only stopped by the shops because I was with… some people, and they wanted to look around."

I notice the little jag in the flow of his speech. It's almost like he rethought what he was going to say when he mentioned being there with other people. We get to the door and he takes hold of the doorknob, but puts his body in between me and the entrance as he turns to smile at me.

"Did I answer everything you need to know?" he asks.

"Other than showing me that paper," I say.

"Right." He hesitates. "Alright, come in."

He opens the door and I step into the apartment. I don't know what I was expecting, but the fact that it's a perfectly normal, a bit disheveled but clean and comfortable apartment, feels a little like a letdown. There's a reason he was so hesitant about letting me inside and I automatically assumed it was something to do with his apartment. But it looks like that wasn't the case.

"Just wait here," he says. "You can sit down. I'll be right back."

He goes down the hallway and I hear a door open and close. Apparently, he is secretive about more than just his living room. Feeling odd just standing there in the middle of the living room, I walk over to the couch and sit down. It takes a few minutes for him to come back, but I don't see anything in his hands.

"Did you lose it?" I ask.

Kade gives me a sheepish expression I think is meant to look regretful. "It turns out I left it at someone's house."

"Who?" I ask.

"I'd rather not say. It's kind of a messy situation," he says.

"Speaking of which, you never told me why you decided to come live in this housing complex," I say.

He sighs. "When my soon-to-be ex-wife kicked me out, this was the first place I found with availability and cheap enough rent for me to get the down payment, last month, and security deposit on really short notice."

"I still need to know who has that roll."

"My girlfriend," he says. "The reason for the soon-to-be ex."

He is locking up even more. I know I'm not going to get anything else about his girlfriend out of him, but I have a good feeling I don't really need that information from him. Sometimes I have to temper myself and tread more carefully to prevent people from fully blocking me out rather than staying at least somewhat open to the possibility of talking to me again. It isn't always easy for me.

It's rarely easy for me.

"Okay. Thanks for your time."

"You might be able to find the other roll, though," he says.

I pause, processing what he just said. "The other roll?"

"Yeah. The two transactions. I bought two rolls. The other one wasn't for me. One of the girls who lives around here saw me in there, but the others were leaving, so she asked if I'd grab one for her and she'd hit me back."

"Which girl?" I ask.

His face twists up a bit like he's thinking hard to pull the information forward, but he shakes his head.

"I can't remember her name. I don't really hang out with them. Not exactly my crowd, if you know what I mean. I have a hard enough time. I don't need to be the creeper who is around all the young girls all the time. But around here, you run into your neighbors often enough you get familiar with them," he tells me.

"But you must have dropped it off with her and gotten your money back."

"Nah. I left it outside the door for her to pick up and she was supposed to send me money over the phone, but she hasn't yet."

"And it was two transactions?" I ask.

"Yeah. Not too far apart. Just a few minutes."

"Thanks. I'll check into it. I appreciate your cooperation."

He says something as I'm leaving, but I'm not paying attention. There are too many other thoughts going through my head. I have to force myself to file them away and get through one more interview.

I make my way to the apartment where the last two girls of the group live together. They show me one still-wrapped roll of the paper and two partial rolls, along with a stack of gifts. I ask them about their shopping experience and they give me an explanation much like the one I heard from Kylie, Nancy, and Presley. They decided to spend the day together and went shopping at a few places. That particular boutique wasn't their destination, it was just one of the places where they stopped among many others.

I've sat on enough couches today, so I'm up walking around their living room when the nativity scene they have sitting on an end table catches my attention. It looks handcrafted and very old. It stands in stark contrast to the collection of reindeer statues, snow globes, and oversized glitter ball ornaments arranged on the other end table. It's like each of the roommates got one of the tables and decorated it with their own view of the holiday. Since these are college students, however, I'm going to take a dip back into my own early higher education days and assume there's some sort of statement going on about the duplicity of the holiday season and how far society has divided, or something along those lines.

I touch the top of one of the globes. The glass feels cold against my fingertips, reminding me of the thick cardboard encasing the unknown woman's lungs. The way Molly talked about running into the girls rather than being with them—and how they aren't close because they don't have anything in common, going against what Kylie told me—is still sticking in the back of my mind.

"Who all was together that day?" I ask. "The ones who went from place to place together shopping."

"Presley, Kylie, and Nancy," Lila says.

"And Helen," Cory adds.

"How about Molly Garson?" I ask.

"She was there," Cory confirms.

"Not for the whole time, though," Lila says. "She didn't ride with us."

"That's right. She met up with us later in the day. She said she had plans first, but would meet us down in that area," Cory explains.

"So, it was the plan for her to come along with you?" I ask.

"Yeah," Cory replies. "At least, that's what it sounded like to us. I'm not sure if all the others knew she was going to meet us. She doesn't really know Presley or Helen. We kind of all end up together at different events and activities and things, though."

"How about Kade Murray? He lives at the Triangle building out front. Does he end up at the same kinds of activities and events as you, too?" I ask.

"Sometimes," Lila shrugs. "He doesn't come hang out with us or anything, but we've talked a few times. He's a nice guy."

"Did you see him at the shop when you were buying the paper?" I ask.

They both shake their heads. "No."

"It was getting pretty busy when we were leaving, though. I guess he could have come in without me noticing," Cory says.

"Yeah," Lila agrees.

"Have either of you ever been to Sherwood?" I ask.

"I have," Lila volunteers. "You have, too, Cory. Remember? That market the other day."

"Oh, that was Sherwood? I didn't know where exactly we'd ended up." Her eyes snap to me. "Is that what this is about? That heart?"

"I didn't even think about that," Lila said. She groans, sounding vaguely ill. "We got there right as it was starting up and left two hours or so later. We weren't even there when all that was going on. But I heard about it on the news the next morning. I couldn't believe it. We walked by that tree a dozen times while we were there. It makes me sick to my stomach to think there was a human heart wrapped up in a box right there and I just walked by it without knowing."

"Did you see the silver box sitting there?" I ask.

She shakes her head. "No. I didn't notice."

"So you don't know if it was there when you were there?" I ask.

"No. I'm sorry. I wish I could help more," she says.

"It's alright. You can only tell me what you know. I'm just trying to narrow down the window of when that package was put under the tree. I appreciate you letting me know you were there that night."

"If I'd realized that's what you were asking us about, I would have told you earlier. I wasn't trying to hide it or anything."

"I know. The things you think will come to mind don't always do. Don't worry about it. Anything you can think of that you might want to tell me about that night? Anything you saw or heard that seemed strange to you then, or that seems strange to you now that you look back on it?" I ask.

The girls look at each other again. It's the kind of look that people who have gone beyond just close friends to a bonded place where they feel secure in each other. Like they store some of their own thoughts and memories in the other's brain. That's what they're doing now, poking around in the information they have outsourced to the other to see if there's anything about the market in Sherwood that could mean anything.

"I can't think of anything," Lila says.

"There was that one woman we saw," Cory says. "Remember? You said you thought she was weird."

"What woman?" I ask.

"I don't even know. Honestly, it was probably nothing. Just us being bitchy," Lila says.

"Honestly, sometimes just being bitchy is completely valid," I say. "That's when you notice things that other people might just dismiss."

"There was this woman," Cory starts. "She was walking around by herself like she was looking for someone or something. She had a bunch of stuff in her hands. I didn't see what all of it was, but I know there was a big bag and a few smaller things. She went over toward the tree and was there for a while, then walked away. Then when we went by the tree again a little later, she was there again. Just kind of standing near the platform."

"But then those people came up and took a picture with her."

"That's right," Cory says. "They just walked up to her, got a picture, and walked away. Then she went back to leaning on the platform. She had at least one of her bags with her."

"What did she look like? Do you have any idea who she was?" I ask.

"A definite adult, but young. Like around your age, maybe a couple years younger. Very dark hair."

I can tell she's dancing around the idea of making an assumption about the woman's ethnicity. That's not new to me. Especially when it is a younger person doing the describing, they feel there's a fine line they feel like they're walking, and they don't want to even come close to crossing it. Then there are the people who throw themselves whole-heartedly into giving all those details. That's a whole different situation.

But even when a possible witness is not saying anything, they are telling me something. The fact that Cory and Lila are doing their best not to say the wrong thing tells me most likely this woman was not white.

"What else can you tell me about her?" I ask.

"She was wearing a lot of pink," Cory says. "Like… a lot of pink. Maybe that's why the people wanted to take a picture with her. I don't know who she was, but later we saw her in the vendor area."

CHAPTER ELEVEN

"There's something going on between Molly and Kade. Neither of them would say it, but they both danced around it. Molly mentioned that she was there with her boyfriend, but she had just told the others that she had some plans and would meet them. There's apparently a disconnect over how good of friends any of them really are with each other, but if she is close enough with them to agree to meet them there for some shopping, why wouldn't she mention her boyfriend to them unless it's someone she wouldn't want them to know about?

"And who is the ideal candidate for a boyfriend a girl in college wouldn't want the other girls around her to know about but a married man almost twice her age? Kade was really careful with what he said about who he was with at the caverns, but then later admitted he has a girlfriend who is the reason he is getting divorced. And both were very hesitant about me going into their apartments. Molly flat out refused. She was a lot more resistant to me than Kade was, but he didn't want to let me in, either. When he finally did, he was really insistent about me staying right there in the living room," I say. "He didn't even want to answer the door. He faked being in the shower because he took so long to answer and I wouldn't give up."

"Do you think he was hiding something?" Sam asks.

"I don't know if it was a matter of him hiding something, or her hiding anything for that matter, or just wanting to keep as much distance as they could. But I'm still curious about the discrepancy in the transactions. His financial information only shows up one time. But he says he made two transactions. And Molly says she didn't buy anything, but her information shows up."

"Could you tell what she was wearing?" Dean asks.

I frown. "What she was wearing?"

"Yeah. Did she look like the kind of girl to carry a purse? Or clothes with a lot of pockets?" he asks.

"Are you trying to decide if her personal aesthetic matches the silver wrapping paper?" Sam asks. "That way lies madness, my friend."

"No," I say, shaking my head. "He's wondering if she might not have been carrying her own stuff."

"Exactly," Dean says. "If they were going through the caverns, they might have also decided to go down the hiking trails that are right there before going to the shops. That's a lot of wandering around carrying things if she doesn't have a purse or pockets, or if she just didn't want to carry a bag. She could have handed them off to her boyfriend to carry."

"And he would have put them in his pocket with his own cards," I say. "He could have just accidentally grabbed her card and used it. That explains that discrepancy, but it still leaves me with the question of who asked him to buy the other roll. If it was one of the girls I already spoke with and who had bought their own paper, someone lied to me. I asked each one of them what they did with the paper and they each either showed me the unused paper or told me how it was used. But obviously, those are not the only girls living in this complex. It's entirely possible there was another one there who asked him to buy the paper for her. Either way, there is an unaccounted-for roll of this paper somewhere."

"I think you might need to take a step back from the paper," Sam says gently. "I don't really see how this gets us any closer to finding the killer. If this is murder, that is. We're spending a lot of time on some pretty minor details and we don't even have anything concrete."

I let out a long breath and rake my fingers back through my hair. "I think you're right. It seemed a good lead, but now I feel like I'm off in some weird direction."

"So, what now?" Dean asks.

Almost as though on command, the front door opens and Xavier walks in. He's grinning from ear to ear and carrying a corndog nearly as tall as he is. It's made of plush yarn, and I can only guess it's another gift from Cupcake.

"Actually, two of the girls did share something interesting with me. Apparently, they took a little road trip and came to the market the other night. They said they got here when it opened and were only there for a couple of hours. They were gone well before anything happened with the package. But, one of them remembered noticing a fairly unusual woman near the tree a couple of times while they were there."

"An unusual woman?" Sam asks. "What did they mean by that?"

"They described her as around my age and wearing a lot of pink," I say.

"Xavier's yarn woman?" Dean asks.

"Sounds like her. They said she was just kind of standing around the tree, near the platform, and that a couple of people came up and took pictures with her," I say.

Xavier narrows his eyes at me angrily. "Cupcake didn't have anything to do with this. You can't possibly be thinking about accusing her. What reason would she have to do this?"

"That's always the question we have about any perp," I point out.

"She wouldn't…"

"X, calm down," Dean says, detecting the changes happening in him as he starts to spiral toward panic.

"I'm not saying I think she did anything," I say. "What I mean is, they noticed she was taking pictures with people. And neither of them reported seeing the silver package there any of the times they apparently saw Cupcake."

"So, it wasn't there at the beginning of the event," Dean says.

"Or it was there, and they just didn't notice it because they were too busy noticing Cupcake," Sam offers.

"We asked people for pictures and video, but we got a lot from right around the time of the illumination. We know the box was there then. What we need to know is when it was put there. If Cory and Lila noticed a couple of people taking pictures with Cupcake, then maybe other people did, too," I say.

"I wouldn't be surprised," Dean says. "You should see how many followers this woman has. As soon as she posts anything, there are tons of people making comments. I'm actually really surprised she didn't say anything about doing the market. Her fans would have swarmed the place."

"That's why she didn't say anything," Xavier says. "She told me she gets overwhelmed by all the attention sometimes. When she first got started, she mostly posted for her own amusement. But before she knew it, she just shot into the public eye. She says sometimes she misses just being able to do a little market and talk to people who aren't there just to specifically see her."

I nod. "I can imagine that's pretty tough. I'm barely a public figure in this town and I… do not envy her."

"She told me it feels like going to markets and things has now become more about her than about what she makes. So when she saw the market in Sherwood, she thought it would be the perfect opportunity to just go without it being a big deal. But she does appreciate her fans, and she isn't just going to run away if someone asks for her picture. That way she still gets to spend time with her fans without having people lined up around the block to see her."

"Do you think there might have been other fans there that night?" I ask.

"It's likely," he says.

"We need them," I say. "Every picture we can find."

"Look at her social media," Xavier says. "When people take pictures with her, they tag her. They'll all show up under her profiles."

"Can you pull it up for me?"

He nods and takes out his phone, tapping through a few commands and then handing the phone over to me. I scroll through the most recent images until I see a series of pictures with her near the platform of the tree. In some of them I can clearly see that the package wasn't there. In others, the people are positioned in such a way that they block the gift display all together. By the amount of light and some of the details in the background I can tell that the time has shifted in the pictures. They weren't all taken in sequence, which means they cover a wider span.

"Do you think it's possible there are more?" I ask. "Is there a way to search for them other than her being tagged in them?"

"She could ask for them," Xavier says. "Have her put out a call for any pictures and video from that night that she is in and see what comes up."

"Do it."

Xavier takes his phone back and his fingers fly across the buttons. I look over at Dean and Sam. "If she can get us pictures of the whole time she was near the tree and we can confirm the silver gift wasn't there during that time, we can further narrow down the timeline of when it showed up. Other people were taking very specific pictures of their family and friends positioned in any random spaces. The pictures of Cupcake were taken because she was standing there. They are going to cover much more of the area and the time."

"Did you live in a dorm when you were in college, Emma?" Dean asks.

"A dorm?" I ask.

"Yeah. I was just thinking about all those people from the college living in the same neighborhood and what that must be like. I didn't exactly have the usual college experience, so I wonder about what other people experienced," he says.

"I lived in the dorm for a little bit at the first school I went to in Richmond, but after I changed schools I lived in the house my father bought. The same one he lives in now. I don't really know that I'm the one to talk to about the dorm experience. I didn't really spend a lot of time in it. I was at the library or at a friend's apartment most of the time," I say.

"Well, I lived in the dorm when I was in college," Sam says. "And it was an awesome experience."

It makes me feel ridiculous to even think it so I don't say it, but I don't want to hear Sam talking about that time of his life. That was during the years after I told him I couldn't be in his life anymore when I tried to live the life I thought I was supposed to, the one that didn't include him. At the time, I thought I was doing the right thing. I thought I was making the decision that was going to be the best for both of us.

For me it was going to mean being able to devote myself completely to the Bureau. I'd be able to put my gun on my hip and go into even the most dangerous circumstances without a second thought. I wouldn't hesitate because Sam's face crossed my mind. I wouldn't think about the fact that I could leave him a widower or that I was neglecting him and our marriage when I was thinking of nothing but the case that was in front of me. But I also wouldn't have to worry that I wasn't giving my everything to the cases I was investigating because I was thinking about him.

And for him it would mean releasing him so he could find the kind of woman who would be able to do that for him. I wanted him to be happy then as much as I want him to be happy now. I knew I could make him happy. But I didn't believe then that I could make him happy and be a good agent. I would have to sacrifice something. I felt like the Bureau was calling me. It was my birthright. I'd lost my mother and believed I'd lost my father. I needed to fight back in the only way I thought I had the power to fight. Behind a shield.

It meant years of us being apart. It means years of his life happening without me. I know it happened. I know there were other women during that time. I know he has memories that I'm nowhere near. He's entitled to them and I don't begrudge him any of them. But that doesn't mean I enjoy facing them.

"I didn't go to a four-year school," Dean says. "I went straight into the military. After I was discharged because of my injury, I went to community college to give myself some cred when starting my private investigation career. Mine definitely didn't have housing like that."

He sounds wistful talking about his brief time in college.

"Have you ever considered going back to school?"

"No. It wasn't exactly the experience most people think about when it comes to college, but it was fine. It was what I had. And, honestly, it wasn't ever going to be the typical college experience. I was already older than the students starting, and I was very focused on getting my career going. Even if living in a dorm had been an option for me, I don't think I would have gotten the whole experience out of it. I wouldn't have gone out partying. I wouldn't have let myself be in that place. Not then."

"I'm not just talking about the dorm," I say. "I mean you were saying you didn't go to a four-year school and you were only really at the community college to make yourself look good in your new career. You're well-established in your career now, obviously. Have you thought about going back and studying something else?"

"There are some things I wish I had taken when I was in school just because they fascinate me. Maybe one day I'll do some online classes. Or maybe I'll just do a deep dive into Xavier's library. I'm sure I'll find all kinds of things in there. For all I know I could find some first editions or some primary resources for historic events," Dean says.

I laugh. "That's very possible."

Xavier comes over. "She's going to make a video. See what she can get people to send in."

"Fantastic."

CHAPTER TWELVE

Them

VISITING THE ELABORATE CHRISTMAS DISPLAY AT THE MALL WAS deeply nostalgic for me. Every year as soon as the decorations started going up, I wanted to go and explore the beautiful world they created. It was easy to trace back. When I was a child, going to the mall was one of my family's steadfast traditions. No matter what else we did during the season, no matter what other plans we had in place to get the holidays started or to celebrate, visits to the mall were non-negotiable.

When it was time to visit Santa, we'd walk slowly along the corridors of the mall, looking through the windows at the displays inside. I would gaze at everything, not wanting to miss a single one of the special new things that had shown up just for the holiday season, wondering what I should add to my list. My mother always encouraged me to make multiple copies of the list. She told me it was an important lesson for life. To have a backup. I needed to make more than one copy just in case Santa lost the one I gave him or because they needed to reference it to make sure the gifts from my parents didn't overlap with what was going to appear under the tree Christmas Eve.

I never did it. I felt absolute confidence and security in those visits to Santa. While other children fidgeted and got restless when they were waiting in line for their turn, I stood there calmly, going over exactly what I wanted to say to him. After all, he was a very busy man. There were a lot of people who wanted to see him and who were going to be telling him things. I needed to make sure I was clear and concise so that he would retain what I said. And when it was my turn, I sat on his lap and talked to him in full seriousness, walking away with unshakable belief in my heart that I had just touched magic.

It was so real to me. It wasn't just about the gifts. I wasn't just thinking about Santa as a man who was going to stuff my stocking full of candy and stack up gifts under my tree. He represented so much more. He was proof that dreams could make things happen.

Those days exploring the mall were always such a special time. They seemed so much simpler and happier. There was never a question that Christmas was going to be happy. I never worried about getting what I wanted or having fun with my family. I didn't grow up with that horror story of the Christmas everything went wrong the way most people did. I always went into the season filled with joy and knowing I was going to have the most wonderful time.

I never wanted to let go of that feeling, so I found ways to make sure I didn't have to. Coming to the mall remained a special tradition even after I grew up. I no longer went to see Santa, though I wouldn't ever fully outgrow the sense that that man represented the magic in the world. I knew the truth. I knew my mother wanted copies of the wish list I gave him to make sure she was buying the right things to give him credit for. He turned into magic of a different kind.

His magic became that warm, fuzzy feeling that came as soon as the first signs of the season started to appear in stores. His magic was the way Christmas softened hearts and brought people back together. It was the ability to create that fantasy for younger generations. I never wanted any of that to go away, and it didn't have to.

I didn't sit on Santa's lap anymore and I didn't write wish lists. But I still went to the mall every season. There was just something about walking around among the other shoppers, looking at the decorations, listening to the music, smelling the food. It all centered me, grounding me right back into the childhood Christmases that were the most important part of every year.

It was harder now. Far harder than when I was a child and even harder than the earliest years of my adulthood. It wasn't as carefree and simple, and I couldn't just go through the holiday season filled with the sense of wonder, joy, and fulfillment the way I once did. But I still wanted to love it. I still didn't want to let go of that magic. I wanted to believe it was real. I wanted that fun and happiness.

That was part of why I chose this place. It was part of my Christmas celebrations my whole life and I didn't want to lose that. Even if the holidays would never be what I wanted them to be. I could never fully outgrow my desire for the joy, for the memories and the nostalgia. This was a gift.

I'd planned extra time for this one. The market had been far busier than I anticipated it to be and everything felt more rushed. I hadn't been really prepared for that and because of it, I felt like I was under scrutiny. I thought somebody saw me. I took extra time getting ready for the one at the mall. I didn't want to rush so much and miss something important. I wanted the chance to roam around for a little while and immerse myself in those feelings again.

No one was paying any attention when I walked through the display again to the back section they'd designed to make it look like a beautiful living room, complete with fireplace. This was my favorite area of the display. When no one was looking, I slipped a stocking onto one of the fireplace hooks and walked away.

CHAPTER THIRTEEN

THE DRIVE TO THE MALL IS FAMILIAR.

Not just because it's a mall I've been to, but because that tingling, stinging feeling that comes at the beginning of a case, when I don't even know what the case is yet so my imagination is going wild, is running down the back of my neck. It's from one of my memories that aren't memories, the feeling of having come this way to respond to the terrifying killings happening within the mall. I know that was one of the cold cases that I had been looking into because it fascinated me, and that was finally solved when I was under.

But knowing that in the full reality of my thoughts doesn't take away the feeling. Those impressions are so strong and so vivid, I can still feel every bit of fear in the parking lot and see blood smeared across the glass. I can close my eyes and see every one of the brutal killings from the bullets sprayed down from the mezzanine on the unexpected partygoers gathered around the fountain, to the body trapped on the escalator and mangled in its mechanism.

The mall is a very different place now, and I force myself to push all those thoughts out of my mind as I park and head to the store that has been transformed into Santa's winter wonderland. This special location was designed to bring Christmas joy to all who visit the mall. This is where memories are meant to be created. It would be an amazing place to come to enjoy Christmas festivities, but I'm not here to enjoy. I'm here because I've been called to see something that was found by one of the employees.

The rest of the mall is still functioning like nothing's happening. Shoppers mill around, trying to cross off items from their lists, contemplating special surprises, and wondering if they've done enough to prepare their homes for the upcoming celebrations. Some look thrilled to be here, brimming with joy and excitement even as they try to navigate their way through dense crowds. Others look frazzled and overwhelmed, like they already know they are so far behind it's unlikely they will catch up and they aren't enjoying the process of even trying.

This store, though, is desolate. What was once one of the large anchor stores went out of business several years ago. The mall ownership immediately swooped in, not wanting to face sagging profits, and transformed it. Now it takes on different themes and experiences throughout the year. Spring and summertime specialty experiences bring in shoppers during traditionally slower times. Come fall, the hotly anticipated Halloween overlay combines the ultimate decorations and costume shop with a maze and haunted escape room.

But it's the Santa's Winter Wonderland Christmas Experience that is the most popular event throughout the year. The entire sprawling space is full of highly immersive decorations and photo backdrops. Craft stations invite children to make little gifts for their families and write out their letters to Santa on templates they can then color in. The completed letters can be dropped into special mailboxes to be sent right to the North Pole. Of course, there are also treats for sale along with specialized shopping integrated among the different elements of the experience.

This is definitely somewhere a person who loves Christmas could completely lose themselves for a while. I have to stop myself from just wandering around and taking it all in. The fact that it's empty helps to temper some of the wonder. There should be people here. There are lingering signs of the visitors who had been here just before I was called. But they were ushered out and the security gates lowered to keep anyone else from coming in. I step up to one of them now and show my badge.

"Agent Griffin, FBI," I identify myself. "Carrie Buchanan is expecting me."

The security guard recognizes the name of the store manager and lifts the gate to allow me under. I'm impressed at how well they were able to contain the situation, and how quickly. This entire store was cleared out, but there doesn't seem to be any sort of panic happening throughout the rest of the mall. Which means no one has caught wind of what one of the employees found.

Carrie is waiting at the center of the store for me. She is one of those rare people who at high school reunions people say she hasn't changed a bit and they are actually telling the truth. I know I look different than I did then. Sam certainly does. Both of us are fully recognizable, but the years have etched themselves on our faces, our bodies, how we carry ourselves.

Seeing Carrie standing there, however, is like looking back and seeing her standing next to her locker during senior year. As soon as she sees me, she takes several steps forward, reaching both hands out toward me. I grasp one of them in mine.

"Emma, thank you so much for coming so quickly," she says.

"Of course," I say.

"The employee who found it said she was going to call the police, but I thought it would be better if it went directly to you in case..."

Her voice trails off, but I know the rest of that sentence. In case it is what they fear it is. Another body part to add to my investigation. I nod to signal to her that she doesn't have to say anything else.

"Can you bring me to it?"

She scurries down the aisle that has been covered with thick, highly damage-resistant vinyl to make it look like a cobblestone pathway and lined with sparkling glitter fabric to make snow drifts. I follow behind her and soon we're at the back of the store.

"This area is supposed to be a house on Christmas Eve. Families like to come and take pictures here and there are some unique stocking stuffers and other little gifts available here. The thing is, none of the stockings that are hanging by the fireplace are supposed to be filled. Remember, this is Christmas Eve, so they are still waiting for Santa's arrival. One of my employees noticed that one of the stockings looked strange."

She points to the display where the item was found.

"She said the first thing about it that stood out to her was that it looked like it was out of place. Like it was too crowded among the others. But then she realized it also looked like it had something in it. She took it down and looked inside, and there was a small, wrapped box in the toe of the stocking. That definitely shouldn't be there."

"Did anyone report seeing somebody hanging the stocking up or putting anything in it?" I ask.

"No. We asked around, and nobody saw anything. We've been trying to take precautions around here, not wanting to be part of these twisted crimes. We have this new, specialized, custom wrapping paper to wrap all of the prop gifts that are put under the Christmas trees and around the store. We have them fixed to the platforms so that any odd packages are immediately noticeable. All of the trees have hidden cameras around them. We didn't expect something that didn't have anything to do with one of the trees," Carrie says.

"You've been doing all the right things," I assure her. "This isn't something that you anticipated, and you didn't cause it. Let me see what they found."

Carrie gestures and a girl even younger than those I interviewed at the housing complex comes over. Her bright green eyes are red and puffy. Makeup is streaked down her cheeks from where she has obviously been crying. She grasps and twists her fingers in front of her nervously.

"Olivia, this is Agent Griffin. Tell her what happened."

Through a voice still high and thin with emotion and shock, the teenager tells me about noticing the out of place stocking hanging on the faux fireplace. According to her, this isn't the first time they have found an extra stocking hanging there. Apparently, some children get very wrapped up in the theme of Christmas Eve and want to hang their own stocking by the fire.

That's one of the reasons she regularly checks the display. They make sure no extra stockings have been added and none of the ones that are supposed to be there have been removed. If there are any discrepancies, they fix it to make sure the display looks exactly as it is supposed to at all times. This time, however, when she got closer to the fireplace to remove the extra stocking, she noticed it wasn't flat the way the others were. She picked it up and felt the heft of something inside it. Glancing in, she noticed a small, wrapped box.

"And the paper isn't the type that's being used around here this year?" I ask.

Olivia shakes her head no. "All of the paper in the store is solid colors with custom glitter patterns. White, blue, red, and green. Once everything happened, we took all the silver paper out of the store and eliminated any other types of paper so we would recognize any out-of-place gifts right away.

"That's why it bothered me so much when I looked into the stocking and saw the little box wrapped in silver paper. I… I recognized it from the other night. I immediately called Carrie to show her."

"Did you touch the box?" I ask.

"No." Olivia shudders slightly.

"Okay. Thank you."

The stocking is lying on a table in the living room scene, and I can see the small bulge of the box in the toe. It is obviously a much smaller box than the other two that have been found. I pick up the stocking and hold open the top so I can glance inside. Sure enough, the box is wrapped in the same silver paper.

"Alright. I'm going to bring this to the sheriff's department so it can be photographed before opening it. I'll give you a call when we know anything."

Forty minutes later I'm standing in a conference room with Sam and his crime scene photographer preparing to open the mysterious box in the stocking. The photographer snaps several images of the stocking itself, then a sequence as I take the box out of the toe of the stocking and set it down on the table.

I'm wearing gloves as I carefully unfold the paper from the edges of the box and slide the box itself out from the paper. Unlike the one containing the lungs, this box is not taped shut. There is a small flap and I slide my finger under it to open it. Even the experienced photographer gasps slightly when the top of the box opens to reveal a set of eyeballs.

A tag nestled between them reads *"the future I see."*

CHAPTER FOURTEEN

CALL CARRIE ON THE WAY BACK TO THE MALL FROM SAM'S OFFICE to ask her to gather all of her employees together so I can speak with them. She has them sitting around a table in the employee lounge when I arrive.

To make sure she can be there for her employees as a source of support and guidance, I take Carrie aside first when I arrive.

"The package had eyeballs in it," I tell her. "They are most definitely real. They've been turned over to the medical examiner for testing and preservation."

"Oh, my god," she gasps, seeming to sway slightly on her feet as if she might pass out at the thought.

"Listen to me. I know this is disturbing and you might feel like there is nothing any of you can tell me, but we're going to break it down from the beginning and see if there's anything else. I want you to think of it this way. This is the first time one of these packages has been found somewhere with such close quarters. The village market was very busy, but it was also a large space and everyone was kind of doing their own thing. It makes it much more difficult to really pay attention to everything. The second package was found under the tree of a hotel lobby, which is less expansive than the green, but still people rushing back and forth, focusing primarily on themselves and what they are doing.

"This location, though, is very personal. It is far more closed in. The store itself is huge, but because of the way the sections are organized, every set feels cozy and personal. That makes it far more likely someone saw something or there is some sort of evidence to review."

"I just thought I was doing everything I could," she says. "I tried to put measures in place to ease people's minds and create the feeling of a safe, secure holiday. I wanted to show we are paying close attention to everything and that people who come here can celebrate in peace. Even with all the precautions, though, there has been a definite decrease in the crowds compared to other years. Even comparing it just to the beginning of this season, there are distinctly fewer people coming. It has been really sad to see. I hate that the holidays are being tainted this way."

"I know," I say. "I do, too. I hate that whoever this is chose this place to leave this package. But I'm going to do everything I can to find out who it was so you can reclaim this space. If it's okay with you, I'm going to talk to your employees for a little bit."

"Absolutely. I've instructed them to cooperate fully and be completely honest with you. I told them that if any of them know anything, or saw anything, they are to come forward with one hundred percent truthfulness, and that even if telling you something they saw or know might go against work policies here, their jobs are still safe," she says.

I go back into the lounge and find the employees in silence. They each sit in their chairs at the table, staring into the distance or at their hands, obviously rolling the situation around in their heads. Going to the head of the table, I wave at them. I notice with the exception of one woman, all of the employees seem very young. This was meant to be a simple, fun, and approachable seasonal job for kids still in high school and it's turning out to be a nightmare.

"Hey, Carrie, is this your entire staff?" I ask.

"No," she says. "A handful aren't in today. Some of them have other full-time jobs and only do this in the evenings and on the weekends."

"Can you get in touch with them and let them know I'll need to speak with them?" I ask.

"Of course."

I look back at the employees sitting around the table. "For those of you who don't know me, I am Special Agent Emma Griffin. I'm with the FBI. I'm not going to sugarcoat this situation at all. And I'm letting you know right from the beginning that I will be discussing things with you that are considered sensitive and confidential. Please do not discuss any of this with anyone who is not in this room right now. That is very important to my investigation.

"First, I'm going to get right down to it and tell you there was something in the package in the toe of the stocking. This makes it absolutely critical that each of you is honest with me. I'm going to ask everybody what you've been doing around here, what's your job, and if you noticed anything that might have something to do with these incidents. Either here, at the fair, or anywhere else."

The employees are immediately cooperative. They answer my questions and give me full rundowns of what they were doing before each of the body parts was found. I listen closely to what they're saying, waiting for one of them to mention the gift tags. I decided to keep the tags and the words on them out of the media. The first one existing is fairly common knowledge because it was revealed on the village green, but I haven't told anyone what the others say, yet. Or even that the other packages had the tags in them.

I want to keep that detail close to the vest so it can be used for leverage later on. It isn't a big leap for anyone to make to guess that the other packages also have gift tags in them. It's the words that matter. I don't want to reveal what these tags say so if someone mentions those words, I can take notice.

The employees of the store aren't allowed to have their cell phones out for any reason other than a true emergency during their working time, which means none of them have pictures or video of the time surrounding the stocking appearing at the fireplace. I decide to use the tactic Xavier suggested for Cupcake. I will have a public plea go out on the news to anyone who visited the store today and has pictures or video to send them in. Every image I can find that shows the fireplace can help me to create a timeline that will eventually narrow it down to when that stocking was put in place.

I leave the store later with a tight ball in the middle of my chest. I know the stocking being here means something. This wasn't just a random decision. Whoever this is chose to leave this package here, and the others at their locations, for a very distinct purpose.

CHAPTER FIFTEEN

TWO DAYS LATER, THE SITUATION FEELS MORE DIRE. CHRISTMAS continues to draw closer and we still don't have answers. Teams are out searching for bodies, for signs of other evidence, anything. Keegan has run multiple tests on the body parts, but they haven't really provided any additional information. None of them seem to have any trace of medications or other drugs, and there's nothing to indicate a cause of death.

One wall of my living room and one of my dining room are taken up by pieces of butcher paper where I'm constructing the timelines for the night of the market and for the day the eyeballs were found in the stocking at the mall. Cupcake's fans came through for her. She put out a call for pictures and video, and both came flooding in. It turns out even though she hadn't advertised that she was going to be at the market, there were still plenty of her fans there who were beyond thrilled to see her. There are nearly a dozen pictures of her posed with various people beside the platform of the tree, and several pieces of video as well.

Some fans were either too shy to approach her to ask for pictures, or just felt like they didn't want to invade her privacy, so they decided to take them from a distance instead. Apparently, it didn't occur to them how awkward and creepy it comes across to have pictures and video of someone unaware they are being watched and documented. Thanks to the collection of images, however, I've been able to create a much smaller window in which the box could have been placed on the platform.

There were three distinct times when Cupcake went over to the platform. According to her, these were the times she was taking breaks from her booth. One came shortly after the market started and she had just finished getting fully set up. Another was a couple of hours later after a particularly aggressive rush of customers. The third was just before the guys and I got to the event. It isn't easy to see the platform in all of the images, but there are enough of them for me to confirm that the package was not in place at any of the times when Cupcake was at the platform. This means the box was put into place within a fairly tight window of when it was discovered.

I considered asking all of the vendors for their financial transactions and trying to run checks on the identities of anyone who purchased from them during the narrowed down window, but I have decided against it for now. That would be a truly unreal amount of information to try to process, and because of the lack of surveillance footage, anyone who paid with cash would be completely untraceable.

There's also simply the fact that I find it highly unlikely this person perused the offerings from the vendors and bought things while carrying around a human heart in a box. Though I am under the distinct impression this person intended to blend in with the rest of the people at the event and look like they were just there enjoying themselves, they wouldn't want to make themselves too visible. Going up to a vendor or one of the artisans and engaging with them about their products, going so far as to buy something, would make an impression. That is far from what this person wants.

I spoke with Molly Garson again yesterday, this time opting to have the conversation over the phone rather than trying to get into her apartment. There may come a point in this investigation when I need to compel her to allow me inside, but for now, and until I have any kind of evidence that would indicate that kind of necessity, I need to keep this distance and not corner her.

I could have beaten around the bush a little bit and tried to needle her into admitting her relationship with Kade on her own. Instead,

I decided to respect her bold, somewhat brash personality and come right out with what I knew. As soon as I offered the explanation behind the phantom transaction that would show she owns a roll of that paper, Molly gives in. Willing to save herself the hassle of trying to explain away the lack of paper she has never had, she admitted she and Kade have been seeing each other. She didn't want the other girls to know because it doesn't look great, and she knows they would all have something to say about it.

She admitted that she called Kade as soon as I left her apartment the other day and they talked about what they were going to say and what they weren't. They were still talking when I got to the door and she told him he had to answer or it would look more suspicious. She was right about that, but probably should have stopped there rather than advising him to fake having been in the shower. That action makes them look shady and untrustworthy. Molly was able to confirm to me that the group of girls who were there shopping together weren't the only ones from the housing complex who were at the shops that day.

There was one of the special shopping day events going on at that stretch of cute little shops near the caverns, just like Kade said that there might have been, which drew many people. Molly said she saw a handful of others there that day, including in the little shop. But she didn't see anyone ask Kade to buy the extra roll of paper, so there was no way to confirm who it was.

It makes me feel better to know Nancy, Presley, Helen, Kylie, Cory, and Lila weren't lying to me about the rolls of paper, but now there's another possible contact. I want to be careful in asking the public for more help this close at the heels of asking for the pictures and video. It may seem messy and disorganized, which can be emboldening for a perp.

My phone rings as I'm rewatching a video for what feels like the hundredth time, trying to determine if a hazy form that moves along the very edge is something to pay attention to or if it is just another customer walking through the Winter Wonderland display. I pause the video and answer.

"Hey, babe."

"Emma, you need to come down to the station," he says.

His tone is tense, his voice tight.

"Why? What's going on?" I ask.

"Milo and Cora Gable are down here. They came in to report their granddaughter Trisha missing."

"I'm on my way."

It seems like Sherwood is the kind of town where everybody knows everybody and especially as the wife of the sheriff, I should be on a first-name basis with every resident, but that's not really how it is. It's a small town, but big enough that while everybody knows all the big stuff that's happening and you're very likely to end up in the gossip of any and everyone living here, there are still plenty of people I've never met. The Gables are just such a couple.

The older pair sit next to each other in the chairs across Sam's big desk from him. They are turned toward each other so they can grip their hands together, and when they look at me as I walk in I can see both of their eyes filled with worry.

"Mr. and Mrs. Gable, this is my wife, Emma," Sam says.

"We've heard about you," Mrs. Gable says. "You can call me Cora."

"Hi, Cora. I'm so sorry to hear about your granddaughter."

She pulls in a tight breath, a tissue clutched in one hand coming up to press against her nose as a tear escapes one eye. "She never does this. Never."

"Does she live with you?" I ask.

I get an extra chair from the other side of the room and drag it over so I can sit at the end of the desk near both Sam and the couple.

"No," Milo says. "She lives with her father in Marlon."

"That's not too far from here," I say. "About forty-five minutes? An hour?"

I do my best not to show a reaction to the fact that this is the same location as the college and housing complex.

"That's right. But she comes to visit us at least once a week, usually more. Her father called us this morning and asked why she wasn't answering her phone. We haven't seen her in days, so we didn't know what to tell him, but he told us she had come this way three days ago. She never showed up and neither of us ever heard a word from her."

"Was that unusual? Her showing up to visit you without calling first?" I ask.

"No," Cora says, shaking her head. "Our home is her home. She has blanket permission to come whenever she wants and stay as long as she wants. She never has to let us know she's coming. And that's how it usually is. We've kind of come to expect her on a fairly steady basis, but it's not an exact science. We put fresh sheets on her bed and fill up on groceries every so often when it feels like she's coming.

"This time, though, we weren't expecting her at all. The last time we saw her she said she was going to be spending some extra time with her boyfriend because he was going out of town for a while over the holidays. But we've been following this case. We know…"

Her voice goes thin and chokes. The tissue presses to her lips and her eyes squeeze closed. Her husband tightens his hands around the one of hers he's still holding and looks at me firmly.

"We know there have been several incidents and no bodies have been found. We don't want to think she could be one of them, but we've tried everything we can think of to find her and haven't been able to," he says.

"What have you tried?" I ask.

"We've called her phone until it started going straight to voicemail. We've called all the friends of hers we know. Those who answered haven't heard anything from her and don't know any of the plans she had. We called her boyfriend but haven't been able to get in touch with him. We don't know if he already left town or not. We even went on her social media and posted on her page that we can't get in touch with her and asked for help tracking her down if anyone had been in contact with her in the last three days. There's been nothing," he tells me.

"Alright. What's her boyfriend's name?" I ask.

"Tyler O'Rourke."

"Can you write down his contact information for me? Every way you know how to get in touch with him. And everything you have for Trisha, too. Also, can I see a picture of her?"

Sam opens the top drawer of his desk and takes out a small pad of paper and pen. He hands it to Milo, who takes out his phone and begins transcribing information from the screen to the paper. Trisha's grandmother takes out her phone and pulls up a picture of a sweet-looking early adult woman with golden blonde hair and milk chocolate eyes. I lean toward Cora and meet her very similar gaze.

"I can't give you full information about the case because it is still obviously a very active investigation. But I promise you I will do everything I can to look for Trisha, and as soon as I have any information I'm able to share with you, I'll be in touch," I say.

"Thank you so much," she says. "Please find our girl. She's everything to us."

"We're going to find her," I say.

Sam walks the couple out and comes back. I'm pacing his office, typing out a message to Trisha on my phone.

"What do you think?" he asks, closing the door behind him.

"I think they have every reason to be worried," I say. "But we know she couldn't be the donor of the heart. Keegan says that belonged to a male. The lungs also couldn't be hers. She is too young. And the eyes we found were blue. The picture Cora just showed me showed Trisha has brown eyes. None of the body parts correspond with her. But she's still missing and we need to have someone looking for her. Have you reached out to her father?"

"Not yet. I'll do that now," he says.

"Great. I didn't get the impression there was a very good relationship between the grandparents and the father, so I don't know how much I trust that they are sharing information reliably."

"Cora and Milo are Trisha's mother's parents. She died a few years ago from cancer. They were never very close with her father, James," Sam says.

"Do you just know everything about everyone?" I ask.

"I'm sheriff. It's my job," he says. "But, no. They told me when they first came in to talk about her. They said they were worried James wasn't going to do anything about her being missing because she's an adult. She lives under his roof right now, but he doesn't seem to have a whole lot to do with her other than checking in every now and again."

"Alright. You get in touch with the Marlon PD. I'm going to try to reach out to other people in her life and see what I can come up with," I say.

Ten minutes later I've sent a dozen messages and haven't heard back from anyone. Sam comes back into his office and hands me a cup of coffee he brought from the lounge.

"I spoke with the detective out of Marlon. I filled them in on what's going on here. He had already heard of our case and doesn't have a great feeling. I explained that Trisha doesn't fit the demographic for any of the body parts, but they still feel like it would be a good idea for you to keep her case in mind as we are investigating. They'd like to work together," he says.

"Absolutely. At this point, any missing person is going to be on the radar. We need to keep checking the databases and cross reference with surrounding areas to make sure we aren't missing somebody. But since we know for sure that she is missing, we need to double down. We are already at a disadvantage with it being three days since she was seen or heard from, so we need to see what we can find out about her and her movements before her disappearance."

"I'll get in touch with her father and see what he can tell us about her habits. I highly doubt he does, but I'll find out if he has any access to her finances. If we can look at her banking records, we can see when the last time was that she used her debit card and where it was," Sam says.

"Great. I really doubt he has that kind of access, too, since she's an adult and he doesn't sound like the most hands-on parent, but it can't hurt to ask. If he doesn't, we can ask for a warrant. We need to act fast here," I say. "There could be a really simple explanation and we'll find her just fine. And on the other hand..."

"We might not."

Sam and I split tasks trying to track everything we can about Trisha Gable. The fact that she has her mother's last name doesn't surprise me. I didn't get any details about the family dynamic, but the brief explanation I did get is enough to show there is obvious tension. I'm slowly piecing together her activities in the days leading up to the last time her father spoke to her. There doesn't seem to be anything that stands out too much, nothing all that unusual for a woman in her early twenties. But it's the fact that there isn't anything standing out that may be cause for concern.

If there were unusual spending habits or she seemed to be communicating with people no on else in her life knew about, then that could possibly point to what happened to her. Everything seems completely normal, though, which means she encountered something that bluntly and suddenly disrupted her regular flow of life.

I can't find anything else unusual in her life. Until suddenly, I do.

The voice on the other end of the call I get while I am trying to research and eat lunch at the same time sounds nervous and curious.

"Agent Griffin?"

"Yes, this is Agent Griffin. Can I help you?

"This is Kayla O'Rourke. I'm Tyler's mother. You called earlier and said you were trying to get in touch with my son."

"Yes, Mrs. O'Rourke. Thank you for calling me back. Like I said, I have been trying to get in touch with Tyler so I can talk to him about Trisha," I say. "But I haven't had any luck. Do you happen to know how I might be able to reach him? Or can you give him my contact information and tell him to reach out to me? It is very important," I say.

"That's just the thing, Agent Griffin. I can't reach Tyler, either. I haven't heard from him in days," she says.

That makes me frown. "You haven't been able to contact Tyler for days?"

"No. He was supposed to be visiting an old friend, so I didn't think anything of it when I didn't hear from him. He's an adult and doesn't have to call home every day. But, when I got your message and heard something is going on with Trisha, I got concerned. I tried to reach Tyler, but I couldn't, so I called his friend Devin. He told me Tyler never showed up at his house. He got a message from Tyler saying he couldn't make it on the day he planned, but that Devin would see him soon. No one has heard from him since," Kayla says.

She's obviously trying to control her emotions. She was hoping I would be able to tell her something that would put her mind at ease. Because she was contacted by an FBI agent, it was probably in the back of her mind that her son might have been involved in some sort of criminal activity. But even if I was calling her to tell her that her son was now in custody, at least she would know where he was. At least she would know he was okay. But I can't tell her that.

"Mrs. O'Rourke, I need you to listen carefully. I'm going to give you my e-mail address. Send me absolutely everything you possibly can about your son. Contact information for everybody you have. His address, his regular schedule, where he works, his gym. Everything you can think of that will tell me about him and his regular life, I need it. We need to find your son."

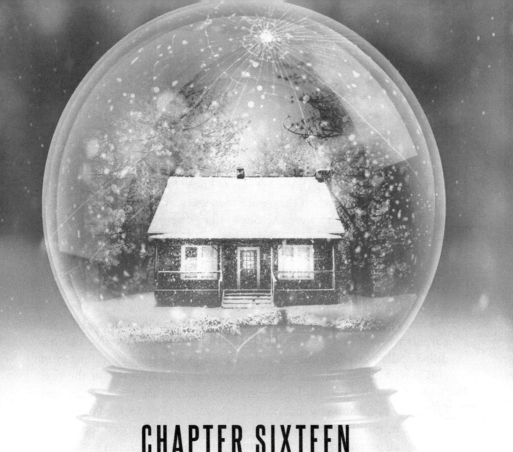

CHAPTER SIXTEEN

C YRUS, CYNTHIA, GEMMA, PAUL, AND AVA PRETEND THEY DON'T
hear their parents calling after them as they run out into the woods
behind their grandparents' house. They have escaped the indoor
boredom of all the adults in the family and are now running to go ice
skating. It's one of their favorite holiday season pastimes and the stuff of
many of their most wonderful memories together.

The entire family always gets together at the grandparents' house
for the Christmas season, and while the adults are inside cooking, playing card games, and talking for what seems like endless hours, the teenage cousins venture out into the woods to find the tiny pond that freezes
over every year into a skating rink. Getting to the age where they are old
enough to join up with the pack is a rite of passage within the family.
And all of them silently wonder and dread when the year is going to
come that makes them too old to continue on with the tradition and
forces them back into the house with the other adults.

All of them try not to think about that. They don't want to imagine a Christmas without the rush of running through the cold woods and the excitement that comes every time they find the pond nestled just past where it feels like they are never going to find it and it may have all been a dream.

The parents of the family hate that their children go out there. They say the ice hasn't frozen hard enough and they could fall through. But even as they are saying it, the teenagers know that those exact parents did the same thing when they were teenagers. And at the time, it was the grandparents who were the ones telling them they shouldn't do it because it hadn't yet been cold enough and the ice wasn't thick and strong enough yet. And before that, there was a time when the grandparents were the ones doing it and it was their parents telling them to stop.

At some point each generation of young people wondered who was the first person in the family to come play out on the pond and if their parents warned them not to do it. Or if it was so long ago that parents didn't really warn their children of such things. Maybe they weren't even children at all who found the pond and ran around on it for the first time. Maybe that was the big secret of the family, that it was adults who found the pond and saw that it was iced over, so they decided to make a game of it. But then their children were born, and they developed that fear that all parents do, so they started warning their children not to play on the ice and the tradition was passed down from there.

None of it really mattered to the teenagers when it was their time to go out into the woods and find the pond. They felt confident and comfortable playing out here. It wasn't like they were actually ice skating. Not really, anyway. They didn't have skates that would cut down into the ice and let them glide over it. They just put thick socks on over their boots and slid around on the surface.

It wasn't always perfect, even if they said they knew it was safe and nothing could ever happen. There were years when the weather was warmer and the pond really didn't have the chance to freeze over before Christmas, so when the kids went out onto it they'd notice it starting to crack. When they saw that, they'd immediately get off and spend the rest of the time just sitting by the bank looking out over the sparkling surface and thinking about Christmas.

But this year has been particularly cold. Days before the family descended on the house there was an extremely cold snap. That had to have made the ice strong and thick. They've been waiting since the day after last Christmas to finally get to enjoy the ice again and they believe it's going to be just fine.

They drop their bags to the ground and lay out thick towels to sit on while they pull the socks over their boots. They always scramble to see who is going to be the first one to step foot out on the pond. They all wanted to be that one, and yet they also didn't mind so much if one of their cousins got to it first. If it was going to crack, they didn't want to be the one who went through.

Cynthia is the first this year. She adjusts the socks and steps down off the edge of the bank onto the ice. She puts some of her weight on it and waits for the sound of the ice giving way but doesn't hear it. That's all she needed to know. She launches out onto the ice and is soon sliding and slipping, laughing as she fights to keep herself upright. One by one, she's joined by her cousins. She laughs as they shakily gain their balance on the slippery ice. An only child, it's the times she's with her cousins celebrating Christmas, Easter, or the Fourth of July at her grandparents' house when she feels what it's like to have siblings.

She wouldn't necessarily want to have them around all the time. She knows how hard it is for the ones who have multiple siblings. But she treasures the time she does get with them. It feels like she's getting the best of both worlds.

Cynthia usually stays around the edges of the ice ever since she got old enough to come out onto the pond with the others. She knows the ice is the thickest and strongest here, and it is closest to the bank, so if she gets tired it's easier to get off and flop down on her towel for a break. Paul, the oldest, has his dark green canvas backpack with him, which means tucked away in there is the big silver thermos of hot chocolate their grandmother made for them while the parents were telling them all the reasons why they shouldn't go out onto the pond.

Cyrus's mother, Cynthia's aunt Patsy, once chastised her mother for it, asking why she would encourage them like that when she was always the one to tell her and her siblings and cousins they weren't allowed to go out. Grandma just smiled, knowing her daughter wasn't listening to the words coming out of her own mouth and didn't realize she was giving herself away by admitting she had thought nothing of going out onto that pond. And not too long ago in the greater scheme of things. Grandma then told her it wasn't up to her to tell the grandchildren not to go do something they loved.

Being a mother is about worry and stopping children from doing things. Being a grandmother was just about loving on them and finding ways to make them happy. And on a cold December day when their cheeks were wind-stung and their fingers numb, nothing makes her grandchildren happy quite like a big container of homemade hot chocolate.

This year, Cynthia feels brave. She isn't the youngest one out on the ice anymore. Ava just got old enough that they decided she could come, and so Cynthia feels like she needs to be braver. She can't have explored less of the pond than the youngest cousin allowed out there. She ventures out toward the center where they've been constantly warned the ice would be thin and weak.

She turns around to look for Paul and get his approval when she hears the sound that makes her stomach feel soft and her knees a little shaky. The ice is cracking. She tightens up all her muscles like when she took ballet and the teacher told her that the more pulled up she was, the less weight would be pushing down on her feet. Cynthia pulls up with everything in her and inches back away from the center. But she has already gone too far. The ice cracks more.

"Everybody off!" Paul shouts. "It's cracking."

Cynthia looks down and sees the crack coming toward her like a snake. She can't move.

"Come on, Cynthia!" Cyrus yells.

When she doesn't move, he runs toward her and takes her by her hand, yanking her backward. She starts moving, but the shift of her body makes him lose balance. Cyrus tries to regain his footing but slips and falls onto the ice. He's down on his belly and as he pushes himself up he sees a pair of eyes staring back at him. His face is just inches away from a man beneath the ice.

Cyrus screams in terror and tries to scramble away. The hard impact of his movements causes the ice to crack even more. He can't get back to his feet and he can feel the ice giving way.

"It's a man!" he screams. "There's someone under the ice!"

"Somebody call for help!" Paul shouts.

Cynthia tries to move toward Cyrus again, but Paul waves his hand aggressively at her, telling her to get back while Ava snatches her phone from the bag and tries to call her parents. There's no service.

"My phone won't work this far out!" she cries. "I can't call anyone."

A crack so loud it reverberates through the trees brings her to her feet and she takes off like a shot through the woods toward the house, screaming for her parents, her aunts and uncles, and her grandparents. She felt so grown up at the beginning of the day. Far too old for the adults to warn her not to go out onto that pond. Far too mature for anyone to think she can't handle a little bit of fun with her cousins. Now she needs them. She needs a real adult, someone to tell her it's going to be fine and handle what's happening.

At the pond, Paul continues to make his way slowly out across the ice toward his brother. He can feel the ice moving and shifting beneath his feet, but if he moves slowly he can get there with less of a chance of falling through.

"Don't move, Cyrus," he says. "Just stay where you are."

"He's right there," the younger boy says in a shaking, terrified voice. "Right under the ice. I can see his eyes."

"Just stay where you are. I'm coming."

Ava runs through the forest not caring that the bottoms of her feet are getting cut up by frozen roots and rocks on the ground. Her throat is raw, but she keeps shouting. The louder she is, the more likely they are to hear her before she's reached the house. It will make them come out and they'll come with her. They'll get back to the pond faster.

Gemma follows close behind Paul. She can't let him go out there on his own. Out on the ice, still lying on his belly, staring not into the dead man's eyes but at his chest now, Cyrus trembles and cries. The tears freeze on his skin and his nose feels like it's closing. He can hear Paul coming up behind him and wants to get to him faster, so he pushes back with his hands to slide across the ice.

That pressure is just enough to break through the ice. The skating rink opens up beneath him and Cyrus falls down into the bitterly cold water. The last thing he hears is his brother screaming his name as he disappears beneath the surface. The cold of the water is painful immediately and Cyrus forces himself to open his eyes so he can see where he is and how to get back up through the ice.

The man's body is close enough that if Cyrus moved his hand just slightly in front of him, he would touch his arm. Panic rushes through him and he starts to thrash, unable to control his movements or his attempts to cry out from beneath the water.

"Help!" Ava yells as she reaches the grassy stretch of her grandparents' backyard. "Help! There's a body at the pond! There's a dead man in the pond!"

Her uncle Brad finally comes out of the house, a confused and concerned look on his face. He's wiping his mouth, the remnants of his lunch clinging to his thick moustache.

"Ava? What's going on? What are you yelling about?" he asks.

"There's a body in the pond," she says, stopping and bending over to try to suck icy air into her lungs. It burns and makes her stomach ache, but she keeps doing it, trying to stop the swirl of her head. "Cyrus found it."

"A body?"

He doesn't sound convinced.

"Yes. He said it's a man."

"What's going on?" Ava's father asks, coming out of the house behind his brother-in-law.

Ava rushes toward him. "There's a body in the pond. You have to come help."

"She says it's a man," Brad says. "If that thing is frozen over, how could there be a body in it? Your grandpa goes fishing out there all the time when it's warm. He would have seen someone floating in there."

"There is," Ava insists. "Cyrus wouldn't make that up."

"Honey, did you see it?" her father asks.

"No, but he says it's there. And he screamed. Really loud. He was afraid. Cyrus isn't going to be that afraid out there if he didn't actually see something. Please, we need help," she says, starting to feel desperate.

"Ava, if this is some kind of joke ..." her aunt Melanie warns.

"It isn't a joke." Tears are starting to spill over her eyes now and she can't get her chest to stop aching with every breath she pulls in. All she can think about is her cousin out on that breaking ice and the sound of his horrified scream when he saw whatever was in the water. "Please, help. We have to hurry. The ice is cracking."

That's enough to galvanize the adults. Her father and Uncle Brad run back inside to get on their shoes while her mother, Aunt Melanie, and Aunt Patsy gather up towels and shove them into Ava's arms. Her father is the first out the door and down the path, not even waiting for her to go ahead of him. She wonders how he is going to find his way, forgetting he is just a teenage cousin grown up past the age of going to the pond. His feet know where he's going.

Paul tries to calm his brother down as he lowers himself down to the ice and starts to inch across it on his stomach, feeling in front of him for the strongest areas. Cyrus has to stop panicking. The more he panics, the harder it's going to be for his body to withstand the cold and keep him alive until they can pull him out. He needs to keep his head above the ice. If he dips too far below, they won't be able to grab onto him.

Every time he bobs back up, Cyrus looks more tired and his voice has more of the gurgle of cold water deep in his throat. Paul wishes he could get up and run to his brother. This feeling of helplessness is like someone scooping out his gut. He's listening to his terrified little brother drowning and there's nothing he can do about it but try to slide to the edge as fast as he can without risking falling through and them both drowning.

He continues to talk to his brother as he goes, hoping the steady sound of his voice will help him settle down. Finally, Paul reaches the opening in the ice and reaches out to grab onto Cyrus. He slips through his hand at first, but then the second time he grabs him, he's able to yank him up and partially out of the water. But he's too heavy and Paul is too tired to get him all the way up.

His brother is slipping, falling back down into the water as he clutches desperately at Paul's shirt to try to keep himself up. Paul feels like his energy is gone and there's nothing left to pull his brother out when two more hands grab onto the younger boy and pull him out. Paul falls back and feels hands take hold of him as well. They are several feet away from the hole in the crumbling ice when he realizes his uncle and father have saved them.

Ava is on the bank, sobbing on her knees, her arms wrapped around herself. Gemma is sitting on the ice, seemingly transfixed with the events unfolding in front of her.

"Wrap them up!" Brad demands. "Get them back to the house."

"The man," Cyrus mutters through blue, frozen lips. "The man under the ice."

Brad and Frederick look at each other. While it angers them to think the kids would play such a dangerous, cruel joke on the adults, they also don't want to think that there's actually the body of a man beneath the layer of ice on the pond. This is a place they know so well. They spent many summers swimming and fishing here when they were young adults, and they often still do.

It has been a lot of years since Frederick's wife introduced him to the frozen pond and they hadn't come out here many times after they got married, but he still holds onto many special memories from those visits. The thought that something so wonderful could be forever marred by something so gruesome as a corpse is unfathomable.

Frederick starts back across the pond. As he approaches the edge of the opening in the ice, he notices something dark bobbing just beneath the surface. It's being held down by a chunk of ice that broke off and is now floating in the water. Rather than coming at it from the same angle, he stays on the more solid ice and works his way around in a circle, spiraling gradually toward the open area.

"Somebody slide me a stick," he calls back when he gets close enough to the edge.

A chunk of branch comes toward him on the ice and he grabs it, using it to shove aside the piece of ice. As soon as he does, the body finally floats to the surface, as if carried there by a bubble of air. He sees his shoulders, his mottled blue skin, his open eyes.

They didn't believe Ava when she came screaming for help, but here it is. Right in front of him. The body of a man with a stomach-churning dip in his chest beneath the shirt clinging to him with the water.

CHAPTER SEVENTEEN

THE MAN STILL HAS HIS EYES.

They are focused upwards in a wide, terrified stare. Now that he's lying undressed on the medical examiner's table, the hole in the middle of his chest is blatantly obvious. There is nothing where his heart should be.

"I was pretty skeptical that the heart was going to belong to Tyler O'Rourke because he's so young," Keegan tells me. "But there is always the possibility of misidentifying the age of an organ without more extensive testing. That means it might have been possible, but now we know that isn't the case. I will do a DNA comparison just to confirm it, but considering the age and apparent health of this man, along with some evidence of injury and damage to the chest cavity, I would say with complete confidence this is where the heart came from."

"Was there any identification located in his clothing?" I ask.

"Yes. It held up pretty well to the exposure to the water. I had it dried, and it will be delivered with my initial report to the Sheriff's Department within the hour."

"Perfect. Thank you, Keegan."

I leave the ME's office and make my way over to the hospital where the family who discovered the body is waiting. The responding officers gave Sam an overview of what happened which he shared with me, so I know the young people, a group of cousins together to celebrate the holidays, are deeply upset by the entire experience. The boy who first saw the body through the ice then fell through into the bitterly cold water panicked, which nearly caused him to drown. He then watched the corpse of the man come to the surface and get dragged up onto the ice.

The traumatized thirteen-year-old hasn't spoken since getting out of the water.

He was admitted to the hospital to safely raise his core body temperature back up and for observation. It's a common misconception that people are automatically safe after getting out of the water. They don't even consider the phenomenon of secondary drowning. Particularly common among those who thrash or experience a violent near-drowning, secondary drowning occurs well after the person is back on dry land and can be quickly fatal.

The rest of the family is gathered around him to provide support and love, apparently taking up both of the family waiting rooms on this floor of the hospital. I stopped in with them first so I can get their version of what happened. It's a fairly straightforward story and I have no reason to believe that any of the teenagers or the older generations of the family aren't telling the truth.

I'm immediately inundated with questions about the man beneath the ice.

"Who is he?"

"What happened to him?"

"Is he the man whose heart was cut out?"

"Why was he on my parents' land?"

I don't have full answers for any of the questions yet. I assure the family I will let them know as much as I can as soon as the initial investigation is finished but that, yes, it does seem this man is the one whose heart was found beneath the tree. As of now, I have no idea how he got onto their parents' large tract of land or under the ice. But that's something I'm going to try to find out.

I can't ever really say that I'm sure of anything until I have unequivocal proof, but I am as sure as I can be that this family had nothing to do with the death, mutilation, or concealment of this man's body. It's an unfortunate turn for their family's holiday season, but hopefully they will be able to put it behind them and get back to their celebration together. Selfishly, I'm happy for this development. Finding this man's body is a massive step in the investigation. Before I only had body parts belonging to at least two people, but no idea who those people were or where the parts came from.

Now I at least have one.

This man will have his name said and his story told. I will find out what happened to him.

And now I can't let go of the pricking awareness at the base of my skull that there is still a woman out there whose lungs have been removed, and that I don't know if the eyeballs belong to her or a third victim. And the missing young couple could be wrapped up in all of this as well.

But one step at a time.

One person at a time.

I will start with this man. Which means finding out exactly who he is.

The boy, Cyrus McClean, is silently watching the TV in his room when his mother brings me to him. She walks up to the side of the bed and runs her hand over his hair. She leans down and kisses his head. I can't even begin to imagine what she must be feeling. It isn't just relief. That can't touch the experience of a mother who nearly lost her young child and who is still able to touch him and kiss him. This will never leave her. Even when he walks out of the hospital and the years tick by, the scar will still be there deep within her. She might not think about it all the time, but there will be moments when she glances in his direction or she hears him laugh and all the emotion of this second will rush back and threaten to overwhelm her.

He's old enough that he will carry it with him as well. His family will do everything they can to help him through and to make it as easy for him as they possibly can. They'll try to remind him of all the fun they've had out on that pond and boost his spirits for Christmas. He might rebound out of it. He might just need today and tomorrow will wake up rambling and talking just like any other teenage boy. He might have no problem going back to the pond and be even braver now than he ever was before.

Or this could change him entirely. It could be months before he speaks again. He could become withdrawn and terrified, not wanting to leave home much less venture back into the woods. He may never step foot near that pond again and have traumatic reactions to Christmas lights or the smells of the food they ate right before they left.

Like my visceral reaction to jellybeans. Or never wanting cut roses in my house.

I'm glad he has such a large family around him willing to do whatever they can to help him through.

"Cyrus, baby, this is Agent Griffin. She's going to be investigating what happened today," Patsy says.

"You're not in any trouble," I make sure to say carefully, not wanting the boy to think I'm here to investigate him in any way. "I just wanted you to know that I think you are very brave. It isn't easy going through what you did, and you should be very proud of yourself for how well you handled it. The doctors are going to take good care of you and before you know it, you'll be home celebrating Christmas. And I am going to do everything in my power along with my friends in the FBI, and my husband who is the sheriff in Sherwood, and my own cousin who is a private investigator, to find out what happened to that man and make sure his family gets the answers they need."

His head turns slightly so he can look at me. It's a long silence, but finally, he speaks.

"You have a cousin?" he asks.

It's the kind of question a child asks without thinking about what they are actually asking. It isn't that they don't understand what it means or that they aren't aware of simple concepts like family links. Instead, it shows just how deeply valuable his cousins are to him. When he hears me mention my cousin, he wonders if it's possible I could have the same kind of closeness with him that he does with his own.

"I do. His name is Dean. He's a little younger than me. But he is amazing at his job, and he has helped me catch a lot of bad guys. And we have a very dear friend who is the most brilliant person I've ever met who can help, too."

"What's his name?"

"Xavier."

"Why is he so smart?"

I let out a little laugh. "That's a really good question. And I have asked myself it many times. The only answer I can come up with is just that it's how he was made."

"Does your cousin like baseball?" he asks.

"Yes," I say.

"How about Xavier?"

"He does." Well, he likes the societal ritual of sporting events and the collective gatherings of groups cheering on hometown heroes to play games. But we don't need to get into the details.

"How about your husband?"

I smile. "He does, too."

Cyrus nods. "I like baseball. My cousins and I play it during the summer when we come to visit our grandparents."

"That sounds like fun."

His eyes are starting to flutter. "It is. I'm really tired."

"You should take a nap."

I think he's asleep before I finish saying it.

"I can't believe you got him talking," his mother says as we leave.

"I didn't do anything," I say. "He just didn't want to talk about what happened, that's all. We like to think we have control over our brains, but that is definitely not always the case. Sometimes our brains decide they don't like something or aren't going to do something, and that's just the way it is. There's nothing we can do about it but wait. Family means a lot to him. That's why he picked up on my cousin. That's great to see. If you guys are here with him, I'm sure it will help."

She nods and sniffles, looking like she's not even sure what emotion she's feeling and how she's supposed to handle it.

"We're going to help him get over this."

"He will. Don't worry. I'll be in touch."

"Thank you."

I leave the hospital and head for Sam's office. By now the information from Keegan should have arrived. I take a quick detour to grab Sam something to eat to make sure he has some lunch in the midst of the chaos of the day. He's on the phone when I step into my office and he mouths a 'thank you' when I place a massive pulled pork sandwich with coleslaw in front of him.

I sit down across from him with my own lunch and wait while he finishes his conversation. When he hangs up, he thanks me again and takes an impressive bite of the sandwich.

"So," he says when he gets the bite down. "Keegan brought me her initial findings and the victim's identification. I knew you were going over to the hospital to talk to the family that found him, so I thought I'd take it upon myself to do a little research. His name was Jesse Santucci. Both of his parents are listed as deceased and he was an only child. I was able to find out he was a professor at the college just outside of Marlon."

"The college?" I ask. "The one where all those people from the housing complex go?"

"That's the one," he says. "Apparently since classes are out of session and he doesn't teach intersession classes, there wasn't anyone to report him missing."

I think about this for a few seconds. "Hey, babe. You still believe there are no coincidences?"

"Do I even have to say it?" he asks, picking up his sandwich again for another huge bite.

"That's what I thought."

I stuff another bite of my own sandwich into my mouth, then stand up and walk around the side of the desk to give Sam a kiss. He hurriedly swallows down another bite so he can reciprocate.

"You just got here. Where are you going now?"

"Back to the housing complex in Marlon," I tell him.

"You just talked to all of them," he says.

"I didn't talk to all the students who live in that complex, just the ones with the wrapping paper. And I only talked to them about the paper, not about the dead professor. It's going to be a lot more efficient for me to go and talk to all of them at the same time. I'll be able to get a lot of information at once. It's also a chance for me to make the notification of his death since there is apparently no next of kin. I'll see you tonight for dinner."

"Love you."

"Love you."

On my way to the complex, I call the property manager and ask if there is a way for him to communicate with all students of the college at once. He confirms he can send a mass text and often does that for events and activities targeted to the student population.

"Fantastic. Can you please contact all of them and ask them to gather in the common building in one hour? Let them know they'll be meeting with Special Agent Emma Griffin from the FBI and it pertains to one of the professors at their school," I say.

The manager confirms he will send the message immediately and I thank him, hoping the short notice won't diminish attendance too much. I need to speak to as many of them in the immediate aftermath of uncovering Jesse Santucci's death as possible. The most comprehensive and authentic information comes when the initial response to the death is still fresh because people are less likely to overthink what they say or remember.

They are wrapped up in how they feel and will respond to questions authentically rather than putting too much thought into it if they think that what they are saying sounds right, or questioning what they remember. This is also the time when it is far more likely to get someone to trip up and reveal something they didn't intend to because they haven't yet had the time to come up with what they want to say.

A few people are already in the common building when I arrive and I purposely avoid interacting with them. I don't want to give any information until as many people as possible have arrived. I go through my notes and jot down a few more as I wait for the others to filter in. After giving them ten extra minutes, I finally step in front of the group clustered in the various pieces of furniture arranged on one end of the building. Looking out over the group, I see five of the girls I interviewed the other day. Kade is not there and neither is Molly. I take note of that and push ahead.

There's no reason to be coy or suspenseful in a situation like this. Being straightforward and getting right to the point means getting over the difficult hill fast so I can focus the rest of the conversation on the information I need.

There was already an air of confusion and tension as everyone filtered into the room, but as soon as the news about Jesse Santucci's death is out, emotion erupts throughout the gathered students. Some begin to cry; others are stone-faced like they don't know if they want to show a reaction or what reaction they should show.

I give them a few minutes to process what I just told them. I know it isn't easy for any of them to hear, even those who didn't know the professor. Being gathered up into the common room of your housing complex along with all the other students to be told one of the teachers at your school was likely murdered is a trauma and life disruption none of them were prepared for. This isn't the way Christmas is supposed to be. And for those who are on their own for the first time, this isn't the way that it's supposed to be, either.

"I'm so sorry for your loss," I tell them to get the conversation going again. "I know this is a difficult situation even for those of you who were not students of Professor Santucci. I want you to know the investigation is active and we are following all leads as aggressively as possible. But I could use your help. Particularly those of you who were his students, either currently or in the past, and knew him personally, which can be extremely beneficial in this kind of investigation."

As I'm speaking, I notice Molly coming through the door and join the group from the back. We meet eyes right there, but a girl beside her takes hold of her arm and tugs her close, leaning in to whisper in her ear, inevitably sharing the information she just missed. I watch her reaction. Molly's face goes pale and she swallows hard, licking her lips she looks over at the other student like she's waiting for more details. She whispers something and the other girl shrugs.

Molly looks around. The expression on her face is one of tense, frantic energy, like she feels trapped and wants to get out of the space where she's standing. But when she meets my eyes again, she stays still, looking as though she's trying hard to force herself steady. She knows I saw her. She can't just leave now.

I listen as the students talk about the teacher, giving me insight into his friendly, supportive personality and teaching style. He was clearly a favorite among his students, and many went out of their way to arrange their schedule around making sure they could take his writing or literature courses.

"What about his wife?" one of the students asks. "Has anybody told her?"

"His wife?" another asks, sounding confused.

"He was married?" someone responds.

Muttering questions ripple through the group as many of them react to the apparently new information that Professor Santucci was married.

"He didn't wear a ring," another says. "I had no idea he was married."

I notice Presley nodding. "I met her a couple times when she came to campus. Kristie. It's not like I got a lot of time to talk to her, but she seemed nice."

Kylie brushes a tear from under her eye. "She was really sweet. When I was his teaching assistant she would come and bring him treats and stuff on days she knew were going to be busy."

"I never even heard him mention her," another student says. "I guess I didn't have a lot of conversations with him about life, but I'm surprised."

I have to admit I'm surprised to hear about Santucci's wife, too. When Sam was looking for a next of kin he wasn't able to find anyone. He should have easily come up with a record for his marriage so we could notify his wife. It's strange that the records wouldn't come up, but that doesn't concern me as much as the fact that his apparent wife hasn't reported her husband missing. That tells me Kristie Santucci is either missing as well, or she had something to do with this.

I'd only come here with the intention of talking about Jesse Santucci, but as the reaction grows more intense, I decide to switch gears.

"I know this is a lot for all of you, but I do need to talk to you about some other information that has come to my attention." Their eyes lock on me, staring intently, some of them looking like they aren't even breathing. "I want to make myself clear. I am not making any sort of declarative statement with the information I am about to give you. I have not come to any set conclusions and I am not making any assumptions. This is simply a matter of cross-referencing cases to determine if they may be linked.

"Please do not take what I am about to discuss with you as a statement of anything. The reason I want to discuss this with you is it will be released into the media soon and I believe it would be better for you to hear it now while we can discuss it. I don't know if you will have any information to give me, but if you do, it could prove very helpful."

I take a moment to survey the room carefully, making sure I catalogue everyone's reactions to what's coming.

"The local police and I have recently received missing persons reports for Trisha Gable and Tyler O'Rourke."

The room erupts in gasps and cries. Despite the warning I just gave, I'm immediately peppered with questions and horrified assumptions start building. This is how damaging rumors are born. One person coming up with their own idea about what happened leads to someone else thinking that is fact and spreading it, which turns into those who hear it embellishing the story with their own details and assumptions until the story takes on a life of its own. I hold up my hands to stop them.

"Quiet, please. Again, I need you to understand that I am not saying anything other than the fact that they have not been in contact with family for several days. That's it. I am not saying anything happened to them. Right now, they are missing and we are trying to find them," I say.

"Then why tell us about them at the same time you're telling us that Professor Santucci is dead?" Presley asks. "That makes it sound like you think the same thing has happened to them."

Several voices shout loud agreements.

"Stop!" I shout to quiet them. "I will say this one more time. I am not implying anything. I am not one to make implications. I make statements. Right now, I am making the statement that there are two people missing and those people happen to overlap in some ways with Jesse Santucci's life. They are from the same area. That is enough to take note and keep both situations in mind at the same time."

"Tyler went to school with us," Helen says. "I met Trisha, but I don't know if she was a student or not."

"Okay. Thank you. That's helpful. Does anyone here know if Trisha was a student?" No one responds and I make a mental note to check with the Gables about whether she went to school at the local college. "I know I've kept you here for a while, so you are free to leave whenever you want to. For those of you who have something to share with me about Professor Santucci I haven't heard yet, or if you know Tyler and can tell me about him, I would really appreciate if you stayed around a little longer."

The crowd in the room thinned out, but many stayed. I get a few bits of information about the teacher, including that he enjoyed jogging with the suggestion of the trails we should check, and that he was heavily involved in extracurricular and social activities, including being a part of the events planning committee. Most recently, he helped plan a winter gala for the faculty and staff, as well as a select group of students invited based on personal and academic merit.

Once I have that information recorded, my attention turns to the people still here wanting to tell me about Tyler. I'm surprised to see Molly has stayed behind and is still sitting in the chair she perched on when she slipped into the back of the group.

"I knew Tyler freshman year. We were in an art class together. He was just doing it for the elective credits because he thought it would be a really easy high grade. I'm a double major, but one of them is art, so I get really aggravated by people who fill up the classes thinking they're just going to sail through because they don't take art seriously. We ended up clashing when we first talked to each other, but then we were cool," she says.

"Did you keep in touch after that?" I ask.

"Not specifically. We didn't, like, call each other and make plans to hang out or anything. But we ran into each other at events a couple of times and he came to a show that had some of my art on display."

"But there was never anything very personal about your relationship?" I ask.

"If you're asking if we ever had sex, no. It wasn't like that," she says.

"That's actually not what I was asking, but thanks for that detail. I was more asking if you knew him well. Did he talk to you about things that bothered him or his relationship with his girlfriend?"

"We weren't really like that. Like I said, we were cool. We'd talk during class, and I helped him out with some of his projects because he was a good guy, but that was really the extent of it. We never had any particularly deep conversations. If one of us was having a bad day or something we could vent, but we didn't bond over our past traumas or anything. And as far as I know, he wasn't dating anybody during that time. At least, I don't remember him ever mentioning a Trisha," Molly tells me.

"Alright. Thank you," I say.

"That it?" she asks.

"Yep. If there's anything else I can think of about anything, I know where to find you."

She lets out a heavy sigh. "I know you do."

She walks away and I can't help but notice that everything about her seems deadened compared to when I last spoke with her. She doesn't have the same sharpness, the same abrasiveness. She hasn't become suddenly pleasant, but there's a heavier feeling about her now.

I next speak with a couple of guys who tell me they were Tyler's roommates for a year. Their sophomore year the three of them had a close relationship and did just about everything together.

"And you aren't close anymore?" I ask.

"Not really," Jace says. "I mean, we're still friends, but we're just not tight like we used to be."

"What happened?"

Ben shrugs. "I don't really know. He just changed. He got quieter and didn't want to hang out with us as much anymore. He started leaving the apartment all the time without telling us where he was going and would be gone for a day or two before showing back up and acting like nothing happened. He just seemed like a different guy."

"Do you know if he was drinking heavily during that time or using any kind of drugs?" I ask.

"We were all drinking," Jace says. "It's college. I think it's a whole lot more likely somebody's drinking than they aren't. I don't know anything about drugs."

I lean slightly toward him like I'm going to share some insider information. "Just so we're clear, I'm FBI. Not DEA. If I'm doing a case that has to do with drugs, it's because it involves really heavy hitters. Manufacturers, traffickers, cartels. I don't care about kids who dabble on their own time."

They both nod.

"I think he might have been doing something," Ben says. "I don't know what. I never saw him do it, and he never told me anything. But I've had other friends who got wrapped up in things like that and they changed in a lot of the same ways. It's part of why I pulled back from him and didn't really argue when he wanted to move out. I didn't want to go through any of that again. It's too hard watching people struggle and not be able to do anything."

"I completely agree," I say. His head hangs slightly, and I can see the regret flickering through his eyes. "Listen to me. No matter what is happening with Tyler, it's not your fault. You didn't do anything wrong and there's nothing you could have done to change it. You were there for him as much as you could be and that's all anyone can ask of you. You can't be expected to sacrifice yourself for someone who isn't willing to save themselves."

"You're gonna find him, right?" asks Ben.

"I'll do my best. And if either of you has any idea of where he could be, what could have happened, or any information that could point me in the right direction, don't hesitate to call me. Right now, we need all the help we can get."

Jace nods, the emotion still flickering through his face. "Okay."

The next couple of conversations are similar, with the handful of students who stayed behind sharing with me that they had friendships at various levels of closeness with Tyler over the years and they all noticed him undergoing changes in the most recent years. Though none of them could pinpoint exactly what it was or even really when it happened, they knew the changes greatly influenced his personality and the people he kept up with.

My last conversation is with Nancy and Kylie. They walk up to me gripping hands like they are trying to give each other strength. I know both of them had Jesse Santucci as a professor several times and were fairly close with him as a result. They are taking his death hard, but it seems learning about Tyler's disappearance is compounding it.

Nancy fights her way through telling me that she and Tyler were in a few classes together and he had always walked her to her car afterward because they were night classes and he wanted to make sure she got to the car safely. But that stopped in the last couple of weeks of their last class together. He suddenly cut off talking to her completely, then missed the last week of the class. She doesn't know what happened to him or why he would change so dramatically, but she was worried then and is even more worried now.

Kylie is the last to speak. Others have lingered in corners and off to the sides of the room in smaller clusters, talking in quiet tones as they try in their own social comfort spaces to wrap their heads around everything they learned tonight. It's obviously getting to them, even the ones who didn't say anything to me and who I'm not sure knew the professor or either of the young couple. Even without the personal connections, the brutality of the deaths and the painful uncertainty and fear of the disappearances has shaken them up and their understanding of the world around them, when they walk out of here they will never be the same.

"I know both Tyler and Trisha," she tells me. "At least, I did. Not as a couple, though. I met them separately. We used to be very close, especially Tyler and me. But we haven't really spoken much over the last year."

"What happened that put the distance between you?" I ask.

"Just life taking us on different paths, I guess is the best way to put it. Not one specific thing. Just growing up and becoming different people," she says.

"A couple of others told me they noticed some changes in Tyler's personality and maybe his lifestyle over the last couple years. They didn't have precise reason, and some even said they couldn't figure out really what happened, only that he began to withdraw and was acting differently toward them. Is that what you experienced, too?"

She nods. "Yeah. That's how I would put it, too. I'm not sure what happened, if it was pressure at school or something going on in his personal life, but somewhere along the line a switch flipped and he wasn't the same person anymore."

It's interesting to me that several people have said the same thing about Tyler. I can't help but wonder if it was that personality change, and whatever it was going on his life that acted as the catalyst for it, that led to his disappearance. Even without the people who are, or were, in his social circles being as familiar with Trisha, her going missing at the same time as him isn't all that strange. They were a couple, and if he was wrapped up in something that might either cause or require him to disappear, she could easily be collateral damage. Or an accessory.

CHAPTER EIGHTEEN

"**H**ONESTLY, WHETHER OR NOT WE CAN FIND HIS MARRIAGE license is really my least concern right now," I say. "I'm much more worried about the fact that we can't seem to find his wife."

"I know, babe. I'm doing the best I can," Sam says. "When the school checked his personnel file to get his wife's phone number, they also gave me his home address."

"Perfect. Give it to me and I'll go over there," I say.

"Not by yourself," he says.

"It's a wellness check, Sam," I counter. "I'm just going over to a woman's house to make sure she is alright and possibly break the news to her that her husband is dead, likely murdered. I don't think that's going to require a lot of back up."

"Emma, you know as well as I do this is not just a wellness check."

"And you know as well as I do that doesn't change anything," I say. "You can come with me if you want, but I'm doing this now. Time isn't exactly a luxury we have a lot of right now. We know there's a woman somewhere who had her lungs cut out of her and possibly a third person whose eyes have been removed. There are also at least two missing people. We need to find out if Kristie Santucci belongs to one of those categories, or if she is sitting home wondering where her husband is."

"Or when she's going to need to start acting like the grieving widow and hoping people believe her alibi," Sam says.

"Another reason to get there as soon as possible," I say.

He sighs. "I can't go. Call Dean."

"He's working on his own case right now. I don't need an escort. And I don't need someone beside me with a gun," I say. "If for some reason that changes and something indicates I might need some help, then I'll call."

"You will?" he asks.

His voice is a little playful and tongue-in-cheek, but I can hear the real concern in his voice. The need for confirmation is not entirely misplaced. I haven't been the best at accepting help in the past. It's been getting better, but Sam doesn't like acknowledging that. I'm fairly certain he thinks if he recognizes that too much I'll just decide I've hit my quota and regress.

And in all honesty, that assessment might not be so entirely off track. I know why it's important to have backup, but I also know I am stubborn and impatient as all hell and really don't like to wait or depend on someone else when there's something I feel like I can do on my own. Especially when it is time sensitive.

"I will."

I leave the station with the Santucci home address typed into the GPS on my phone. It's a bit of a drive, bringing me past the housing complex and the college and into the next town beyond that. I grab a snack for the road and turn on my favorite podcast to keep me company. It makes the drive go by faster and I'm soon driving slowly through a neighborhood of midrange homes tucked back on wooded plots, creating the feeling that each is fully isolated from the others. This does not strike me as the kind of neighborhood where people get together for block parties or a chat over the fences while they do their gardening.

This is a neighborhood for people who want their privacy. The kind that would make it very easy to go missing and not have even your closest neighbors notice. I arrive at the house and sit in the driveway for a few moments just looking at it, trying to notice anything off about the house itself, the yard, or any of its other surroundings. Nothing looks out of place or like there was any kind of struggle here recently. There's a car in the driveway and the front porch light is on. It's still daylight, but there are a few people in my neighborhood in Sherwood who leave their lights on like that most of the day during the winter months because the sun sets so early and they don't want to be caught without it.

I get out and go to the front door. Ringing the doorbell gets me no response so I knock. Everything inside the house remains quiet, so I knock again. When I still don't hear anything and the door stays closed, I try the doorknob. It's locked, so I start moving around the perimeter of the house, looking into windows to see if there's anything amiss inside. I don't notice anything, but when I get to the back of the house and try one of the doors there, it opens.

Still standing outside, I put my head inside and call out to Kristie. There's no sound in the house, but a strange smell is enough to bring me the rest of the way inside. I announce and identify myself, making sure to speak clearly so no matter where she, or anyone else, may be in the house, they will know I'm here and won't be taken by surprise if I enter a room.

The door brought me into a bedroom that doesn't look like it's used very often. Likely a guest room set aside either to actually be used for guests who may show up for long weekends or for holidays, or simply because there are more bedrooms in the house than they need for themselves but they didn't want to leave it empty. I step the rest of the way inside, purposely leaving the door open. When entering an unfamiliar property or one that has any chance at all of being involved in a crime, it is important to maintain as many potential exits as possible. Leaving a door open this way also provides a point of reference for any backup I might call, showing them exactly where I entered or clearly demonstrating that someone closed the door when I indicate it has been left open.

I walk through the bedroom and take out my gun before opening the door. There's nothing in the hallway in front of me and I repeat my announcement of my presence. The smell is stronger, making my stomach turn a little. Continuing through the house, I still get no response, but when I enter the kitchen, I see a cutting board on the counter with several pieces of chicken breast laid out on it; the obvious source of the smell, as they seem to have been there for a few days.

Pausing, I take out my phone and call the local police to let them know what's going on. While I wait for them to arrive, I continue to look through the house. One of the closed doors opens up to a studio filled with stacks of t-shirts, various forms of design and print equipment, and packaging materials. I notice a stack of business cards at the corner of a desk against one wall that have the name Kristie Santucci.

It's the first thing I point out to Officer Collin Maguire when he responds several minutes later.

"It looks like she runs a home-based business. If that's her only career, she likely doesn't have any coworkers or anyone to notice she's missing. Considering her husband has now been found dead, this is particularly significant," I say.

As soon as I've finished clearing the house with the officers and making my statements, I start making calls. I need to find as much information about Kristie and her movements as I possibly can so I can trace when she might have disappeared and when her husband may have died or been murdered. My mind is split as I go into the investigation. The initial compulsion of most investigators at this point would be to think of Kristie as another victim and approach the investigation with the aim of finding her and deciphering what happened to her.

But there is the other part of my brain as well that is considering the possibility she may be involved. She could have either committed the crime herself or have had someone else help her and is now attempting to lie low. It would not be the first time I've dealt with one partner who has killed their spouse and then disappeared to garner sympathy. That isn't as unusual a set of circumstances as people would want it to be.

That nagging possibility remains in the back of my mind as I gather every bit of information I can about Kristie and Jesse Santucci and their marriage. It doesn't strike me as all that unusual that many of the students didn't know about his marriage despite being in his classes. College professors may carry on more personal relationships with their students than teachers of younger ages, but that doesn't mean they are close or that Jesse frequently discussed his private life with them. If he was the kind of man who simply prefers not to wear a wedding band and he also didn't have specific reason to talk about his life outside of his career with his students, they wouldn't have much reason to know.

That doesn't seem to be any indication of the state of their marriage, though. As I learn more about them it seems they were an idyllic couple. Combined with the fact that the lungs that were found seem to be from a woman older than Trisha, my instinct is that Kristie is not a clever culprit hiding away, but another victim.

With almost nothing to go on, my only option is to delve into the details of her life, tracking her online activities, getting warrants for her banking and other financial accounts, and scouring the house to find everything possible that may tell me when she disappeared. It seems like these people just vanished and I need to find out when and where they last were so I can start narrowing down what happened to them.

CHAPTER NINETEEN

WHILE I WAIT FOR THE INFORMATION I'VE REQUESTED TO COME through, I pivot my attention back to Jesse Santucci's body. It's crucial I find out how he ended up there.

Obviously, someone didn't just cut the ice open, put him under there, then put the ice back and seal it over. That would be a great Scooby-Doo plot twist, but it's not realistic for an actual real-world mystery. I'm staring at the photos of the pond and the place where the body was pulled out when Xavier comes and sits beside me.

"I don't understand how he ended up under the ice of a skating rink," I tell him. "Whoever put him there didn't just stuff him in and pour water back over until it froze up."

"That wouldn't work," Xavier says. "Technically speaking, it is very possible for someone to put the body there intentionally. Remember, it wasn't really a skating rink. It was a naturally occurring pond that froze over. A skating rink is very shallow. No room to stuff anybody. But this body of water has plenty of space for a body to be stashed away.

"It's a small pond and only has a moderate ice layer. Small ponds like that freeze much more quickly than larger bodies of water because of the heat generated and held within the water itself. They freeze from the top because the ice is lighter than the rest of the water, and when the water starts to freeze, it rises up to the surface and then solidifies further there.

"Depending on factors such as air movement and overall consistency of temperature, it would be quite possible for someone to cut a hole in the ice, deposit the corpse, and then put the plug of ice back into place, pouring water over the seams to seal them back up. But that would require some specialized equipment and a good amount of time without anyone being around to see or hear it."

"Which would be extremely unlikely considering the proximity of the pond to the house and how often those kids went out there to run around on the ice," I say.

"Which brings us to my conclusion… technically possible, but for the sake of accuracy, not possible. Like… technically it is possible for me to walk across a tightrope. But could I actually?"

Xavier squeezes his lips together and gives a slow shrug.

"Alright, so we're going to go with the far higher chance that this was not where the perpetrator intended the body to end up. They didn't actually pinpoint this pond and decide it would be a good place to leave a man with no heart so that a bunch of kids could find him. Which means him ending up there was an accident," I say.

"At the very least, a byproduct of circumstances," Xavier says.

"So, what are those circumstances?" I ask. I look back at the pictures, then him again. "I think we need to find out more about this pond."

Firmly bundled up against the deeper cold, Xavier and I venture into the woods to the pond. There's still crime scene tape clinging to a couple of the trees and the large hole in the ice is visible from the edge where we remain safely standing.

Xavier shakes his head when he sees it. "Walking out onto this ice was not a good idea."

"Probably not," I say.

"No probably. Not a good idea. Look at the color. The entire pond is white," he says.

"Aren't most skating rinks white?" I ask.

"Again, not a skating rink. This is a pond. Naturally forming ice. Clear ice is the strongest. It is pure water frozen solid. When you see cloudy or white ice, that means air bubbles have been incorporated into it. It is only about half as strong as clear ice. This ice should never have been walked on. It looks like it went through several temperature changes as well as a tremendous amount of agitation."

"What do you mean?" I ask.

"Ice that is frozen, melts, and then refreezes traps air and is not as strong. That can happen with naturally occurring ice because of outdoor temperatures, wind temperatures, wind movement, anything that might change the surface temperature of the ice or the temperature of the water beneath. Remember, the water itself is going to be warmer than the ice, and if it becomes warmer, it will damage the structural integrity of the ice by weakening the bottom portion of it. The top looks solid, but the white coloration is an indication that the bottom is no longer as strong and unlikely to be able to support much weight or movement," he says.

"Alright, so the pond froze, unfroze, and then froze again," I say.

"Not fully," Xavier corrects. "It didn't become solid, go fully liquid again, and then form another cap of ice. A layer of ice requires a couple of weeks to form at the very least, but then it's fairly well established and even if it is weakened by brief bouts of higher temperatures, it will remain in place until the full thaw."

"But it did get weakened by higher temperatures," I say.

"Yes. But it doesn't necessarily have to be the environmental temperature. The water flowing into the pond could have been warmer. Look." He gestures across the pond. "There's the access point. That stream feeds the pond."

We walk around the perimeter of the pond to get to the stream I hadn't noticed before. It dips down a small hill and feeds into the pond through a rocky area.

"It's definitely wide enough for a body to move down it," I say. "But could that happen? The water is moving, but it seems like it would take a lot more than that to actually transport a fully grown man."

"If there was a lot of rain in a short period of time, it could make the water move very quickly. Since there's a hill, the gravity would help once the body got there. It's not much of a decline, but gravity is gravity," Xavier says.

I nod. "Alright. We need to look into the weather patterns recently to see if there might have been a time of heavy rainfall after Jesse went missing. We also need to find out where this stream goes. If that's how he got into the pond, he was put into the water somewhere the stream connects."

"Well, entering extremely cold water does cause immediate paralysis and the victim often takes in a sudden deep breath, leading to drowning. But it doesn't generally cause spontaneous expulsion of the heart."

I stare at Xavier. He stares back.

After taking a series of pictures of the area and speaking some notes into my phone, we leave and head for the library to start our research. Looking over the land use plans shows that the stream feeding into the pond branches off into three other streams that lead into other bodies of water, all fed by a spring.

There was a stretch of heavy rains a few days before the Christmas market at the village green, and looking further into the weather of the entire area shows this town experienced the same intense rainfall along with somewhat higher temperatures that very suddenly plunged. With that in mind, my theory of how Jesse Santucci's body ended up beneath the ice of the pond solidifies.

His body must have been dumped into one of the bodies of water connecting to the pond and was moved downstream by the heavy rainfall. The pond had already formed a layer of ice, but the warmer weather impacted the strength of the ice by slightly thawing the bottom of the layer. The body entered the pond and the deep freeze that happened just after sealed it in place. It's the perfect combination of factors that came together to put him right where he would be found as he did. The question is what the person who left his body thought was going to happen to it.

Did they somehow know it would move and end up in a deeper body of water?

Or did they think it would stay right there and not be noticed?

Or did they intend for it to be found there all along?

Studying the movements of the water and the wind over the time prior to the heart being found helps us to narrow down the likely spots where the body was put into the water, eventually bringing me to the largest of the three streams. Standing in the grass on a cold, overcast day looking at the gray water sends a chill along my spine. The area gives off a miserable feeling. It's quiet to the point of desolation, giving off the sense that there was no one else for miles.

Looking around at the shrived grass and bare trees, though, it occurs to me that it may be that very feeling that makes this place appealing. It has this foreboding appearance and chill because it's December. In the spring, however, it will come to life. The grass will turn lush and green. The leaves will sprout once again on the trees. Flowers dotting the banks will burst into bloom. Even the water will look fresh and clear. It will be a beautiful place, and the lonely, isolated feeling could easily become private and serene.

I look closely along the edge of the water, trying to find any indication of other people being here any time recently. It looks untouched until a couple dozen yards away from where I parked, where I find an area of grass that looks slightly matted. Moving it aside with my toe, I find tire impressions in the dirt. They are only partial and not particularly clear, but it shows that a vehicle did come this way fairly recently.

I walk from that spot toward the water and then along the edge, moving away from where I have already been standing and looking out over the wide stream. It's faint, but I spot it after a brief search of the area. Right there, on the rocks near the mouth of the water, is the faint spatter of what I know all too well to be blood.

"It looks like we found the right spot," Xavier says, looking down at where I'm pointing.

"He wasn't just dumped here," I say. "It looks like this is where he was killed. Most of the intense rain would've washed the blood away, but clearly it didn't get all of it. Some of it must have dried into the rocks before the rain started. At least that answers the question of how his body was transported. It isn't easy to pick up the dead body of a grown man and move it around. But if he was killed and his heart was cut out right here, all the killer would have to do is push or roll his body into the water. But it still doesn't answer the question of who."

After the scene is processed and I've gotten the photographs I want, I go back home to continue trying to track Jesse Santucci and his wife. The chirping sound of my phone telling me I have a text stops me following a rabbit hole on a website of reviews posted about professors by their students and colleagues. I finish reading a long-winded negative review of Santucci that describes him as being unfair in his grading and showing clear preferences among his students before picking up my phone.

The message is from a number I don't recognize, but the message itself tightens my chest.

The professor hasn't lived happily ever after.

CHAPTER TWENTY

T HE MESSAGE IS EQUAL PARTS CHILLING AND INTRIGUING. I TRY TO run the number through reverse lookup sites to find out who it belongs to, but there's no name associated with it. It's from a texting app, which brings the number up as being a landline rather than providing me any sort of identifying information. I read the message over and over. It's short and seems to have little nuance, and yet, that draws me into it even more.

I know Santucci was a literature professor, which makes the wording of the message appropriate. It could simply be a crass reference to his sudden and unexpected death. But I don't think so. Even if someone wanted to make that kind of comment while making a cheeky hint at his profession, there would be plenty of other more creative and meaningful ways to do that. This reference is pointed. It's the end of every fairy tale, celebrating the romance between the characters, which tells me it's actually about his marriage. Maybe there was something going on in his relationship that I haven't uncovered.

When I was interviewing the students at the housing complex I heard several times how sweet Kristie was and how wonderful their marriage was. The same was reiterated among colleagues I spoke with. It sounded like while many people didn't even realize he was married, those who did had a very clear image of their relationship and saw it as very successful and happy.

The idea that their marriage might not have been everything envisioned by people on the outside looking in could be a very important part of unraveling this case. Someone wants me to think about his marriage differently than others have wanted me to. They want me to know there were problems. It brings my mind briefly back to the possibility his wife could have been responsible for his death, but that still doesn't feel exactly right. Which means someone else knows about the issues going on between them and thinks they are important to the case.

If there's someone else involved in the relationship, or even more than one person, this could point to motive. I need to look deeper into their marriage and find the truth of what it was actually like. I need to know what might have been going on between the two of them in recent months so I can expand my circle of possible persons of interest to include those who might have interfered with what was apparently, at least at one time, wedded bliss.

Generally, one of the first things I would do when trying to find out about the life of a murder suspect is to speak with their close family. Most of the time this starts with their spouse and their parents. These are the people who know them and their lives the best, and usually will provide me with the most in-depth and reliable information about the person and their life.

But this time I don't have those resources available to me. I found out very quickly after learning about Jesse Santucci's disappearance and death that his parents are both deceased. He did not have any siblings or other close family, leaving only his wife as who would be considered kin. Since Kristie is also missing and, like her husband, doesn't have parents or siblings to speak to, I'm stuck without that valuable source of information. My next step is to revisit those in the next level of his circle, friends and coworkers.

I already spoke with several of them at the very beginning of the investigation, but that was for a general overview rather than with anything specific in mind. This time I'm pointed, going into the conversations with the direct goal of finding out as much as I can about Jesse and Kristie's marriage so I can try to decipher the strange message and also figure out what that might mean for the investigation.

I make it a point not to mention the strange text message when I approach the first man I'm interviewing, a man named Steven who shows up on Jesse's fairly sparse social media more frequently than anyone else. I don't want to give away that I have my suspicions, or that someone is giving me information that might make me feel suspicious. Instead, I want him to tell me genuinely what he thought of their marriage.

I word the questions carefully to give him as much room as possible to truly tell me how he feels and what he thinks about the situation. Often when having these conversations with suspects, witnesses, or the people on the periphery who fill in the blanks, investigators can inadvertently present questions that are restrictive and prevent the person from actually saying what's on their mind. I try to ask questions that have widely open ends so they can fill them up as much as possible.

Unfortunately, even with my open-ended questions, Steven doesn't have much to tell me in response. I already spoke to him at the beginning of the investigation, but this time, I go into the conversation with a notification that Kristie is missing. Steven seems shocked by the revelation but doesn't give any kind of editorialization. He doesn't offer the kind of questions I've come to expect in situations like this.

When people find out that someone is missing, they often start asking questions that have no answer as they work on processing what happened.

"*Where could they have gone?*"

"*Did someone take them?*"

"*Why would they do something like this?*"

"*How could they hurt their spouse like this?*"

"*How could something like this happen to such a perfect couple?*"

After those questions usually comes the set of questions that very well may have answers but that aren't immediately obvious. The kinds of questions that dig a bit deeper and tell tales the person might not realize they are giving away.

"*Did you check with his cousin?*"

"*Did he go to his usual tennis lesson on Wednesday?*"

"*Has anyone asked their couples therapist if she knows anything?*"

"*Did he find out about her affair?*"

Steven didn't ask any questions. No rhetorical ones. None with answers that could guide the investigation, whether he knew it or not. He simply blinked at me and said he couldn't believe they were both gone. I didn't correct him, even though there's still no solid verification that Kristie is dead. Precision isn't the most important thing right now.

Whether she is alive or not, right now, she is, in his mind, gone, right along with his good friend.

Without the questions to prop up the conversation, I have to take a fully straightforward approach.

"How would you describe their marriage?" I ask.

He doesn't look taken aback by the question but takes a second to form what he wants to say.

"It was great. Far better than a lot of the marriages for people I know. They're both really wonderful people, so they're great together. They've been together a really long time. They met in college and connected over the loss of their parents and being only children. Then they found out they have a lot of shared interests. They really loved the outdoors. They'd go hiking all the time. We used to joke that most women think of a fancy restaurant as the ideal romantic date, but Kristie wanted a campfire and a sleeping bag," he says.

"So, they were getting along well and didn't seem to have any problems?" I ask.

"They were getting along great," Steven says. "And they've never had problems, at least not that I've ever heard of. I wouldn't say they never argue, because everybody argues. But it was just the occasional disagreement or not seeing eye to eye on something. They didn't have long drawn-out battles or hold grudges against each other or anything."

I get much the same information from the next couple of people I speak with. They all saw Jesse and Kristie as having the perfect marriage and insisted that nothing bad was happening between them, or had happened between them in recent months. According to a neighbor I spoke with, they would both be completely lost and devastated without the other, and she honestly hoped Kristie was dead, too, because then she wouldn't have to try to cope with the loss of her beloved husband. She promptly apologized for the comment, looking horrified that she said it, but I reassured her I understood what she meant.

Facing an actual possibility of death makes assertions that are fully accurate seem extremely uncomfortable. The truth is, for tightly bonded married couples, death would be better than having to live without each other. At least in death, they would be together. Saying that when both partners are healthy and well sounds romantic and strong. Saying it when one is cold with a hole in his chest where his heart should be and the other is missing can come across as morbid and insulting.

It isn't until I've started working my way through the people who worked with him at the college that I get some traction. The first couple of colleagues said the same things I'd already heard, but then I meet

Mike Escher, an intro-level math instructor who seems incredibly eager to gain approval and very pleased to feel like he's giving me insider information only he has. Because of the puppy-dog yipping style, I am cautious about listening to what he has to say, aware he might be embellishing to keep feeding that feeling of being important.

"I've heard that Kristie and Jesse liked doing things together in the outdoors. Is that something you knew about them?" I ask.

"Oh, yeah," Mike says. "Yeah, I knew that. They really liked going camping. I showed Jesse how to make a campfire one time to help him do it more efficiently and he really appreciated it. It totally changed how he camped from then on."

"Did you camp with him?" I ask.

"No. He didn't quite have the skills I do so I think he was intimidated."

"Oh, really?" I ask. "Everyone else seems to think he was really comfortable in the outdoors and knew what he was doing. They spent a lot of time out there."

"Well... yeah. I mean, yeah, he did."

I decide not to keep going down that path before I end up learning how to make a campfire. Instead, I lean right into the couple again.

"So, what else about them? They liked the outdoors, but that's not a whole relationship. What else did they do? How did they get along? Were things good between them?"

Peppering him with questions is meant to throw off his game a little. This man is clearly someone who likes to be in control. He wants to hold the conversation and determine where it's going to go and what gets emphasized, like he's playing pinball. I'm not going to let that happen. Just as he's about to answer, the door opens and a woman comes in. She looks surprised to see me standing there and stops in her tracks, backing up a step.

"Oh. I'm sorry. I didn't realize someone was in here," she says.

"It's fine," Mike says. "This is Emma Griffin. She's an FBI agent investigating Jesse's death."

"Oh, wow," the woman says.

"Emma, this is Doris Gaiman. She's the beating heart of this department," Mike says.

I take that to mean she is administrative personnel of some type. I remember the administrative assistant Dinah from my early years of college and how she essentially ran the entire department. Every member of the faculty deferred to her and would have been completely lost without her there to help them with everyday tasks and logistical nightmares that came up.

"Hello. It's nice to meet you," I say.

"You as well," Doris says. "We are all devastated by Jesse's death. I can't even wrap my head around it. He was just here. I took a picture with him at the Christmas gala. It just doesn't seem real."

"I know how that feels," I say.

"Emma is asking about Jesse and Kristie's marriage," Mike says.

There's a note in his voice that sounds like he's speaking in some kind of code, like he means something more than just the words he's saying. She clearly understands the implications because her head bobs slightly and she utters what I'm coming to understand is her favorite word.

"Oh." She looks at me. "Well, if you ask me, there was something going on there."

"I am asking you," I say simply.

She and Mike exchange another look. "Jesse has never been very big on talking about his marriage to a lot of people. Those of us who have known him a long time know her, obviously, but he's not the type to go around sharing stories about his personal life or showing off pictures of him and his wife together."

"How about his wedding ring?" I ask.

"He used to wear one, but he broke his hand a few years back and they had to cut it off in the emergency room. After that, he said it made him anxious to wear one because it brought back the memories of that injury, so he doesn't," Doris explains in response.

It's a plausible, if interesting, explanation.

"What else?" I ask.

"Well," she says, "I don't have any real specifics I can give you, but I thought there might be some tension in their relationship a couple of months ago. But things were getting much better recently. They looked happy at the gala. He'd given her some jewelry as an early Christmas gift to wear and she was showing it to everyone. They danced and laughed. It looked like they'd gotten to a much better place."

"But you don't have any idea of what might have been going on to create the tension in the first place?" I ask.

They exchange another glance.

"Again, nothing specific," Mike says. "But there's a pretty short list of things that cause tension in most marriages and he never complained about money."

It's a delicate approach, one that is intended to give me a hint without associating him specifically with spreading rumors. Even without the details, I feel like I've found a solid lead. If the couple was going through a rough patch because of one of the common causes of difficulty in marriages, and it didn't have to do with money, it seems they are just giving more credence to my thought that someone else was involved in the marriage between Jesse and Kristie Santucci. Someone who didn't get the ending they wanted and decided to create one of their own.

CHAPTER TWENTY-ONE

M Y KITCHEN FILLS WITH THE AROMA OF COFFEE BREWING, AND A bowl of fresh cinnamon roll dough is rising by the edge of the stove when my phone rings early the next morning. I've come to learn that phone calls that come in when the sky is still milky blue and edged with pink are almost never a good thing. In fact, I can count on one hand the number of times I've actually gotten one of these predawn calls and it ended with me smiling.

This is no exception.

"Agent Griffin, this is Savannah. I need you to respond to Orchid Park immediately. The back walking loop near the azalea gardens."

The young deputy's voice is tense and harsh, very different from what she usually sounds like when I talk to her at Sam's precinct. She's a determined, intense officer striving to push through the ranks and with eyes on the head of a homicide division in a bigger city one day, but she's also a friendly, bubbly woman who never misses an opportunity to stop for a quick chat when I'm at the office. I've had the chance to work with her before when I've helped Sam out on cases, but I've never heard her sound quite like this.

"What's going on, Savannah?" I ask.

"We found Tyler O'Rourke."

I want to feel hopeful as I'm driving as fast as I can through the first rays of sunlight, the coffee pot turned off mid-brew after filling my mug with what had already been made, and the dough stuffed in the refrigerator to slow down the rise. I want to think that because she said he was found and didn't give me any more details before hanging up that there's a chance Tyler is still alive and was simply found after being held for several days. Maybe she ended the call because she is assisting the medical first responders in helping him.

But I can't muster that kind of hope. She would have said it. She would have told me he's alive and the circumstances of him being found. There's no reason to maintain suspense. I know he's dead. It's just a matter of finding out how he died.

The park where Savannah directed me is a popular spot among locals of several surrounding towns. Though it is technically located in Sherwood, it is frequently claimed to be owned by Marlon and two others as well. People flock to the sprawling space to walk wooded trails, jog on paved paths, have picnics, and just enjoy quiet time. There are frequently dozens of people roaming the park by the time the sun is up, getting their exercise first thing in the morning and taking some time to center and prepare for whatever challenges lie ahead for them.

For two of them, that includes coping with the reality of stumbling on the body of Tyler O'Rourke propped in the corner of a gazebo bench, his head rested against a support beam like he was taking a nap. It wasn't until they walked around to the side of the gazebo and one glanced back over her shoulder that she noticed the rivulets of dried blood down his cheeks and on the front of his shirt.

By the time I get there, it seems everyone who was in the park this morning has now gathered around the gazebo and is gawking at the horrifying image. Savannah, along with two other officers, is doing her best to hold them back, commanding they keep their cell phones in their pockets and trying to collect them off to the side so that they can be interviewed.

The people standing around aren't just frustrating, they can be a major hindrance to the investigation itself. The initial review of a crime scene is a very delicate process. Every possible avenue of evidence needs to be considered, which includes trying to identify footprints and small clues that could have been left behind by the culprit such as fibers, hairs, or dropped items. Having this many people gathered around compromises the validity of any possible evidence found. Just by walking in the area, they are potentially contaminating the entire scene.

I push through the crowd and Savannah rushes toward me.

"Sam is responding to another call, but he will be here soon," I tell her. "What can you tell me?"

She leads me into the gazebo to where a blue tarp has been set up on a metal frame between the body and the crowd to block their view.

"Two women were taking their usual walk down this path early this morning. They've been coming here to do this walk three times a week for the last few years, and they've gotten to know some of the regulars who take walks at around the same time. One person they see fairly often is a young man walking his dog. When they first noticed the body, they thought it might be that young man. Ellen Garfield, the woman on the right over there, was worried when he didn't seem to move or make any acknowledgement of them going past, so she turned around to look at him and make sure he was alright. That's when she noticed the blood and that it wasn't that young man," she says.

"Alright. Any apparent cause of death yet?" I ask.

"Not yet. The medical examiner and CSU are on the way," she replies.

"I want to talk to the two women who found him and then get statements from everyone who is around. Even if they weren't anywhere near this section of the park today according to them, I want a full description of what they've been doing, who they saw, if they heard anything. Everything."

Savannah gives a sharp bounce of her head and starts toward another of the officers. I'm headed for Ellen Garfield and her companion when I hear my name. Turning toward the sound of the voice, I see Nancy, Kylie, and Lila clustered close together at the edge of the crowd. I cross to them.

"What are you girls doing here?" I ask.

"Taking pictures," Nancy says. "For a project I'm working on."

"A project? The semester is over."

"It's for my portfolio. I'm studying fashion design and I have to build an entire portfolio before graduation. My collection is inspired by the changing of the seasons, so I've been taking pictures of the same areas of the park during different months over the last year for reference," she explains.

"What's happening?" Kylie asks. "Why is that tarp up?"

"Is it true that someone is dead over there?" Lila asks in a half-whisper, her eyes welling with tears. "Did someone have a heart attack while they were jogging?"

"This isn't a heart attack," Kylie says. "The FBI doesn't respond to heart attacks. He had to have been murdered."

"Why did you come here today?" I ask.

Nancy's teary eyes meet mine and widen. "Why are you asking that? Do you think we did something?"

"I'm just asking you the same questions everyone else here is going to be asked," I tell her. "I'm having the officers get statements from everyone around here right now and everyone else they can find in the park. Right now we're not releasing any information. We need to establish a timeline as quickly as possible and the easiest way to do that is to find out who was in the park, why they were here, and what they were doing. It will streamline the investigation.

"It's especially important in situations like this when there is an unexpected death in a public area and people enter the scene without investigator knowledge. We could find trace evidence that links to someone who was here, but by getting the statement ahead of time, we can explain why something like hair or a footprint is present and eliminate their involvement."

"Unexpected death?" Kylie asks. "So, not a murder?"

"If it wasn't murder, there would be no evidence being collected," Helen points out.

"Is that Molly?" Nancy asks.

I follow her gaze and see a figure walking away, her head tucked down as she hurries down the path. I gesture at the nearest officer, and he descends on her, stopping her progress and guiding her back toward the area. I can see it is, in fact, Molly. She looks just about as miserable as she has every other time I've seen her, but this time she's more fidgety, rocking back and forth with her hands stuffed down in the pockets of her oversized black hoodie. The temperature is too cool for her to be wearing only that, which makes me wonder how long she's been here and if someone is parked nearby waiting for her.

"He'll get her statement from her," I say, trying to direct the girls back to the conversation we're having rather than letting them get distracted by Molly being there apparently without them knowing. "Let's just go back to why you decided to come here this morning. I know you said you are working on a project, but what led your decision to choose today rather than any other day?"

"It was me," Kylie says. "I'm leaving for a trip in just a couple of days and I'm starting to get emotional about being away from everybody, especially everything going on with Professor Santucci and Tyler and Trisha. It's really weighing on all of us and I wanted to spend more time with them before I go. I know that Nancy is working on this project and thought it would be a good opportunity to do something useful while also spending time together.

"I've always loved this park and it seemed like a nice time to visit. I've seen some of the pictures she's taken, and they are so amazing, so I wanted to be a part of getting the ones for December." She shakes her head. "I'm so sorry I did. I can't believe this is happening."

I don't like the answer and I tuck it to the side in my mind as I ask them basic details about coming to the park and they tell me they rode together and had only been there a short time. They hadn't even taken the pictures yet. They show me texts from last night planning the visit and Nancy pulls up a debit card transaction for gas only twenty minutes before I arrived at the park. Satisfied for now, I let the girls go.

There's almost nothing to go on. I walk around the tarp and see the body for the first time. He's stiff and discolored, likely from the cold. The blood on his face has long since dried. I don't see any kind of highly visible wound or weapon nearby that might indicate how he was killed. The blood on his face is concerning, but for right now I don't know if it is related to his cause of death or something else. There's a twisting feeling in my belly telling me I already know why the blood is there. I just need to wait for confirmation from Keegan.

The CSU arrives and starts processing the scene. Keegan gets here minutes later and looks over the body.

"I'll let you know," she says as the body is loaded onto a gurney to be wheeled to a waiting vehicle.

I didn't even have to ask her a question. She already knows what is on my mind.

As the team is continuing to go over the area with a fine-toothed comb trying to find anything that could generate a lead, I look around, for the first time really taking in how isolated this section of the park is. It isn't visible from any of the parking areas or the larger clearings. There aren't other trails just through the woods like there are in other parts of the park. It's the deepest part, which means the least likely to be surveilled.

It seems the opposite would be true and a place like this would make sure there was security coverage, or at the very least a trail camera, active near the least frequently used areas of the park to cut down on the possibility of crime. But that's simply not something that crosses the minds of people in this area. When they think of a park, they think of serenity and wholesomeness. They don't want to consider that there's any such thing as a seedy underbelly anywhere near where they live.

I know too well there's nowhere exempt from crime or tragedy.

In fact, it's the places that seem the calmest and most unassuming that often attract the most horrifying of events. The people who commit these crimes know they are less likely to be detected in what others view as safe havens. Those areas like this park that are easily accessible even at night and that have no type of surveillance equipment.

The innocence of Sherwood is really showing. It isn't that I think we need cameras covering every inch of the world at all times. I believe in privacy and the need to be able to live life without someone watching us. But there's still the strong pull in the center of my chest and the back of my mind every time I realize a place has absolutely nothing to provide even the smallest amount of help when terrifying crimes happen. The pull that says if they knew they were being watched, the criminals would often choose not to do what they do. Or at the very least, we'd have details like when the crime occurred, how many people were involved, what they looked like, and exactly what happened.

Those are the kinds of details that knit together the beginning of an investigation. They are what can make the difference between a case that is solved quickly and without further loss of life, and one that lingers on and results in further deaths.

But at the same time, I want to hold onto that feeling of comfort that comes with not thinking about the negative things of life. When my mind hasn't gone into the dark spaces where it generally resides during the harsh trenches of a case, I cherish the times when I can be somewhere and not see a camera or a flashing red light. I love when I can go an entire day without reading a warning sign. Having pockets in this world that still allow for moments of peace is a beautiful thing.

It leaves me struggling over whether we in Sherwood should continue to hang onto the innocence, or if it's time to bend to the horror and start monitoring more of our surroundings in an effort to protect the people within it.

CHAPTER TWENTY-TWO

Them

WATCHING TYLER BE FOUND WAS HARDER THAN I THOUGHT IT would be. I know I did what I had to do, but I was surprised by how intense the experience was. Just standing there watching brought up all the feelings and emotions I wanted to get rid of. It was like every person standing around me wondering what had happened was another needle plunging into the center of my heart.

Everything I was trying not to feel rushed into me as soon as I stepped foot into the crowd and watched the whole thing unfold. I have to fight hard against the demeanor I'm trying to maintain. No one around me can know what's happening. I can't let them see it in my eyes if they look my way. I need to reflect the same confusion, the same horror as they have. What they see is a blue tarp blocking their view. They assumed it was a body. Then they heard it was. They don't know who it was, or why it was there.

I need to portray the same.

They can't think even for a second that I might know more about it than they do. I can't let them have any suspicion. I need to blend in with everybody else and seem just as bewildered as they do, just as taken aback by my morning being so suddenly and intensely shattered. But it isn't easy. I still feel everything I don't want to. I want to say his name. I want to yell and spit and tell him exactly why he ended up where he is.

And as I shove those feelings down and continue to look around me at pale, stricken faces, I wonder if this is, in a way, cleansing me. I'm going through all these feelings now because they are leaving me. Now that I've done what needed to be done, I am ridding myself of the suffering and it is being purged from the depths of my being.

I can't stay here as long as I want to. If I had my way, I would watch every second of the investigation to see what they think and which direction they go. I know at some point, I'm going to have to leave. It would draw far too much attention if I just lingered here. But for as long as I am able to stay, I watch Emma Griffin. It's easy to see the confusion and frustration on the face of the pretty FBI agent. It drew her eyebrows together so hard that when we spoke, I could see deep wrinkles in her forehead.

But they disappeared as soon as she forced her face to relax. As I watch her, I can't help but think about her life and how good it must be. She's probably never dealt with anything like I've gone through. But this isn't going to be easy on her. Emma Griffin's work is far from finished. There's so much left for her to discover and do.

And I'll be right here to watch.

This isn't about her. It doesn't matter to me who takes on the investigation. But knowing the Bureau is already involved makes my stakes higher. I have to tread lightly, to plan carefully. Everything has to come out exactly as I've wanted it to, or this was all for nothing. I'm a step ahead. Maybe two. She doesn't know and I'm going to keep it that way.

CHAPTER TWENTY-THREE

TYLER LIKELY DIED FROM AN INJECTION OF SOME KIND OF VERY fast-acting poison. The full toxicology report will have to come in before Keegan can know for sure what killed him, but that is her strongest theory.

The blood dripping down his face came from his eyes being removed. Apparently, the poison didn't act fast enough for his heart to stop before they were cut out.

It's an image I don't envy Keegan finding and one I try not to hold in my mind as I walk into the house of Kayla O'Rourke, Tyler's mother. Her name had immediately conjured images of girls I went to school with, and I'm not surprised to see a woman very close in age to me when she opens the door to invite me inside. She had to have had Tyler when she was a teenager.

She isn't a small woman, but the grief weighing on her makes her look somehow frail and vulnerable. I want to take her arm and guide her into the living room even as she is directing me there. We sit down and she looks at the worn coffee table in front of the couch like she's hoping somehow in her fog she has remembered to brew a pot of coffee or tea, or at least put out a couple of glasses of water. Instead, there's nothing there but rings left behind from easier times.

"Can I get you something?" I ask. "Do you want some water before we talk?"

She turns big eyes toward me. Clear blue and framed with a fringe of thick, long lashes, even through the lines that have formed around them and the heavy dark circles surrounding them, they are beautiful. I immediately think of the eyes found in the box at the Christmas shop in the mall. Tyler's eyes.

"I...sure," she says.

She doesn't tell me where the kitchen is, but the house isn't complicated, so I walk out of the living room and turn down the hallway to find it. I don't know which cabinet to look in for a glass and feel strange just going through all of them, so I try for a more direct approach first. Opening the dishwasher, I find a small assortment of clean dishes sitting in the racks. It makes sense that she wouldn't be too concerned about putting her dishes away fresh out of the dishwasher when she was dealing with her son's disappearance and then the news of his death.

I fill the glass with water from the dispenser in the refrigerator door and then fill another for myself. Kayla is leaning forward, her elbows rested on her thighs and her face in her hands when I get back to the living room. She sits up straighter when she hears the glass touch the table. One hand shakes as it wraps around the glass and brings it up to her lips. She swigs the water down like she hasn't had anything to drink today. I wouldn't be surprised if that turns out to be true.

"First, I want to tell you how sorry I am for your loss. I don't have children, so I can't tell you I know what you're feeling. But my mother as well as dear friends were murdered, so I can in some way imagine the pain you're going through. I apologize for having to come here so soon and talk to you about this when you are still trying to process the news," I say.

"It's alright," she says, sniffling and shaking her head. She squares her shoulders and bends her neck back and forth a couple of times like she is preparing herself for some sort of athletic feat. "I understand. You have to get the information from me as soon as possible so you can move ahead with your investigation."

"Exactly," I say.

"I want you to do everything to find out who did this to my son," she says with the kind of fierce, rumbling anger that only a mother can have in her voice.

"I will," I promise her. "I have already started the investigation. But I need your help. I need you to tell me everything you can about your son, his friends, anything he was going through in his life. I'm sure you are already aware that his death is not isolated. It is part of a larger, complicated situation that I am working to unravel. Right now, anything I can learn about him could be helpful. Since we don't yet have a direction to go, we don't know what could be beneficial and what likely isn't."

Kayla takes another sip of water and a steeling breath before talking. She tells me about her son, the smart, well-rounded, driven young man who chose to attend the smaller local college close to home rather than the larger, more impressive university that had accepted him because it would be less expensive and would also allow him to help take care of his elderly grandmother. She talks about Tyler's close relationship with her mother, starting when he was just a baby, and her mother took care of him while she worked to support him. She was very young and single, but determined to give her son the best life she could, and part of that was having him at home with his grandmother rather than in daycare.

That started a bond that only grew stronger as he got older and continued until his disappearance. She gushes about Trisha, how sweet and lovely she is, and how much she likes her. She hoped so much for a future for the two of them. She knew they were still young and it was still early in their relationship relatively speaking, but she could see in their eyes that they were the real thing. These two were perfect for each other and she didn't see the point in them waiting too long to make things official. She'd never had the opportunity and she wanted so much to see it for Tyler.

I don't want to ask the question I have to, but there's nowhere else to go in this conversation that's going to have any benefit if I don't.

"Can you think of anyone who had something against Tyler? Any grudges or arguments?" I ask.

Kayla's face twists slightly as the question settles on her. "No. Tyler is… was such a sweet boy. There wasn't anything about him anyone could hate. Especially not enough to do something like that. There were friends he had drifted away from, but that happens as you get older. And former girlfriends, as most young men his age have. There were also a couple of Trisha's former boyfriends. But it wasn't ever anything dangerous or threatening.

"He had words with one of Trisha's old boyfriends when that guy tried to get Trisha back and was being rough with her at a party they all went to, but it didn't amount to anything. He's in jail now for being difficult with the wrong person and getting into a much worse fight."

"You said he drifted away from some of his friends? Why is that?" I ask.

She shrugs. "I don't think anything bad happened or anything, he just wasn't in the same place in life anymore. They graduated high school, they went their separate ways. But I don't understand. Why are you trying to make this a personal attack on Tyler? There are other victims, right? That professor from the college? Why would there be another death like that if this had anything to do with Tyler specifically?"

The question itself isn't all that strange. It's actually one I would probably ask if I was put in anything close to the situation she is in now. But there's something about the way she asked it that sticks with me. It makes me feel like Kayla O'Rourke isn't necessarily telling me the full truth. She's holding something back.

Even though I have that feeling, I don't want to press her any further. She is going through such an incredibly traumatic experience right now she is fragile. I need to be careful or I might end up causing her to withdraw or even contribute to a further downward spiral. Kayla needs to work through these first stages and settle more into this new reality for her before I try to get any more information out of her. When she's ready, I'll talk to her again.

"It's just a standard part of investigations like this," I offer. "I have to look at it from every possible angle."

That seems to mollify her, and we chat for a few more moments about nothing significant and then I excuse myself.

"Thank you so much for your time," I say as I stand up. "I really appreciate your willingness to speak with me and for being so helpful."

"Of course," she says. "Like I said, I want you to find out who did this to my Tyler. No matter what it takes."

I take out one of my business cards and hand it to her. "If you think of anything you didn't tell me, or if you have any questions you think I could help you with, please don't hesitate to call me. That's my cell number so I always have it near me. Day or night."

"Thank you," Kayla says, looking down at the card for a second before bringing her striking blue eyes back to me. "For everything."

I drive away from the house with an even more intense heaviness sitting on my spine at the base of my skull. The weight of my thoughts won't lessen and only seems to be getting worse the deeper I go into this investigation. The heart and the eyes have been accounted for and I have two bodies to show for it. But they are both men. The women are still missing. I don't have any doubt they are dead. Even the most cynical part of my mind that continuously whispers they could be working together to eliminate both of the men is no longer loud enough to convince me. It is clear beyond question both Kristie and Trisha have been murdered.

It's just a matter of finding them. Unfortunately, I am also waiting for something else. Another body part. We have a heart, a pair of eyes, and a pair of lungs, but four people. The lungs I am convinced belong to Kristie Santucci, which means there's something missing from the girlfriend, wherever she is, and it's our task to find it.

Unless she is miraculously still alive and just being held, her severed body part and the rest of her are out there somewhere, just waiting to be found.

CHAPTER TWENTY-FOUR

I DON'T GET THE NOTE BACK INTO MY DESK DRAWER IN TIME BEFORE Sam sees it later that evening. I've done my best to keep it out of sight and not pore over it, but every now and then, I can't help but revisit the sinking feeling I got in my stomach the first time I read the words.

I didn't save you for you. I saved you for myself.

"You're looking at it again?" he asks, coming into my office.

"It just came into my head today. I don't know why, I just felt like I needed to see it. I know it doesn't make sense, but I just felt like I needed to read it," I say.

"You've already read it," Sam says. "A dozen times. Probably more. You know what it says. And you also know how I feel about it."

"Yes, I do," I say, putting it back in the drawer and closing it firmly.

"Then you know I'm going to ask why you still haven't turned it over to police."

It's what he's been harping on since the night I found the note outside our house. He thinks I should have immediately called the police as soon as I read the note. It's an obvious threat, but I still haven't felt the need to get anybody else involved.

"I don't need to turn it over to police. I have my very own sheriff," I say with a hint of a smile, hoping it will distract him, but it doesn't work.

"That's not the same thing and you know it. Having a sheriff as a husband doesn't preclude involving police in threatening situations," he says. "This is serious, Emma."

"I know that, Sam," I tell him, all humor gone from my voice. "I know this is serious. I'm the one who was out there in that parking lot, remember. I'm the one who was staring that man down, knowing he wanted to cut me to pieces the way he had the other women. And I'm the one who watched him get forced out of the way by a car only to later find out it was by someone who wanted to seek their own revenge against me rather than a good Samaritan who didn't hang around long enough to be acknowledged and thanked.

"That's serious. I'm well aware of it. But I don't know what you think is going to happen, or even what police I'm supposed to give it to. This is far beyond the scope of your department, or the department in any of the places where I've been. A special agent is being threatened, which means this situation is the territory of the Bureau. And I am the Bureau."

"You can't investigate a case that you're a part of," Sam counters.

"Since when has that stopped me?" I ask. "I know this is dangerous. Someone is very clearly trying to scare me and make sure I know they're able to follow me without detection and integrate themselves into my life without me noticing. And it goes so far beyond a little note. I feel them around me all the time. I never know the next time they're going to do something to scare me or make my life more difficult."

I was stopped at the airport, rather aggressively interrogated, and everything I own searched, scanned, and questioned all because somebody reported a suspicious person and gave a description that matched me and my movements. They weren't able to discern why the person would have actually put in the complaint or what they might have been afraid of. And clearly, I wasn't doing anything illegal or dangerous. It felt so much like another example of this person creeping into my life and exerting their power over it. But I can't be sure of that. I can't be positive it is actually related, and it wasn't just a really jumpy person making a report for no reason. FBI agents are permitted to carry our firearms on planes without question and don't have to go through regular security, so it's possible someone saw that, didn't understand, and panicked.

But it could also be whoever wrote that note. They were just trying to aggravate me and show off their ability to manipulate and control.

They were able to completely disrupt my travel and put me under the suspicion of the entire security force at the airport.

It has to be the same person. And the same person who has followed me and left things on my car to make absolutely sure I know they're there. I know there are plenty of people with something to hold against me, and plenty who have promised they were going to get some sort of revenge that I disrupted and ruined their life, and so they are determined to do the same for me.

But all of them are locked securely away in prison. In a feverish moment soon after getting the note, I had Eric check in on the status of every one of the people who have grappled with me, survived, and been put away. I wanted to make absolutely sure people like Jake Logan, Anson, and Jonah Griffin were still fully under control and hadn't escaped. I've faced the reality of an escape before. I know it can happen even from facilities that seem totally locked down and impossible to breach.

Hearing confirmation from each of the facilities holding these brutal men that they were still in their cells with eyes on them within moments of having the conversation made me feel better in a way.

At the same time, it was gut-wrenching because it's come to the point now where I believe keeping their identity concealed is as much a part of their twisted game as anything else. Being pursued, being stalked, and harassed is nothing new for me. It has happened several times before and as long as I am a part of the Bureau, I will live with the constant reality that it will likely happen again.

But what sets this apart from the other times I've become the targeted obsession of a sick criminal mind is that after all this time I still don't even have a hint of why this is happening. Even when I wasn't given an indication of who was responsible for my stalking, or the torturous games I was forced to play, like with Anson, after a bit of time, they would tell me what it was that caused them to come after me, or what they intended to get out of it.

But this time, I have no idea. What they've done has been at once so brutally overt, but also hidden in the shadows. No explanation. No message. Nothing to tell me why they zeroed in on me or what it is they want me to do. It's both more unnerving and more infuriating this way. Without some sort of direction, I'm just waiting for the next thing to happen.

Which could be another attack. Another assault aimed at ending my life.

I know that's why Sam doesn't want me trying to handle this on my own. He wants someone else involved, someone who can make him feel like I'm safer. But he's not thinking clearly. He's seeing only the very personal reality that his wife has been nearly killed twice in a span of just a few months and continues to be harassed and threatened by the nameless, faceless person responsible. He's not thinking with experience and logic. He's not thinking like a law enforcement agent. If he was, it would be obvious that there's nothing police could do to help me even if I did bring this note to them.

There is already an active investigation into my attacks. It has resulted in surveillance footage that shows two different people were involved in my attacks. But that's it. Nothing else has come of the investigation and there's really nothing a police department could do that Eric hasn't ensured the Bureau is doing every day.

If he was thinking clearly, Sam would realize that his department is the closest thing to one with jurisdiction over this issue that exists and he is already right here. He already knows everything. And there's still no direction we are confident walking forward in.

Sam had closed the door when he came in and now it suddenly bursts open. Xavier is standing on the other side decked out in extremely festive pajamas. A stack of identical fabric in his arms tells me he has a very distinct plan and soon we will be a part of it.

Just like I expected, he marches up to Sam and me, shoves pajamas into our hands, and gives a silent but very aggressive point to the door. We've been given our orders. There are obviously questions happening at this point, but we've come to know it's easier in moments like this to just stuff all those questions down and go with the situation. Eventually all will become clear. And if it doesn't, asking the questions wouldn't have helped anyway.

When Sam and I are wearing our matching white pajamas with cats of various breeds wearing Santa hats or sitting in stockings, Sam accessorizing his with a scowl of distinct displeasure, we head back downstairs.

"What's going on here?" I ask as we walk into the living room.

The table is covered with snacks and treats, extra glowing decorations have been set up around the room, and the lights are off. Dean, in his own pair of the pajamas, is sitting in his favorite spot with a cookie in one hand and a cup of what smells like peppermint hot chocolate in the other.

"The season is slipping away from us, and we've lost track of it," Xavier says.

"There have been at least three murders, Xavier," I point out carefully.

"That's no excuse," he says.

Sam blinks a couple of times. "I mean, I would think that's a very good…"

"No. Excuse." Xavier stares him down for a second, then suddenly snaps out of the dark moment and steps aside to give a sweeping gesture toward the TV. "Christmas movie night. We're going to restore the spirit together."

I blink and turn to Sam. "Well, that sounds good to me."

He relents. "All right. I guess I could go for some hot cocoa."

We settle into the couch as Xavier animatedly begins passing out snacks and listing out the itinerary for the evening. It sounds like a wonderful way for us to relax and spend some time together away from everything that's been happening. But after the conversation with Sam, it seems like he's holding me a little tighter than usual because he's thinking about my last movie night. That night in mid-August when he was away was the night I was attacked for the first time and ended up in the hospital. I squeeze him back, wanting to reassure him, but also wanting to tell him to let go of his thoughts, at least for tonight. We're all together. We're surrounded by the lights and smells of the season. For tonight, I want him to get all of it out of his mind and just try to enjoy.

CHAPTER TWENTY-FIVE

WATCHING CHRISTMAS MOVIES LATE INTO THE NIGHT WITH Sam, Dean, and Xavier was the rejuvenation and relaxation I needed, but it's right back to work this morning. Scouring the Santucci household didn't give me anything useful, so I need to come from a different angle to find out more about the professor. I contact the college and let them know I'll be coming by to check his office. I figure he spent a considerable amount of time there at the school, so he likely kept many personal items in his space there. According to the school, it's been closed off since Santucci last left and no one has gone inside, so I should be able to see it just as he left it.

I am especially interested in what I might find there if there was something extramarital going on. He wouldn't want to keep any evidence of that relationship in his home where his wife might find it, but may have felt safe with it in his office. Whatever it might be, I hope to find something to steer the investigation in the right direction.

The representative I spoke to assured me the office would be unlocked when I arrived so I could have access to it at my leisure. I much prefer this to someone unrelated to the investigation escorting me to unlock the door and then lingering around while I search. Even if they don't mean anything by it, it feels intrusive, like I can't fully take in the scene like I would want to. When someone else is standing there, I'm very aware of every move I'm making, everything I am touching. I know they're watching and applying meaning and significance to each thing I do even if there isn't really any significance at all. It is far preferable to have unfettered access to a space and be allowed to go through it without watchful, scrutinizing eyes.

As I'm approaching the office, I realize I'm not as alone as I thought I would be. The door to the office is standing open a few inches, but the light is on. Inside, I can hear movement. My body instinctively braces, and I place my hand on my gun. I have no idea who is in that room, but that alone is enough to put me on guard. For the rest of the world, no news may mean good news, but that doesn't apply to an FBI agent. For us, no information means go on alert first.

I press my hand to the door and ease it open. Almost instantly, a figure pops up from behind the desk as a drawer slams.

"Molly?" I ask, shocked to see Molly Garson digging around in Professor Santucci's desk.

I'm immediately suspicious. Molly has already come across as odd since the first time I spoke with her, like she might be up to something shady, but this just made it considerably worse. She starts stammering, and I walk the rest of the way into the office, letting my hand fall away from my gun but still feeling on edge.

"What are you doing?" I demand.

She looks down at the drawer she had been digging in, stammering as she tries to come up with an explanation. As her eyes come back to mine, she decides to play it off.

"I'm trying to find some notes," she says. "I need to study, and I knew Professor Santucci kept them around here, so I was just looking for them."

"You need to study?" I ask. "You don't have any English classes in between semesters. And for obvious reasons, the professor won't be teaching you when classes start up again."

She lets out a forced, strained chuckle that falls in all the wrong ways. She starts to move around the end of the table like she's working toward the door and I notice her hand move behind her like she's trying to surreptitiously put something in her back pocket.

"Well, I can see you're probably here to do some investigating, so I'll, um, just go," she says. "I don't want to be in your way."

I take a step to the side. I'm not actually blocking her egress, but the positioning of my body makes it obvious I don't want her to go anywhere.

"What did you just put in your pocket?" I ask. "What did you take out of his drawer?"

For a brief moment, she looks like she's going to try to lie her way through this, but then her face goes slack, and her cheeks turn red. She's smart enough to know I'm not just going to let this go. She's going to have to show me what she has one way or another. It would be easier if she just does it on her own.

Molly reaches into her pocket and pulls the paper out again. She glances down at it in her hand for a second.

"I know what this is going to look like," she says. "I just…"

"Let me see it."

She reluctantly hands the paper over to me. It is a standard size piece of stationery rather than the notebook or printer paper that might be expected in a college professor's office. I open it and my blood runs cold. Written in the center of the paper in flowing, old-fashioned-looking script is a poem comprised of the lines of text that have shown up on the gift tags packaged with the body parts.

You are my heartbeat.

The air that I breathe.

The future I see.

And at the end is a new line that chills me.

The greatest truth whispered into my soul.

At the very bottom of the paper are the initials "M.G."

I lift my gaze from the page and back to Molly. She's rocking back and forth, her face getting redder and her eyes welling with tears that seem to come from a wide range of emotions rather than just one. Her eyes flit back and forth from me to the door. She wants to escape. She wants to get out of the room and be as far from me as she can get. I don't blame her.

"You're going to need to come with me," I say.

She nods, not arguing, not trying to resist. I'm not arresting her. That's not what I do. But I am detaining her. With the promise that I will bring her back to her car in the college parking lot, I drive her to

Sherwood and lead her into the small room that many on the force have started to consider mine. It's my preferred space to talk to suspects or persons of interest, and right now Molly is most definitely of interest.

The second Molly sits down, she leans across the table in front of her. "I had nothing to do with Professor Santucci's death or the eyeballs."

I cock my head to the side to give her a questioning look. Like the lungs, the details of the eyes being found has been kept out of the media. The only information that's been released is that there have been two further suspicious packages found and they are believed to relate directly to the heart found beneath the Christmas tree at the market.

"What eyeballs?" I ask.

"The ones found in the stocking at the mall," she says. "I have a friend who works there and she told me about them."

"No one from the store was present when the box was opened," I say. "She didn't see them and we haven't released the details of the contents of the box."

"She didn't see them," Molly agrees. "But she was there when a deputy came through to ask for statements and asked if there was anyone on the staff of the store with blue eyes who has been missing. She came to the conclusion on her own. Is that not right?"

I roll my own eyes. After revealing the contents of the stocking, I asked Sam to have one of his officers go back to the mall store and speak again with the people working there to get a baseline statement before I performed a more in-depth interview. I had specifically instructed him not to mention that the stocking contained a pair of eyes. He apparently didn't believe people would think through his question enough to come to that conclusion. I'll have to have a word with him.

"That might be true, but you are still sounding extremely suspicious. You told me you are dating an older man and then here I see what sounds very much like a love poem that you just took out of his office. I have to assume you understand the significance of the words," I say.

"Yes. But again, I didn't have anything to do with his death. Yes, I am dating a much older man. I already told you that. And yes, I was very interested in Professor Santucci. I was for a long time. But he wasn't interested in me. He made that very clear. And I know he's with someone else. I wrote this poem last year. I gave it to him and when he didn't react well, I told him it was for a literary magazine project for the school and just wanted him to look over it. I don't think he believed me. And anyway, he never gave the copy back.

"When I heard about the gift tags, it really freaked me out. I immediately recognized the first line and then there were other packages and one was eyes… I just knew those tags had my words on them. I thought it would come back on me if this was ever found. But if I came and got the only copy, no one would find out," Molly says.

"How did you know the other tags had those other words?" I ask.

"I didn't know for sure, but it aligned too well. And even if they didn't, I didn't want this around. I figured eventually someone would find it in here and I didn't want at any point for it to be connected to me," she tells me.

"The much older man you're dating… that's Kade," I confirm, wanting to make sure she is only carrying on that relationship and she isn't seeing someone else as well.

Molly lets out a long breath and nods. "Yes."

"Then I don't understand why you would say Santucci being married would stop you considering Kade is married," I say. "Going through a pretty nasty divorce as I hear it, but married."

"I didn't mean he was with somebody as in his wife. He was seeing someone else," Molly says.

"How do you know that?" I ask.

"Sometimes working at the school can have its privileges. I've overheard a lot of conversations and I've also had a lot of access to Professor Santucci and his office. I don't know who exactly it is he's been dating, but there's definitely someone. Sometimes he'd talk about important meetings he needed to go to or appointments he had made that required him to leave campus for a while, then come back smelling like a woman. Not like his wife. I'd met her a few times and she always wore the exact same perfume. I'm sure she'd call it a signature or some shit like that. Seems like another boring detail to me, but obviously he liked her," she says.

"So much that he was cheating on her?" I ask incredulously.

"You can't cheat on someone you divorce," she points out. "They didn't have any children and it isn't like professors are rolling in money. The only reason he would hold onto the marriage is if he still cared about her. It's a pretty outdated idea that people are only capable of having feelings for one person at a time, even if they are married."

"Thank you for that," I say dryly.

"Just because someone develops feelings for someone outside of their marriage it doesn't mean they don't love their original partner anymore. It just means they've expanded. Most people are still pretty monogamous, but not everyone."

"This coming from the person who said she wasn't pursuing him anymore because he was with someone else," I say.

Molly gives me a dark smile. "Like I said. Most people."

I nod. "Why do you think the person he was seeing was from campus?" I ask.

"Just a feeling. The way he would act sometimes. Things I'd see around the office. It's pretty obvious when a guy's getting some attention in the middle of the day."

"Do you think it was a student?" I ask.

"I don't really know."

"If you had to guess."

"I don't like to guess at things. But I'd suggest you maybe take a peek at the other professors and faculty around the department and think about that question again," she says.

It's not the most flattering way she could have gone about that, but it gives me the information I need.

CHAPTER TWENTY-SIX

You are my heartbeat.
The air that I breathe.
The future I see.
The greatest truth whispered into my soul.

I READ THE POEM AGAIN AND AGAIN. THOSE FOUR SIMPLE LINES SEEM so frothy, basic, and mundane to the point of cliché. This isn't the work of someone with honed writing skill. It sounds far more like the inside of a greeting card or the tag attached to a generic plush toy than it does a love poem meant to actually woo someone. It doesn't mean Molly didn't put a lot of thought into it, but it does change how I view it. It gives me a stronger feeling that the poem was not written by the same person who killed the victims.

I can absolutely see Molly having a strong attraction to Jesse Santucci. At some point she may have even believed she was in love with him. But it was the dreamy kind of feeling that so often happens between a young female student and their handsome professor.

Those kinds of things happen all the time, especially with students who spend a considerable amount of time with their professors. They begin to feel an intense attraction and because of the attention that the professor gives back to them, they feel it is reciprocated. The professor's position of influence and power enhances these feelings and these students can quickly get fully wrapped up in their fantasy of the relationship. This can obviously take a bad turn, but I don't see that in Molly. And I definitely don't see it in this poem.

It really doesn't strike me that this is the kind of poem that was written by someone who would get so deeply immersed in the perceived relationship, and upon realizing it wasn't going to happen, turn around and kill the professor. It also has nothing to do with Tyler or Trisha.

I take some time to check through the alibis Molly provided for around the times of the murders and when the bodies were found, as well as the last time anyone saw Trisha or Kristie. I'm confident she didn't have anything to do with the murders, but I still want to confirm it. My checks reveal she couldn't have been involved, which puts the poem in new context. It is extremely strange that she would have written a poem like that only to have it used in this way, but it occurs to me that it very likely doesn't have anything to do with Molly. It's something about the words themselves.

I consider how those words fit with the murders and the body parts they were associated with and the connections are obvious. The heartbeat and the heart. The breath and the lungs. The eyes and the seeing. But the reasoning behind using a poem and removing those parts is not as clear. Did the poem itself inspire the removal of the body parts for some reason? Or was the plan always to remove them and the poem just fit?

Feeling like I may have focused in too tightly on the words, I pull back and think instead about how this poem could have gotten into the hands of the killer. I have to figure out who would have access to it and why they would choose to use it. In other circumstances, it may look as though whoever it is was trying to frame the professor by using a poem that was given to him. But clearly that isn't the case here. There has to be something else.

While searching the professor's office, I collected a stack of personal notes and calendars. I brought them home so that I could go through them more closely. With Molly's words about the professor seeing someone other than his wife going through my mind, I carefully pieced together a timeline of Jesse Santucci's activities during his last few weeks. Even though his apparent infidelity has been hinted at a couple of times, there hasn't been any indication of who he was seeing. I'm hoping sorting out what he was doing in the time leading up to his death will pinpoint who he was carrying on his affair with. Finding that person will give me a critical source of information I can't get anywhere else.

Whoever this woman is, she holds details about the last part of Santucci's life that no one else has. She'll be able to fill in the time-line and offer some inside information to some of his activities. Going through his schedule and notes I find the Christmas gala that has been mentioned to me a couple of times as well as several personal appoint-ments and other activities. I notice something scribbled in the corner of several dates on his calendar but can't decipher what it means.

I take a picture of it and send it to Xavier. He and Dean had to leave for a couple of days but will be back to make sure they don't miss the holiday. I don't want to wait until then to get his opinion on what looks like a tiny symbol. He has an incredible mind for codes and patterns. He may see something in this symbol itself or how it shows up on the calen-dar that I don't. A few moments after sending the pictures, he responds back that it doesn't mean anything to him right off the bat, but that he will keep looking at it.

I'm a little disappointed, but I couldn't exactly expect him to spon-taneously have an explanation. I have other angles to consider, and I'll just wait to see if something comes of that code. With other things to look into, I don't need to focus only on one detail. It's a luxury I hav-en't been able to enjoy much in this investigation and I plan to take full advantage of it.

My next step is to go through Santucci's financial records like I did his wife's. His are more involved than hers, showing that he did a lot more spending than she did. Considering her career was based from home, that makes sense. She likely didn't get out as much as he did, so he was going to be the one who predominantly handled things like quick trips to the grocery store to grab a few things or run simple errands.

I'm not surprised to see a higher rate of spending recently as com-pared to the weeks before. We're getting close to Christmas and I'm sure some of the bursts of spending I see are for purchasing gifts. One of the most important details I get out of the records, though, is the point, two days before his heart was found beneath the tree at the market, when the transactions abruptly stop.

CHAPTER TWENTY-SEVEN

AFTER TAKING NOTE OF THE TIME WHEN ANY FINANCIAL TRANS-
actions stopped, I look at the future plans noted on his calendar. I
call an eye doctor, a barber, and a museum director who were listed
as having appointments with Santucci in the several days after the last
financial transaction. Each of them confirms Jesse Santucci didn't show
up for the appointments he'd made, and they didn't hear from him to
cancel.

This information helps to greatly narrow the window of when he
actually disappeared. Now that I have a much better idea of when the
professor went missing, which closes in on when he was murdered, I
want to trace exactly what he was doing leading up to that moment. I
contact the stores listed on his banking records and ask them for security footage. I want to see exactly what he purchased, his state of mind,
his behavior, and if he was with anyone during that time.

I am happy to come up against no resistance from the stores and
soon I'm driving around town to view the footage. I ask for copies of

all of it so I can review it again later but watch it at each store as well. Accessing the security footage allows me to track his movements from store to store across a few days. He made several purchases, including the jewelry he bought for his wife for the Christmas gala, some clothing items and household basics, and then several Christmas decorations including a large snow globe.

Santucci looks completely calm in all of the footage. None of it seems to indicate any kind of distress, anger, or rush. He's simply going about his tasks. Some of the footage shows more drive than others. When he is purchasing several undershirts and socks, as well as the run to get household goods, he enters the store with a long stride, goes right to the items, and checks out. There isn't any kind of meandering or big decision-making at either stop.

His attitude is different when he goes for the jewelry as well as for the decorations and a couple other small items. He did this shopping in the mall, which means I have footage not just from the stores, but also from the open corridors where he casually strolled from place to place, glancing into windows, occasionally stopping to check his phone or look at one of the kiosks set up in the middle of the floor. His demeanor is calm and unbothered. No one is walking around with him and he doesn't seem to be looking for anybody. He's shopping alone and seemingly without any intention of any other distractions.

When he gets to the jewelry store, he takes his time to look over all the options. The overhead camera angle shows him talking to a clerk, using his hands as though describing either his wife or what she is planning on wearing so they can help him choose the right set. They take several items out of the display case and lay them on the glass so he can get a better look at them.

The camera footage shows not just the jewelry displays but also the edges of some of the displays of crystal collectibles lining the walls. I can see a few people come into the frame and leave or walk back and forth in the mall. None of them catch Professor Santucci's attention. He is focused completely on going over the options for the jewelry before selecting the set I now know he would later gift to his wife before the Christmas gala. The clerk says something to him and he laughs, the grin on his face genuine. He is happy to be making this purchase and likely looking forward to Kristie's reaction to receiving the beautiful gift.

The next set of footage is from when Santucci purchased the snow globe and a few of the other decorations. He has the same kind of casual, unfettered demeanor going through the shops as he did in the mall. The footage of him finding the snow globe shows him walking slowly along the center aisle of a large department store, looking from side to side as if trying to take in as much of the displays as he can.

The store has that kind of over-filled look that happens around Christmas when shops try to offer as much as humanly possible to shoppers in hopes of catching their eye and encouraging impulse buying. The displays have worked on Santucci, causing him to frequently detour to one side or the other, pause at displays, and pick up various items. Many of them go back on the shelves, but some are appealing enough for him to add to his cart. One such item is the snow globe.

He stands in front of a large case of different styles for nearly a minute before reaching out to pick one up. He looks into the globe, wiggles it around to get the glitter snow swirling and falling, then twists the thumb turn on the bottom to listen to the music playing for a couple of seconds before setting it back down. He goes through this similar process a couple more times with different globes before noticing a large one in the corner of the top shelf.

He holds it and looks inside, turning it back and forth to get all the angles of the scene. When he turns it over, he turns the knob, but then also notices a small hatch. Popping it open reveals an open space made into the base of the globe. It almost looks like a battery compartment, but none of the metal components are in place. It's a hiding place, and after running his finger along the inside of it, Santucci replaces the door and sets the globe in the front of his cart. That maneuver interests me. It seems like the feature of the hidden compartment was what really sold that particular globe for him. Which tells me wherever it is, there's something inside that compartment.

I get a little chill watching the clerk take the snow globe and nestle it into a box, surrounding it with tissue paper. It's to protect the fragile item, but it also makes for easy wrapping and gift giving. The parallel between that moment and the way we found the body parts is unnerving to say the least. As Santucci bought that snow globe he likely already had in mind where it was going to be displayed in his house or who he was going to gift it to. I realize as that thought goes through my mind that I don't know which it is.

But that might not be easy to figure out. It's Christmas. There are snow globes everywhere. I think about the ones in my own home and then the different displays in the apartments of the group of college friends living in the housing complex. Each of them had at least a couple of the globes. Unless I find it in his house, it's going to take a bit more digging to identify the globe and where it ended up.

I add the shopping trips and the purchases made at each one to the professor's' calendars. I immediately notice one of the days with the coded symbol in the corner is between the trip where he purchased the jewelry for his wife and the one when he purchased the snow globe. I have no idea if that is truly significant or what it might mean, but I take note of it.

As I'm transferring all my notes to one large document so I can have a visual, my phone rings. I reach over and grab it, tucking it between my ear and shoulder so I don't have to stop.

"Emma Griffin," I say by way of greeting.

"Hi, Emma," a sweet voice says. "This is Cupcake. Remember me?"

I'm always interested in the overtly memorable people who seem to believe they blend in with the world around them and are easily dismissed. Sometimes it is inauthentic, coming across as though they are trying to seem humble, but in actuality, they're hunting for affirmation. But from others, such as Cupcake, it is genuine.

"Of course I remember you."

"You have a lot of really important things rattling around your brain. I didn't want to assume you had any space up in there for me," she says. "But I'm glad you do."

"Absolutely. What can I do for you?" I ask.

"I got more pictures and video from my fans," she says. "Some of them are of me at my booth. I thought maybe you could look at the people around there and it might tell you something."

"That sounds great. Thank you. Just send them to my email."

"Will do. How is Xavier?" she asks. "He hasn't commented on my new video yet and usually he's one of the very first."

"As far as I know, he's fine. Dean had to go out of town for the case he's working and Xavier went with him," I say.

She pauses for a second. There are a lot of kinds of pauses in this world and as an investigator, I'm familiar with all of them. This one feels like the kind that occurs when someone is trying hard to go over their own thought in the head and sift it through different filters before saying it out loud.

"Is he as helpful as I think he would be?" she asks.

The careful wording of the question is very obvious.

"Yes," I tell her. "Well, usually. Actually, probably most of the time, but sometimes it just doesn't register."

She giggles softly. "That sounds right."

I'm fascinated by this woman and concerned for her at the same time.

The pictures and video are in my inbox by the time the call ends. I look over them, not really seeing anything interesting until I get to one toward the end of the set. It isn't Cupcake or the delighted-looking woman posing with her that have caught my attention. At the edge of the image is a hand reaching onto the table to pick up a scarf that looks like it's made of interconnected snowflakes. I remember seeing it somewhere before, but I have to remember where.

CHAPTER TWENTY-EIGHT

THE NEXT DAY FINALLY BRINGS AN EMAIL I'VE BEEN WAITING FOR. Access to Tyler O'Rourke's social media has been provided. He had his profile set to private, so I wasn't able to see anything more than his profile picture, his cover picture, and his name. That gave me nothing to go on, but now I'm able to get into his account and see everything.

Nothing in particular stands out to me as I start to scroll through the unlocked version of his profile. It looks like pretty much everyone else's. Pictures of things he was doing from day to day. Pictures of food. A lot of pictures of him and Trisha together. Memes. He wasn't one for much commentary or effusive captions, but there are occasional entries detailing what was going on in the picture or showing appreciation for something. He left a loving tribute to Trisha on her birthday, and she did the same for him. By all appearances, their relationship was good, and he was living a normal life.

As I trace backwards, I find a stretch of time where there appears to be a large number of deleted posts. There are occasional references to a girlfriend and deleted tags to other people's pictures and posts during that stretch. Obviously, he was in a relationship across those months, and it ended badly enough for him to want to remove all mentions of it. This sudden purging of posts and pictures happened a couple of months before the posts about Trisha started appearing.

This could definitely be cause for anger and hurt on the part of the ex-girlfriend. Especially if she wasn't the one who instigated the breakup and still had feelings for him when he introduced his new relationship with Trisha. Nobody likes the feeling of being cast aside, and being replaced just adds insult to injury. Most people know that kind of hurt and anger, but it doesn't usually escalate to any kind of violence. Particularly the type of violence I've seen in these crimes. I don't know if just a breakup would be enough to warrant killing Tyler so brutally. And even if it was, just like with the professor and the poem, what would that break up have to do with Santucci and his wife that would lead to their deaths?

As I continue to explore Tyler's social media, I come across a picture posted by one of his friends that immediately stands out to me. The images are of the gazebo where his body was found. There isn't any caption or context provided, but it is definitely the same gazebo. I print out a copy of the picture and send it to Dean. I call him rather than trying to e-mail or text the details.

"I know you're working on your own case, and I'm sorry to distract you. But I could really use your help with this," I say.

"Sure," he says. "What do you need?"

"I just sent you a picture. I need you to find out as much as you can about it. You are far better at traipsing through social media and getting details about pictures than I am." I tell him how I found the picture and the significance of it. "There has to be a specific reason the killer left Tyler's body there in the gazebo, and getting the details about this picture might tell me that."

"I'll find out what I can," he says.

I've barely even set my phone down when it rings. It's one of the detectives from the Marlon department.

"Kristie Santucci's body has been found."

Within minutes I'm driving toward Marlon, my mind reeling. The woman's body was discovered behind a dumpster in the parking lot of an abandoned movie theater at the edge of town. It's a place no one is supposed to go, but somewhere teenagers and young adults often visit to party or even to sneak into the theater for what they call urban spelunking. I've come to understand that as meaning breaking into abandoned buildings or accessing old areas to poke around and take in the decay.

Pictures and video from these excursions can be beautiful in a dark, haunting way. They show the vulnerability of the world and the undeniable, unstoppable impact of time.

But it can also be disturbing and exploitive.

Today, it's the backdrop for a gruesome find. The couple that came with the intention of exploring inside came from the back half of the parking lot rather than the front. If they had entered the way patrons once did, they would never have seen Kristie. Her body is fully concealed behind the rusting green box, curled up on one side with her back pressed to the metal.

The crime scene unit is still processing the scene when I arrive. I flash my shield and pass through the tape to see where the body is still on the ground. It's surrounded by bright pink plastic evidence indicators and has been shifted slightly by the medical examiner looking for cause of death. I approach him.

"Ellis Green," he says, holding out his hand to shake.

"Agent Emma Griffin," I say. "What can you tell me?"

"Right now, not a lot. Other than the fact that her chest has been cut wide open," he says.

I don't know if he is trying to joke, or if he genuinely believes that having the identity of a body and seeing that her chest has been cut open is not much information.

"Should I even ask if her lungs are there?" I ask. He purses his lips together and shakes his head. "Perfect."

"At least you have a body part bingo now," he says.

I maintain my stone-faced stare for a disgusted second before stepping closer to the body. I notice a bit of blood on one ear.

"What's this damage to her ear?" I ask.

"It looks like it was torn, like an earring was ripped out of it," he says. "Her ears are pierced, but she isn't wearing an earring in the other ear, either. There's also an abrasion and a small cut to the back of her neck that is consistent with a metal chain of some kind being forcibly yanked off of her," Dr. Green says.

This immediately makes me think of the jewelry set Jesse Santucci bought for his wife that she showed off at the Christmas gala. It included a pair of earrings and a matching necklace. The first thought in a lot of investigations would be that these pieces being missing from her body indicates robbery, but I know that's not true. Kristie Santucci's death doesn't have anything to do with robbery. Her jewelry was stolen, but there is another motive for it.

I thank the crime scene investigation team and Dr. Green, asking them to make sure they keep me fully updated on all developments, and head back home. I want to get a better look at the jewelry. The footage from the jewelry shop showing the professor purchasing it wasn't close enough to provide any details about the pieces, only that they were a set. I pull up pictures of the Christmas gala and search through them. It doesn't take long to find images of the couple together. I expected to find them fairly easily. Not only was Jesse Santucci a very popular professor at the college, but the couple was attractive together. Highly dressed up for the occasion in a sparkling sapphire ball gown that coordinated with his accent tie, they were a striking image.

I find a closeup picture and zoom in as much as I can to see the detail of the jewelry. It's beautiful and familiar. I take a screenshot of it to give to Sam as well as the other departments so they can keep a lookout for the items. I'll contact the jewelry store to try to get a better picture, but at least this shows what the items look like in case they are found or someone attempts to sell them in a pawn shop.

Though he used particularly disturbing humor to describe it, Ellis Green wasn't too far off in his assessment of my relief that I now have the three bodies that coordinate with the three missing organs. At least I have them now and vital information can be taken from them, but the relief isn't complete. Trisha is still missing. No one has seen or heard from her. She's still out there somewhere. The question is where and what condition she'll be in when we find her.

CHAPTER TWENTY-NINE

D EAN GETS BACK TO ME LATER IN THE AFTERNOON.

"Hey," he says when I answer. "I found out a few things about that picture."

"Fantastic," I say. "Why did you find?"

"Well, I started by going back to the point where you found it so I could have an origin. Then I traced who posted it and how many people were tagged in it. It sent me down a long spiral of pictures and posts. It had been reposted several times, so finding the original post took me a bit. But eventually, I found a series of pictures that included that one. There were several others of the park and people in the gazebo.

"It looks like they were taken during an outing with a big group of friends, including Tyler O'Rourke. There are also a few familiar people there. I'm going to send you some screenshots. Look at them and see what you think," Dean says.

The pictures pop up and I immediately notice Molly, Kylie, Nancy, and Presley. They are with several other people I don't recognize and a couple of people whose faces I know I have seen but I don't remember speaking to directly. They must be people who were interviewed by others either when one of the body parts was found or at the park.

The last thirty-six hours have brought a rush of progress in the investigation, from access to Tyler's social media to Kristie's body being found to uncovering the image of the group together in the park, but it hasn't stopped. Within an hour of talking to Dean about the picture, I'm back in the car, driving to the hospital where a growing pine was decorated as a Christmas tree in the courtyard at the heart of the building designed to offer patients, families, and visitors a peaceful, beautiful place to relax, get some fresh air, and think.

Walking through the hospital to access the courtyard is a somber experience. A doctor met me at the door when I arrived and he's now escorting me past whispering staff and wide-eyed patients. They all want to know what's going on and look at me as though I should be able to come up with the answers in that instant. They want me to come into the building already prepared with an explanation of what happened and a reassurance that everyone is safe.

I have no reason to believe anyone in the hospital is in any kind of danger. But I also don't have any other answers for them right now. So, I stay quiet as the doctor brings me through the halls and out the glass door to the courtyard. Several nurses are standing in a semi-circle around the tree, their backs to it as they hold up sheets to create a barrier so no one can see under it.

As I approach, they step aside, and I am able to see the box nestled among Christmas greenery and lights around the trunk. A weight settles in my stomach when I see the familiar silver wrapping paper.

"No one has touched it?" I ask.

"No," Gloria Melvin, a nurse at the hospital who I've encountered several times, tells me. "It was brought to my attention by a parent walking out here with their child and I called you first."

"Good. And you have called Sam?"

"Yes," she says.

Almost as though on command, Sam and Keegan rush through the door and out into the courtyard. The massive windows around the courtyard are getting crowded with faces staring out trying to see what's going on. I ignore them. I'm reassured by the fact that the glass is tinted, making it difficult for them to see any detail. The sheets also provide privacy as I guide Sam and Keegan to the tree and point out the package.

A crime scene photographer is there to document us removing the package and opening it. Resting on the bunched-up tissue paper inside is a severed tongue. One of the nurses glances over her shoulder and gasps when she sees it, her hand flying up to cover her mouth. The reaction causes a furor among the people inside, many of whom try to rush forward and come through the door to find out what is going on. Sam has positioned himself just beyond the door holds his arms wide to stop them, pushing them back inside and telling them they need to remain there and clear of the door.

"Is there any surveillance equipment out here?" I ask. "Anything that might have captured who did this?"

"There are a couple of cameras," Gloria tells me. "You'll have to ask security to show you the footage."

That gives me a boost of hope. I know there is security coverage of most of the interior of the hospital, considering I have accessed that footage to try to find out who attacked me when I woke up from my coma. But I didn't know if they would cover such a private area. While some people come out to this courtyard just to enjoy some sunlight and air or walk around a bit after sitting for a long time, this is also where many come to pray, cope, and grieve.

Having cameras out here could feel intrusive, but it can also be very important considering patients do come out here. If they are a fall risk or otherwise might experience an emergency needing help, having the cameras available allows the security to monitor what's going on in the courtyard so if something happens, they can quickly find someone to respond.

While the tongue is transferred to Keegan's office, Sam and I go inside to the security office. The guard there confirms what I expected. The cameras covering the courtyard area are linked to a separate system than the ones inside. For the courtyard, only about an hour of footage is preserved at any given moment, allowing doctors and nurses to review what may have happened to a patient, but not enough to review what happened hours before.

"Were you watching when the person came in and put the box under the tree?" I ask.

"I was. I didn't realize what I was seeing at the time. A lot of people walk through the courtyard and touch the decorations. I don't know what it is about Christmas decorations that make people want to touch them, but I've noticed a lot of people leaning down to touch the greenery or lights that have been put up under the tree. Maybe they're trying to see if they are real or not. I don't know. But that's what I thought all of them did today. But now I know one of them must have slipped it in," the guard says.

"Did that happen a lot today?" Sam asks.

"A few times. Maybe five or six. There were only a couple during the time I think the box could have been put down. But I can't tell you much about either one of them. Everybody looks pretty much alike when they're bundled up for the cold. Big puffy jackets, boots, hats, scarves, gloves. It makes it a lot harder to tell what a person actually looks like," he tells him. Suddenly something seems to pop into his head. "You know what, though? One of them did have a pretty distinctive scarf on. I couldn't see the whole thing because it was kind of tucked into the collar of the coat they were wearing, but when they leaned down to touch this stuff under the tree, part of it slipped out.

"It was really narrow and kind of lacy looking. I remember thinking it wouldn't keep you very warm. Then they shifted around so I couldn't see it anymore, but that might have been when they put the box down if that was them."

"The box was small," Sam confirms. "It could have been stuffed under a coat or even in a deep pocket, so that's possible."

"This scarf," I say. "What color was it?"

"White or maybe really pale blue," he says.

"And you say it was lacy?"

"Yeah, like holes and stuff. When I think of a scarf, I think of something really thick that's going to keep you warm. This one might warm you up if it's wrapped tightly around your neck, but it stood out."

I thank the guard and leave, knowing what he saw wasn't lace, but snowflakes.

CHAPTER THIRTY

KAYLA'S EYES STILL LOOK RED AND EXHAUSTED WHEN I SIT ACROSS the couch from her again. This time she seems more present in the moment, more capable of communicating with me. She even goes into the kitchen and brews a pot of coffee for us. Holding the mug between my hands feels wonderful, thawing the chill that seems to have gotten into my bones and will be staying there for the foreseeable future.

"Kayla, I know this is extremely hard for you and that you don't want to keep thinking about it. You especially don't want to think about anything difficult that Tyler had to go through, but I really need you to understand how important it is to be honest with me. I need you to recognize that holding something back isn't going to protect him and it won't make anything he went through go away. But it could give me the details I need to find out what happened to him. I'm not accusing you of anything, but I feel like you are holding something back. That you know something you don't want to tell me," I say.

The young mother takes a breath and sets her coffee down in front of her so she can run her hands back through her hair.

"I didn't mean to hold it back. It wasn't intentional. I just don't like to think about it," she replies.

"Tell me," I say.

"When we were talking about people who might want to hurt Tyler or who had something against them, I wasn't really thinking about it too much because of the other people who died. I couldn't understand why somebody who had something against Tyler would hurt anybody else. But when I started thinking about it more, I realized that he did have a strained... situation, call it."

"What do you mean?"

"I don't want to make any accusations, because nothing really bad ever happened, but I know that you've been speaking with some of his former friends, and his former girlfriend. It wasn't a good breakup, but that doesn't mean it was really bad, either. It was just a difficult breakup after a very long relationship," Kayla tells me.

"Who was it?"

"Kylie Pearce."

The name hits me with a rush of both surprise and resignation. An uneasy feeling about Kylie has been forming along the back of my neck and pooling in the bottom of my skull. She's charming and helpful, but there's something about her that has felt increasingly off with every interview and every encounter. The very fact that there have been several times I've made contact with her is enough to seem strange.

But it's more than that. Some of the things she has said to me have stuck in my brain like barbs. I remember standing outside the gazebo while people asked what had happened and Kylie had immediately said "he was murdered." Jumping to the conclusion that a person found dead in those circumstances was murdered isn't all that unusual, but I hadn't referenced the body belonging to a male. She stated that herself. She has provided me with a considerable amount of information, offering details, introducing me to other friends, talking about how sweet Kristie was.

It's all things that are mundane and even predictable on the surface but combined come across as odd.

"What happened between them?" I ask.

"They were together for a couple of years, which is forever at that age. He was in love with her for a while and things seemed good between them, but then they started growing apart. It didn't strike me as anything particularly terrible happening between them. It's not like they had a huge argument and everything just fell apart. It was more that they both were entering a different phase of their lives, and it simply didn't work for Tyler anymore. He broke up with her and she didn't respond well to it.

"She showed up here a couple of times trying to get him to talk to her or take her back. She posted some strange things on her social media. She never outright threatened him. And it didn't go on for a really long time. But it had quite an effect on him for a while. He never meant to cause her any serious pain or negate the relationship they'd had. That wasn't the point. He just wanted both of them to move on and find someone to make them happy."

I can't prove that Kylie has done anything, but I am realizing now how intertwined she was with each of the deaths. I need to look into her more.

Unlike Tyler, Kylie's social media is all public. At this point, I don't want to put a warrant in to get full access to it because I don't want to alert her yet to the fact that I am investigating her. Instead, I search through what is available to see if she has anything that lines up with what I know. I trace back to the same stretch of time where Tyler erased most of his page. I've determined this is when they were together, after both of them started new social media. I'm not sure what happened to their former profiles, but they both began new pages at the same time.

Kylie didn't commit to the same kind of purge of her social media that Tyler did. She kept many of the posts and pictures that existed from the time they were in a relationship, and I'm able to follow along with what was happening between them. I can sense the mood changing and see that some of her posts were starting to get a bit creepy. She posted pictures of him sleeping, comments about going by his apartment at night to see if she could see him through the window watching TV. She said it was because she loved him so much she wanted to make sure he was alright all the time, but there is a heavy feeling of stalking pulling down on the words.

I notice a significant block of time that's empty much like Tyler's and assume that's when the actual breakup happened. It's followed by morose memes about being heartbroken. Sometime after that the content starts referencing song lyrics, books, and movies that are all about being betrayed. It's obvious Kylie was feeling like someone had committed a serious offense against her. Looking over the timeline, this lines up with when Tyler started dating Trisha publicly.

Her use of social media became more sporadic and unpredictable over the next several months until she suddenly started posting again more frequently. Her choice of memes and reposts became much more optimistic, and while she didn't put up any pictures, she frequently made comments about things getting better and feeling good again. As I scroll through, I find a post of clouds with a rainbow going through them and the top spire of a castle coming up from the bottom of the image. Words across it in elaborate scroll speak to waiting for so long and going through so much, but dreams finally coming true.

In the comments section, she followed up the post with a note telling anyone reading it that she was going to have big news soon and they would all be so happy for her. She thanked them for all their concern and told them how much she appreciated everything they did to support and encourage her during the dark time she had walked through.

That elevated mood didn't last, however. Her page went silent for a few days leading up to another stream of angry, despondent posts. This is definitely significant. Something happened in those days that crushed her. I take out the timeline I have already created and start to compare the posts to what I know happened in the lives of Jesse, Tyler, and Kristie leading up to their deaths, and Trisha leading up to her disappearance.

I go backwards a bit and find a post that strikes me. A flowery, poetic caption talks about the serenity and beauty of a stream through the meadow. My mind immediately goes to the place where Santucci was put into the water and I look at his calendar. The tip of my finger comes down on the symbol in the corner of the same date as the post.

CHAPTER THIRTY-ONE

"**H**EY, AGENT GRIFFIN. GOOD TO TALK TO YOU AGAIN.**"

My immediate instinct is to doubt that's authentic, but Kade Murray doesn't really have any reason to dislike me. Our conversation had been perfectly pleasant, even if he had faked being in the shower to try to duck me and had opted out of telling me he was seeing Molly and had been with her the day the paper was purchased. I know now after talking with her that Molly did have some of the paper in her apartment, but it was the leftover portion of the roll that Kade mentioned leaving at his girlfriend's house. She hadn't shown it to me because she didn't want to tell me about her relationship with Kade and hadn't actually purchased the paper. The purchase credited to her I realized was a mix-up of the cards, with Kade accidentally using hers to buy the second roll. Now I need to check to see who he bought it for.

"You, too," I say.

"What can I do for you?" he asks.

"Remember when we talked about the silver wrapping paper and you said you bought a second roll for one of the girls that lives in the complex but you couldn't remember who it was?" I ask.

"Yeah," he says. "I'm sorry. I wish I'd paid better attention. I just said to come by my apartment and grab it later, bought it, and didn't really think about it again."

"So, you knew at that point it was someone who knew where you live?" I ask. "Not just someone in the complex, but someone familiar enough with you that they would be able to pinpoint your apartment."

"Right," he says.

"I know you told me that you don't really hang around with the college kids who live around here, so how would any of them know where you live. Other than Molly, for obvious reasons?" I ask. "Have many of them come over? Is there some sort of directory they would be able to reference?"

"No. There's no directory. But a couple of them have come by to bring over like extra food and stuff when they cooked or baked. Feeling bad for the old, divorced guy, I guess," he says.

"Which ones? Which of them brought over food?" I ask.

"Nancy, I think one time. Kylie. There's a girl named Beth who doesn't really hang with the others much but likes to bake a ton and has brought me a bunch of stuff."

I remember Kylie seamlessly directing me to his apartment after our first conversation.

With my theory now forming rapidly in my mind, I look at the timelines with a more critical eye. Several parallels surface that I wouldn't have put any significance on before, but now are chillingly obvious. I keep coming back to Kylie's gushing comments about everyone getting good news and being happier for her. They were posted on the same day that Jesse Santucci bought the set of jewelry for his wife.

With that at the very front of my thoughts, I pull up the footage of the jewelry store again. I watch through it once and don't notice anything, but when I watch through it again, I pay close attention to the edges of the frame where I noticed the displays of crystal and the door out to the main corridors of the mall. Looking closely, I catch the image of Kylie. She's off to the side and only visible for a short time, but it is definitely her. And she is closely watching the professor.

Chilled by the image of Kylie watching Jesse buy the jewelry, then dipping out of sight before he leaves the store, only to fall into step behind him and trail him again, I pick up my phone and call Molly. She sounds nervous but doesn't try to end the phone call or push me away.

"I just want to make sure I am absolutely clear about this," I say. "Nobody else has copies of the poem that you wrote for Professor Santucci? You didn't write it down and keep them in a notebook, or give them to somebody to read as an editor? Anything?"

"No," she says. "It isn't something that I spent a whole lot of time on. Those words just popped into my mind and so I wrote them out for him. I never gave copies to anybody else and no one knew I wrote it. I only gave it to him."

"When did you give him that poem?" I ask.

As soon as she answers, I realize Molly gave the love poem to Professor Santucci during the time Kylie was his teaching assistant. That means she could have easily seen it and would likely know who wrote it. This would be both offensive and darkly humorous to a girl who I am now realizing was being trailed along by an older, manipulative, married man.

I look back at my timeline to confirm my suspicions and connections click into place. I know I have to act fast.

Kylie looks surprised when I show up at her door, but she doesn't hesitate to open it and allow me inside. I glance at her ears and notice she's wearing the sparkling diamond and pale blue earrings Jesse Santucci bought for his wife. The same ones I noticed the first time I saw her but didn't fully register. I'm sure if I look back on the pictures taken during the investigation, I'll notice them again.

Kylie is standing right in front of me, face and body calm and unbothered, wearing earrings that belong to Kristie Santucci, that were physically torn from her ears just before her death. When I get a warrant to check the apartment, I'm completely confident we will find the broken necklace that matches in her jewelry box.

I don't say anything. Instead, I take out a stack of pictures of the park where we found Tyler's body. I show them to her.

"I'm sorry to just show up like this, but the case is really heating up. I think I might have found something really important to the investigation, and I wanted to get your help. I think you might be able to tell me the significance of it," I say.

"Sure," she says. "I don't know what I can tell you, but if I know something, I'm happy to share it."

"I know. And I really appreciate that. You've been so helpful and cooperative from the very beginning of this investigation, and I don't think I would have been able to find some details if it wasn't for what you were able to tell me. It means a lot. And that's why I came right to you when we found this. These are pictures of where the body was found the other day. Don't worry, I'm not going to show you the corpse. It's pretty disturbing. But I want you to look around the area and see if you notice anything," I say.

I hand her a few pictures actually taken on the day that Tyler's body was found and let her look over them. There's nothing in them. I just want her to think that there is. When she hands them back, shaking her head, I hand her one that looks like it goes along with those but was actually taken an hour ago by Dean. As soon as he and Xavier showed back up, I sent them on the mission and was able to print the picture off my phone just before arriving at Kylie's apartment.

"This is an enlargement of one of those pictures. Look really closely at the dirt and you'll see a necklace. It's broken, but it also has some blood on it. The forensic team collected DNA and we're getting it tested, but it might take a little while. I was really hoping you might recognize it. Does it look familiar at all?"

Kylie stares at the picture, her face looking harder and slightly more pale, but she doesn't give anything away. She shakes her head and offers the picture back again.

"No. I don't recognize it. It looks just like a regular necklace," she says.

Dean had only been able to find a basic chain that he could buy and stage in the dirt. He wasn't able to find one that had a pendant that even somewhat resembled the one on Kristie's necklace, so I'm going to have to work around it.

"There was also a pendant found in the leaves a couple yards away. I don't have a picture of it, but it was blue," I say.

"Blue?" she asks.

"Yeah. Like blue with sparkly stones."

I'm trying to sound a bit flustered, like I can't think straight about the evidence and what it might mean. I don't want to make her too suspicious. This is just to start creating a foundation.

Kylie frowns. "I'm sorry, that doesn't sound familiar. If you want, I can talk to the other girls and see if any of them recognize the description."

"That would be great. Thank you." I force a cough. "Oh. Sorry. I think I might be catching a bit of a cold. Would you mind getting me some water?"

"Of course," she says. "Come on in."

She gestures toward the kitchen, but I hold up a hand and shake my head.

"No. If I am sick, I wouldn't want to get any germs into the rest of your place, especially your kitchen," I say.

She smiles at me. "Okay. I'll be right back." She starts out of the room and I immediately head for the snow globe display I'd admired the first time I was in the apartment. "Are you sure you only want water? Maybe some tea with honey and lemon would make you feel better?" she calls from the unseen kitchen.

"I don't want to be any trouble," I say.

"It's no trouble. It'll only take a minute. It will warm you up and make your throat feel much better," Kylie says.

Her making the tea will buy me a little extra time. I cough again for good measure.

"Thank you so much. I really appreciate it," I say.

"No problem at all."

I wait another second, then snatch the largest snow globe out of the display and stuff it down into the large bag I have slung over my shoulder, replacing it with the one I brought in. They aren't exactly identical, but they are extremely similar. Close enough that it would be difficult to notice the difference without examining it very closely. I have no doubt Kylie will do that, but it won't matter by the time she does.

As I'm walking over to sit down, I take note of the sparkling snowflake scarf draped over the back of a nearby chair. Kylie comes back moments later and hands me the tea. I stay for just a few minutes, drinking the tea fast even though it burns and thanking her before leaving. Kylie watches me from the open door. She doesn't notice Dean out in the parking lot, parked off to the side and a tablet in front of his face.

He's parked several cars down from me and I walk by without even looking his way. He's there to watch the apartment and track Kylie's movements. I don't expect her to do anything for a couple of hours, but just in case, I want to make sure he's there to watch what she's doing.

I hold off on taking out my phone until I'm out of the parking lot. As it rings over and over, I start to get nervous, but Cupcake finally answers.

"Hey," I say. "It's Emma. In that picture you sent me, there's a scarf that looks like a bunch of snowflakes. Have you made a whole lot of those? Is that something you've made for a couple of years and sold or anything?

"No," she says. "That's actually a new design. That market is the first time I've offered it for sale."

"Perfect, thank you. I appreciate it."

I hang up and call Sam. "Kylie was definitely at the market. That snowflake design scarf was only offered that night. She couldn't have gotten it anywhere else. I'm sure her lawyers will say that somebody bought it for her and gave it as a gift, but it's not going to matter. She was there at the market. I got the snow globe. I'm on my way over there."

The drive to the department feels extra-long with the bag containing the snow globe sitting on the seat beside me. When I finally get inside, I set it on the table on the piece of prepared paper Sam has already put in place. The photographer snaps a couple of pictures of it after I write Kylie's name, the date, and a description of the globe as an identifier.

With the pictures taken, I pick up the globe and flip it over. Just like I expected to, I find the small door leading into the hidden compartment in the base of the snow globe. I pop it open. Inside is a folded note. Opening it reveals the poem Molly wrote.

That's all I needed to see for the pieces to fall into place. Now I have an idea of what I believe happened.

I wait as long as I can force myself to wait before calling Kylie. While I wait, I get a warrant for an officer to go into her apartment and get the box of wrapping paper scraps she showed me the first time I was in her apartment. I want the silver paper inside tested for traces of blood.

When I can't wait any longer, I call her.

"I need you to keep this between the two of us, but I didn't want you to hear on the news because I know you knew her. I wanted to let you know that we have found Trisha," I say.

Kylie does her best to react like she is devastated at the news but rushes to end the call. I don't try to stop her. Instead, I immediately call Dean and let him know I've given her the false lead. I stay on the line with him until he tells me Kylie has just come out of her apartment and gotten in her car. He gets behind her to follow her and I drive that way so I can get on the trail.

CHAPTER THIRTY-TWO

I STAY BACK FROM DEAN, KNOWING I'M BEHIND HIM BY TRACKING the GPS wearable Xavier designed for him that allows us to pinpoint each other's locations and movements. This is the first time I've used it to be able to follow Dean, but it is working extremely well. I'm able to stay out of sight but not lose him. He calls me a couple of times to check in and let me know how her driving is changing.

It's obvious she is becoming more anxious, and her driving is getting more erratic. He doesn't think she's noticed that he's following her and has made it a point to look around and check his phone a couple of times when it seemed she was looking in the mirror to make it seem as though he is lost. I'm glad he's putting in the effort. If Kylie is in the state of mind I think she is, she would be very sensitive to being followed. Especially by somebody she doesn't recognize.

We drive along a winding, twisting path for over an hour. At points it feels like we have gone back on our own path, retracing our steps. I start to wonder if she has noticed she's being followed and is trying to get Dean off her trail without it being obvious. But then we start to climb a small mountain. I recognize it as where the caverns are located. Dean calls me when we are about halfway up.

"She's about to go into a resort," he says. "It's one of those old road-side places with the cabins."

"Is it open?" I ask.

"Yeah, it looks…" he hesitates. "Wait. No. It's closed."

"You can't keep following her. If she's going into a shuttered resort, she's going to notice that you're behind her. You need to turn around."

"Are you sure? I might lose her."

"That's fine. You don't want her to notice you. Just park off on the side of the road, I'll be there in a bit. We'll have to follow her on foot and hope we can find her," I tell him.

Knowing I am no longer actually following Kylie, I pick up my speed. I'm going faster than I should on the narrow, winding road, but I need to get there as fast as I can. It takes several more minutes before I catch up to Dean. I see his car parked off on the narrow edge of the road nearly in the trees that line it.

I pull up behind him and we get out at the same time. My gun is already drawn as we run toward the entrance of the old resort.

The old resort looks like it hasn't been sitting empty for too long. It's easy to see why Dean thought it was still open when he first turned into it. But going further, it becomes more obvious that no one has been here in probably a year, maybe a bit more. The grass is overgrown, the build-ings are faded. There are a couple of broken windows and evidence of animals taking over some of the spaces, but it's not completely derelict.

We run, looking around to take in all of our surroundings as much as we can, until we notice Kylie's car parked off to the side of one of the bungalows. I hesitate to call them cabins, though that's probably how they were advertised. They don't have the rustic look or camp-ing energy of a cabin. Instead, they look like miniaturized houses with white-painted wooden siding and little blue shutters.

Dean and I go to the building next door and press up against the side for a second to catch our breath and regroup.

"I'll go into the front," I tell him. "You go around to the back. There has to be a door or a big window or something."

"Got it."

We run around the back corner of the building and then split up. I go up between the two toward the front door and Dean goes to the back. I'm holding my gun firmly in my hands as I climb up the wooden plank steps onto a wide front porch. The blue door is closed, and I'm not surprised to find it is locked when I try the doorknob.

I don't bother to knock or announce myself. I smash through the lock with one hard kick and the door opens. There's a scream, but it's strangely muffled. When I get through the front room and into the bedroom at the back, I know why.

Kylie stands calmly in the center of the room, her hands hanging down by her side. One grips a large knife. In front of her, Trisha is strapped down to the bed. The bedding around her is stained and her hair is matted like she's been thrashing against the mattress for days. Only now, there's no energy left in her to thrash. There's evidence of violence on her throat and her sides. Her face is caked in dry blood.

"I was almost finished," Kylie says quietly without turning around. "You could have let me finish."

"No, Kylie," I tell her, knowing that when she says she was almost finished she means she had almost achieved killing all four of them. "I couldn't let you do that. You need to put the knife down and step away from the bed."

Trisha is still doing her best to scream against the dirty cloth tied around her face and stuffed into her mouth like a gag. But it isn't just the cloth that's muffling the scream. Trisha is missing her tongue.

"They shouldn't have done it. None of them should have," she says. "Everything was going to be perfect. Just like a snow globe."

"A snow globe?" I ask her. "Like the one Jesse Santucci gave you?"

Kylie looks at me over her shoulder. Streams of mascara create black lines down her face and her eyes are ringed with tears.

"We were the snow globe. At least, we were going to be. So beautiful and perfect. Everything I have ever wanted. We were going to have it. It was so close. But it was all ruined."

"Tell me what happened," I say.

Kylie has turned back to look at Trisha, her hand still wrapped tightly around the hilt of the knife. I keep my eyes trained on it. If there's even the slightest twitch of movement in her arm or hand, I will have to act. But for now, I am just going to let her talk.

"I loved Jesse. So much. More than I can even tell you. And he loved me. He told me he did. We were going to be everything to each other. All he needed to do was leave his wife. They weren't happy. He told me that. She didn't take care of him. All she cared about was her business. She didn't want to be the kind of wife he deserved. He just wanted to be loved, taken care of. He didn't want to have to listen to her talk about her troubles at work or how hard she was pushing, because that would mean she wasn't listening to him. I was going to do that for him. I already did. All I cared about was him.

"When I saw him buying that jewelry, I thought everything was about to happen. I had begun to lose hope. I thought maybe he was slipping through my fingers, and I wasn't going to get the dream I saw. But then I saw him buy the earrings and the necklace, and I just knew he was going to give them to me for Christmas. He was going to tell me he was leaving his wife and that in the new year, we could be open to the whole world with how we felt about each other. We'd finally be able to just be a real couple and not have to keep hiding from everyone.

"Then I went to the gala. I already knew he was going to bring her. He was keeping up appearances. The people at work still didn't know they were having problems and he didn't want to cause any drama during the holidays. But they were so cuddly with each other. And then I noticed she was wearing the jewelry. It broke my heart. I couldn't believe he would do that to me. And yet part of me was still holding out hope. We still had plans to celebrate Christmas together.

"When I opened my gift, it was a snow globe. You know what it looks like. You took it from me. That doesn't matter. I never want to see it again. He told me he knew how much I loved snow globes, so he wanted to get me the most beautiful one he had ever seen. And he had hidden a secret. That was enough to make me fall head over heels again and feel all the hope in the world. He might have given her that jewelry, but it didn't mean he hadn't gotten me something else. Something small enough to fit in the base of the snow globe. I was hoping for a ring. What I got was that poem.

"I knew it was stolen. He hadn't even bothered to write something for me. He took what another girl who was obsessed with him had written, copied it in his handwriting, and tried to pass it off as being from him." She takes a breath. "I just couldn't take it. They needed to be gone. I couldn't keep moving forward with my life with them in this world."

"And Tyler? It was the same? You two broke up and he started dating Trisha, so he needed to be punished?"

"I was over Tyler," she says. "Yes, it hurt when we broke up. Of course, it did. But I was so in love with Jesse it didn't matter." She sighs. "No. What Tyler did was worse. He pushed me into Jesse's arms. If he had never broken up with me, I never would have fallen in love with Jesse and none of this would have happened. And if Trisha hadn't thrown herself at Tyler and convinced him to break up with me, we would all be fine. They shattered me. I just wanted to make my world perfect again."

Sirens slice through the silence and the knife falls from Kylie's hand. For a few long moments, we stand there, staring into each other's eyes. Then, when voices shout from behind me, what little tension she still had in her shoulders relaxes, and for a brief moment, a flicker of a relieved smile crosses her face. She doesn't resist when the police cuff her and walk her out of the house. Dean and I work to release Trisha from her binds as she sobs in relief. She's bundled into an ambulance to go to the hospital and for a few moments, he and I are alone in the quiet. My heart is racing. I feel slightly sick to my stomach with the intense rush of adrenaline.

It's over.

Later I go to the hospital to check on Trisha. What she has gone through is tragic and life-changing, but she's alive. The doctors have hope they will be able to save her despite the massive infections she is suffering. I have faith in their abilities and know they'll pull her through. And when they do, she'll learn to live with the disfiguration Kylie caused.

I stand by her bed and reassure her in her sedation. I tell her everything will be alright. It might not seem like it, but it will be. She survived for a reason. She just has to find that reason and fight for it.

CHAPTER THIRTY-THREE

THE WEEK OF CHRISTMAS BLOWS IN ON A SNOW-FILLED WIND.
With all of the horror of the case still fresh and sharply vivid, I sit at the back of the courtroom to listen to Kylie be arraigned. She's dressed like her apartment Christmas decorations now. Tasteful. Pristine. Trying too hard to look like an adult. It hadn't meant that much to me the first time I saw it, but now that I know who she really is, the heavily nostalgic, classic Christmas theming of her home is unsettling. As she put it, she was living in her own snow globe. She'd crafted the image of the beautiful, manicured holiday and had herself and Jesse Santucci like dolls within it. Everything glossy and candy-flavored. Nothing real.

The lawyer standing beside her wants to take full advantage of the holiday season and the sentimental mood it carries. She is clearly trying hard to pull on heartstrings and highlight Kylie's youth and determination to build a life for herself while skating deftly around the true gravity of the charges she's facing. I watch the judge carefully to see if he's buying it. I'm not.

Having a career like mine means being exposed to the full range of emotion within the human experience. There's nothing I haven't seen people going through and little I haven't felt first-hand. I don't just stand on the outside and watch people suffer through the horrendous experience of a loved one being murdered or the gut-wrenching feeling of someone close to them disappearing. The windowpane of unshared reality that stands between them and most agents doesn't exist for me. They stare through that glass, wanting to feel like they are right there and a part of everything so they can empathize with the victims they are protecting, but they still can't touch them.

I am on their side of the window. There is no empty space between us. I'm not saying I know exactly what every one of them feels because every experience is deeply personal. There are situations they go through that I cannot begin to fathom. But we stand beside each other in that space. I've been immersed in searching for someone close to me. I've waded through murder cases I'm entwined in rather than investigating. I know the heartache, confusion, anger, and frustration. I know the feeling of having so much of those built up inside me it's like my lungs can't expand enough for me to breathe.

But with us all standing there together, we can draw in that air.

That has given me tremendous empathy for the victims and their families.

It has also given me the capacity to feel it for the killers.

I can look beyond their crimes to see them as people. I can see the pain they've been through and what has led up to the moment when they made the decision to kill. I can see where their reality has become distorted and their view of the world as others live in it and experience it has cracked. Their grasp on it has loosened and they think they are doing what is fully understandable. Though it doesn't ever take away the impact of what they've done or excuse them for the horror they have exacted on countless people, it does allow me to feel for them as well. They can occupy the space as those broken and tattered by the actions of others. I've seen it many times.

A woman pushed to the brink by the abusive treatment of the man she loved who held her captive and forced her to do his bidding, including participating in and covering up gruesome murders, kneeling in a cornfield wanting to slit her wrists to try to atone for what she had done.

A man driven mad by the loss of his brother and the realization of his extensive, brutal bullying, exacting his revenge on whom he believed was responsible.

A student confused by her own inner turmoil led astray by someone she should have been able to trust implicitly, who was convinced to help along the horrible deaths of others who were suffering.

A girl tormented by the truth of her own past taking back what should have been hers and leaving those who contributed to the torture of her existence dead in her wake.

They were all tragedies, and not just for the victims in the cases. Those stayed with me, continue to live inside me.

Not all of them deserve sympathy, regardless of what they have gone through.

I count Kylie among that number. I am well aware of the manipulation she experienced. Technically she was an adult when she started her relationship with Jesse. Legally, she was old enough to make her own decisions and within her rights to engage in a sexual relationship with anyone she pleased. But anyone looking at that situation can see what was wrong with it. Regardless of her being legally an adult, she was still under Santucci's power. He groomed her, took advantage of her, and strung her along. He pretended he loved her and allowed her to believe they were going to share their lives. He probably never meant it for a second.

In that way, I do feel some sympathy for her. I feel bad that she was lied to and had her heart broken by a man who wielded power over her and used it fully to his advantage. I am angry that he got away with it for so long and wasn't held accountable in the ways he should have been.

But the measures she took were reprehensible. She wasn't out of control when she chose to kill. She hadn't slipped into psychosis and thought she was earning Jesse's favor or was ceremonially ridding herself of the pain that she carried so she could have a better life. Kylie was hurt and upset, and she was certainly not in a stable state of mind when I found her standing over Trisha, but she knew exactly what she was doing and what she had done. It wasn't for any reason but revenge. She wanted to make a spectacle of punishing them, and by doing so had scarred so many people during a time of year when there should only be joy and light.

That was only for her. I have no sympathy for that.

I don't know the full details of Kylie's crimes. No one does yet but her. I doubt even her attorney who is fighting so hard to make her look like a wonderful person who was just led astray and misunderstood really knows all of what she did. None of us may ever know. We'd all like to think that as soon as a criminal is caught and brought into court, they realize the error of their ways and agree to come clean about everything. Or even if they don't have a moral or emotional shift that leads them to confessing fully, a desire to work out the very best deal for themselves and get some leverage in what is an otherwise hopeless situation will encourage them to dole out the details. Unfortunately, that's not how it works.

Sometimes that happens, of course. The trial comes and suddenly the whole story flows out. But there are plenty of other times—more often than not, I'd argue—when no matter what evidence is brought up against them, the killer will never say a single self-incriminatory word. They will never admit to any wrongdoing, will never offer an explanation, will never provide any kind of reasoning. They won't tell what was done or how, and they may even refuse to provide information on where to find the victim's body or other critical details. They've lost all other control in their lives, but what they can do is hold onto that information that they know people desperately want and refuse to ever offer it up.

I have a feeling that is the way Kylie will handle this. She'll never tell us exactly how she committed the murders. I'll never know if my suspicions are correct that she is the one who sent me the text about Jesse Santucci, not able to contain her own jealousy and rage at people worrying so much about Kristie and gushing about their perfect marriage. We won't know the exact chain of events that led to each of her victims falling prey to her grotesque urges.

And I'll simply have to live with that. It isn't my job to be able to explain it all or to provide the full story of what exactly happened. I've fulfilled my responsibilities and even though I'd like to know more, if I never do, I can still feel absolutely confident that I did the right thing and ensured Kylie won't be able to do to someone else what she did to Jesse, Kristie, Tyler, and Trisha.

The judge immediately sees through all the creative wording and emotional pleas of Kylie's attorney and she's sent right back to jail to wait for her next hearing. She'll never walk free again. I'll provide all the testimony and evidence I possibly can to ensure that.

I leave the courthouse satisfied, but with a hurried feeling in my stomach. I feel like so much of the season has passed me by and I didn't accomplish the dream holiday I'd wanted so much to have, but there's still time. Not much. But I'll take what I can get.

The snow is falling steadily, and the ground has lost all the warmth it clung to through the season that made the first day of flakes melt away as soon as they fluttered to the earth. An icy layer is building up now, sparkling and swirling as cars drive at partial speed hoping to take advantage of the rapidly draining time before Christmas Eve. I join them eagerly. There's a lot I still want to get done before the season passes me by.

There are no more holiday markets for the year and I don't have the ability to leisurely explore little boutiques and hidden gems of stores in hopes of finding just the right gifts. I've gotten a few special things, but I'm going to have to join the masses at the department stores to find the rest.

The lines of cars leading into the mall parking lot are unsurprisingly long and slow. It looks like there are far more people trying to creep their way into the lot and get inside to shop than there are available spots. I'm fully expecting to finally get in only to find that the line is moving right back out of the lot because there aren't any spots to park and people are giving up hope.

Fortunately, by the time it's my turn to ease through the entrance to the lot and start the free-for-all search for an elusive empty spot, some of the crush has lessened ahead of me. It's getting later in the day and the snow is coming down harder, scaring away some of the shoppers. It means I'm able to snag a spot fairly quickly. I bundle up tight and tell myself the fact that I'm parked nearly at the entrance to the lot rather than anywhere near the mall itself just means it will be easier to get out when I'm finished.

Inside, the mall is bustling with the last-minute energy of the final days before Christmas Eve. People rush around trying to cross the final names off their lists or find something for people they forgot. Others are rushing to purchase gifts for children with prying eyes they know they can't hide anything from for more than a couple of days. I feel less hurried and pressured than these shoppers seem to be. I have my list of names, but I'm also not looking for anything in particular. I need to fill stockings and add a trinket or two for each person in the family. I also have my eye out for small gifts for important people who have crossed my path and who I may not consider especially close, but who I'd like to acknowledge.

As I'm contemplating something for Detective Noah White in Harlan, my attention is drawn to the glittering display I catch out of the corner of my eye. I'm pulled to it, the breathless, hard feeling in the center of my chest acting like a magnet bringing me closer.

The display of snow globes is more elaborate than the one where I bought the decoy to slip into Kylie's apartment. I am able to step in among several shelves and tables so I'm surrounded by the glimmering glass and snow. Someone has gone through and turned several of the knobs to trigger the music. That was clearly several minutes ago because the songs have slowed and are trickling past, in some moments blending and in others clashing.

My eyes sweep over the various globes and the scenes inside. Some of them are dramatic and elegant, while others are sillier depictions of snowmen, animal families, or even Christmas versions of sports team mascots. There's a little bit of something here for everyone, it seems. A piece of every person's life encapsulated in glitter, water, and glass.

As I'm starting to walk away from the display, one of the globes stops my steps. For a moment, I can't breathe. I can only stare at it. Finally, I reach down and pick up the seemingly simple, unassuming globe. It isn't one of the largest, though it isn't particularly small, either. The base is basic wood, carved into a softly sloping pedestal. And inside, nestled among a thicket of tiny bottle brush trees, is a little building that could have been carved from my own memory.

It looks like a miniature replica of Cabin 13 in Feathered Nest.

Looking into the scene I can see myself walking up to the porch for the first time. I can remember the darkness of the woods and the seemingly endless stretch of trees with shadowy voids between them. I remember the silence. As that thought comes to mind, the music coming from the other globes slows and stops. I hear nothing but my own breath in my ears.

I tilt the globe over and let the iridescent glitter rain down through the water onto the roof of the tiny cabin. It falls softly to the ground and creates a shimmering blanket over the serene picture. It is, as the first time I saw it, a lovely lie. There is nothing serene about the cabin or the grounds surrounding it. I've made my peace with that building and with the woods. I even came to appreciate it and feel a true connection with it the last time I was there.

But I will never forget what happened there.

My heart beats a little faster as I run my fingertips over the curve of the glass ball like I'm trying to touch the cabin inside. I can see myself standing in the doorway. I can see Eli lying on the porch, surrounded in a pool of blood. And deep in the woods, beyond what's contained within the globe, I can imagine what was once a looming house, now burned to the ground.

I hear Kylie's voice in my head.

We were the snow globe.

I carefully turn the globe over to look at the bottom and see that there's no metal knob to turn for music. It's silent. Only the image of soft snow falling over the hidden cabin.

I set it carefully into the front of the cart that has been empty until this moment and continue on.

EPILOGUE

A S THE NIGHT OF CHRISTMAS EVE APPROACHES, SAM COMES INTO
the kitchen where Bellamy, Bebe, and I are baking. He's holding
my coat.

"Want to take a walk?" he asks.

I look at my dough-covered hands and the flour-coated apron I'm
wearing, but then his hopeful face.

"Sure. Give me a second to clean up."

We walk out into the night and stroll along with the soft snowflakes
falling on our faces, taking in the decorations. They are the same lights
we saw taking this walk a couple weeks ago, but they are more beautiful
now. I hold my husband's hand and rest my head against him, letting
him direct us. Soon we find ourselves in front of his parents' house. My
heart swells when I see the entire thing has been decorated. The lights
are bright and the lawn is resplendent with snowmen, reindeer, and
Santas. There's even a fair few decorations I recognize from our house
that I just couldn't find when we took them down.

"Do you like it?" he asks.

"It's amazing. When did you do this?" I ask.

"Between your third and seventy-fifth batch of cookies," he tells me.

I turn into his arms and look into his face. "Why?"

I hope I already know the answer, but I want to hear him say it.

"The house we spend Christmas in should look just like this," he says. "And next year, it will."

"Next year?" I ask.

"The inside needs some renovations and cleaning. We'll need to decorate it and get everything in. But if we stick to it, we should be able to be in by spring."

I smile so wide my face almost splits. It's matched by his cheeky grin.

"What do you think?"

I lift up and kiss him. "Merry Christmas, Sheriff Johnson."

He smiles and gathers me close, kissing me back. When we get home I'll think of a way to tell the others to make it special for tomorrow morning. But for now, I just want to enjoy the snow, and my early look into the future, with Sam.

AUTHOR'S NOTE

Dear Reader,

Thank you for choosing to read *The Girl and the Unexpected Gifts*, the third installment in this new season of the *Emma Griffin® FBI Mystery series*. My hope with every Christmas themed book in this series is that spending time with Emma and her chosen family has brought you joy, kept you on the edge of your seat, and warmed your heart throughout the holiday season. I feel extremely grateful to have a reader like you, and I want to say thank you from the bottom of my heart for being here with me.

I owe Emma and the rest of this beloved cast of characters to your unyielding support and enthusiasm. So, if you could please take a quick moment to leave a review for this book, I would appreciate it enormously. Your reviews allow me to keep living my dream as an indie author and bringing you the thrilling mystery stories that you love.

While you eagerly await the next Emma Griffin book, I invite you to catch up with Emma's cousin in the *Dean Steele Mystery Thriller series!* In the latest book, titled *The Garden of Secrets,* a hunter stumbles upon an unattended fire and discovers a buried hand adorned with a rose charm bracelet. Despite years of effort by citizen detectives, the victim's identity remains unknown. The "Rose Doe" cold case is rekindled a decade later with the discovery of a plot containing multiple graves, each holding the body of a young woman wearing a bracelet adorned with a unique flower. And with no leads in sight, Dean is brought in to bring down the killer on the loose. Intrigued? I bet you are!

I promise to keep bringing you heart-pounding, mind-bending mysteries that will keep you at the edge of your seat, and coming back for more!

Yours,
A.J. Rivers

P.S. If for some reason you didn't like this book or found typos or other errors, please let me know personally. I do my best to read and respond to every email at mailto:aj@riversthrillers.com

P.P.S. If you would like to stay up-to-date with me and my latest releases I invite you to visit my Linktree page at *www.linktr.ee/a.j.rivers* to subscribe to my newsletter and receive a free copy of my book, Edge of the Woods. You can also follow me on my social media accounts for behind-the-scenes glimpses and sneak peeks of my upcoming projects, or even sign up for text notifications. I can't wait to connect with you!

ALSO BY

A.J. RIVERS

Book One— *The Girl in the Mist**
Book Two— *The Girl on Hallow's Eve**
Book Three— *The Girl and the Christmas Past**
Book Four— *The Girl and the Winter Bones**
Book Five— *The Girl on the Retreat**

Season Four
Book Twenty-Two — *The Girl and the Deadly Secrets**
Book Twenty-Three — *The Girl on the Road**
Book Twenty-Four — *The Girl and the Unexpected Gifts*

<u>Ava James FBI Mysteries</u>

Book One—*The Woman at the Masked Gala**
Book Two—*Ava James and the Forgotten Bones**
Book Three —*The Couple Next Door**
Book Four — *The Cabin on Willow Lake**
Book Five — *The Lake House**
Book Six — *The Ghost of Christmas**
Book Seven — *The Rescue**
Book Eight — *Murder in the Moonlight**
Book Nine — *Behind the Mask**

<u>Dean Steele FBI Mysteries</u>

Book One—*The Woman in the Woods**
Book Two — *The Last Survivors*
Book Three — *No Escape*
Book Four — *The Garden of Secrets*

ALSO BY
A.J. RIVERS & THOMAS YORK

Made in United States
Troutdale, OR
11/24/2023